Angel unaware

ELIZABETH SINCLAIR

PRESS.

Jewel Imprint: Amethyst
Medallion Press, Inc.
Printed in USA

Angel Unaware

ELIZABETH SINCLAIR

DEDICATION:

To my angels: my children, Linda, Toni, and
Bobby; and my grandchildren: Rian, Sean,
Meghan, Emily, Charmaine, and Steph.
I love you.

Published 2008 by Medallion Press, Inc.

The MEDALLION PRESS LOGO
is a registered trademark of Medallion Press, Inc.

Printed in the United States of America
Typeset in Adobe Garamond Pro

ISBN# 978-193383631-7

10 9 8 7 6 5 4 3 2 1
First Edition

ACKNOWLEDGMENTS:

Thank you as always to the guardians of my muse, the Plot Queens: Heather Waters, Laura Barone, Vickie King, Kat McMahon, and Dolores Wilson. I couldn't do this without you.

To Vicki Hinze, my best friend and "adopted" sister, for always believing in me and shoring me up with her love and encouragement.

To Helen, Kerry, and Adam for continuing to love my work and allowing me to share it with my readers.

To my husband, Bob, for his faith, love and constant presence in my life.

CHAPTER 1

"Love is what's in the room with you at Christmas if you stop opening presents and listen." —Bobby, age 7

"Dora, Grace is okay. Her fall was broken. No harm done."

Calvin, the Senior Angel in charge of Celestial Maintenance, meant well, but his reassurances didn't make Dora's blunder easier for her to handle. She pulled her knees closer to her chest and stared off into the clear, cerulean sky, her mind full of the image of poor Grace hanging from a cloud by her fingertips, her wings flapping uselessly behind her. This foul-up, just one more in a long line, convinced Dora even more that she had no right to call herself an angel.

Bad enough when she messed up with an angel she didn't know very well. But *Grace* had been her best friend since they'd graduated from the cherubic choir and got promoted into Celestial Maintenance. Gracie had stuck by her through thick and thin, guided her over the bumps in the clouds, and had never let her down when Dora needed her. And this was how she repaid her?

Dora squinted up at Calvin to block out the glow surrounding the tall man, and then swallowed her tears. "What if her fall hadn't been broken? What if that cloud hadn't scuttled by and caught her at just the right moment?"

Calvin laid a large, calming hand on her shoulder. "But it did, and she's fine. We must be thankful for what we get and not brood over what might have been."

His words of wisdom went in one of Dora's ears and out the other, and in no way calmed her distraught emotions.

Emitting a sigh laden with impatience, he squatted next to Dora, took her chin in his fingers, and tilted her face up to him. "You haven't been in Celestial Maintenance long. It takes time to settle in."

Dora pulled from his grasp. "I know. But sometimes I wonder if I ever will. Last week, I polished the shine right off Hermione's halo, and she lost her ability to transport for two days. The week before that, when I was supposed to be mending her sleeve, I sewed the bottom of Estelle's robes closed by accident, and she nearly tripped off the cloud and fell into the middle of Chicago's rush hour traffic. Today, I replaced the levitation feathers in Grace's wings with landing feathers, and she almost broke her neck when she tried to take off. And that's only the tip of a ruptured rainbow." She took a deep breath and then shook her head and swirled her fingertips through the wisps of mist rising from the disturbed cloud on which she sat. "Let's face it. I'm just a celestial screwup."

Calvin cleared his throat and frowned down at her. "Dora!"

She knew how much he disliked that mortal phrase, but today she didn't care what Calvin thought. She just wanted to pull a cloud over her head and immerse herself in it for eternity. How much bleaker could her celestial future become?

Sometimes she felt she'd never get the hang of being an angel. Aside from her friendship with Grace, Dora had never quite fit in among the other angels and suspected some of them laughed at her behind their wings. Her halo was always askew. She had no control over her wings and flew into things on a regular basis. When she sang, entire galaxies cringed. Cloud vapor often sent her into uncontrollable sneezing fits that disrupted her surroundings for hours, and despite every effort she made, she'd never really developed a taste for ambrosia.

In every conceivable way, Dora simply didn't fit into the accepted image of the stereotypical angel or their community. However, the career opportunities up here went beyond being somewhat limited, so if she couldn't be an angel, what could she be?

Dora gazed at the glassy, smooth surface of the Earth Pool and thought about the hours she'd spent gazing into it, observing the humans below. How she'd enjoyed watching them over the last few weeks, buying gifts, singing carols, and decorating trees for the coming holiday, interacting with their families. Would she fit in any better down there?

If she never tried it, she could never be sure that mortality would be any better than an angelic life. Perhaps it was time she found out.

The idea made her brighten slightly. Maybe now was the right time to ask Calvin about an idea she'd been toying with for a long time. "Calvin," she said, her voice echoing her insecurity, "I was thinking . . . maybe I'd be better at something else. Maybe I could—" She cut herself off, still fearful of his reaction to her totally unprecedented request, but nevertheless, a desire that had lain hidden in her heart for decades.

"Maybe you could what, Dora?" Calvin's voice was gentle, encouraging, and perhaps just a tad too eager to move her somewhere beyond his jurisdiction.

Poor Calvin. She hadn't made his job easy. Not a day had gone by in the last century that he hadn't feared the wrath of the Heavenly Council because he'd had to bail her out of some kind of trouble or repair one of her many mistakes.

She stood and brushed the wrinkles from her robe. In her reflection in the Earth Pool, she could see her halo had tilted sideways above her white-blond curls, something that irritated Calvin, who seemed to exist to please his superiors. He lived in constant fear that one of the Archangels would stop by for an unscheduled inspection, and the Celestial Maintenance Department wouldn't live up to expectations.

Not wanting to risk upsetting Calvin right now, she righted her halo, stiffened her spine, and faced him.

"Maybe . . . maybe I could become a . . . mortal?" she asked timidly.

Calvin's mouth dropped open. His eyes grew large and mirrored his outrage and apprehension. The feathers in his wings fluttered into total disarray, a definite signal his agitation level had risen beyond his control.

He glanced furtively around, as if expecting a lightning bolt to be hurled at them. "Oh, dear. I . . . I . . . uh . . . I . . ."

"Please," she begged, clutching the sleeve of his robe. "Please ask them for me. Maybe I'd be better at being mortal than I am at being an angel." She gazed longingly at the Earth Pool.

"That's absurd. You know it works the other way around. Such a request is . . . unacceptable. Totally unacceptable." His hands fluttered nervously, pleating and unpleating the fabric of his robe. "Angels don't become humans. It's just never been done. Never."

As the words tumbled from his mouth in a jumble of thought, Calvin's face began turning bright red, and the feathers on his wings vibrated into even greater disarray. In an effort to calm him, Dora reached out to smooth the feathers, but he retreated beyond her touch.

"Please, Calvin. If you explained how miserably I've failed at being an angel, then maybe the Heavenly Council would allow me to go to Earth to just . . . try it." She smiled her best cherubic smile. "And, if I were down there, I wouldn't be your responsibility any longer." She held her breath and waited. Knowing how eager Calvin was to be rid of her and the trouble that accompanied her, she was not surprised to see him pause to give her request serious consideration.

"Well . . ." he said, looking away, obviously savoring the idea of not having to repair any more of her disasters. Then he shook his head. "No. Absolutely not. If I'm lucky, I'd be laughed out of the Hall of Prayers. If I'm not lucky . . ." He shuddered. Obviously, he couldn't tolerate even thinking about the alternative, much less putting it into words.

She understood Calvin's reluctance. Dora knew that angels didn't venture into the Hall of Prayers where the Archangels, the Heavenly Council, reigned supreme unless they were summoned or they had an urgent problem. Still, this was urgent, at least from *her* perspective. She *had* to convince him to try and, as cruel as it was, she had an idea that might make him see things her way.

Calvin had a vulnerable spot. All the angels knew what it was, and that they could get him to agree to almost anything by using it. Hating to take advantage by doing something she'd always believed to be underhanded, she'd never resorted to it before and abhorred employing it now, but this was far too important to her. His stubborn refusal had left her no alternative.

Dora gazed up at Calvin and squeezed out a few glistening tears. "Calvin, if they let me go down there and try being mortal, just for Christmas, I promise I'll come back and do my job here. You'll never hear another complaint from me. I'll work extra hard to be the best celestial worker you've ever seen." She sniffed and blinked, forcing a generous cascade of tears to escape her swimming eyes.

As the plump teardrops ran down her cheeks, Calvin's eyes widened in alarm. "No! Oh, dear, no! Not angel tears! The last time an angel went on a crying jag, the entire West Coast of the United States was underwater for weeks. Streams overflowed their banks. Houses washed away. Trees ripped out by their roots. People left homeless. Cities without power. Mudslides of mammoth proportions. One of His favorite mountains nearly slid into the San Fernando Valley. I had a terrible time explaining it." Frantically, Calvin dabbed at her eyes with his sleeve. "I'll ask. Just don't cry anymore. But I have to warn you, I'm afraid I already know what the answer will be."

He gazed down at Dora, shook his head, then shimmered out of sight. As he disappeared into the celestial cosmos, she could hear him muttering to himself, "I should not have to be subjected to this embarrassment. I've always been a good angel, always done my job without complaint, always made sure the Department of Celestial Maintenance ran with all the accuracy of the tick of time."

Dora stared at the spot in the sky where Calvin had disappeared. Hope filled her heart. She dragged her gaze to the Earth Pool and looked into its smooth surface. With any luck, she would soon be down there taking part in the lives of the people she so envied.

Since the Archangels did not really favor sending angels to Earth, and because of his fear of reprisal, Calvin more than likely might not present the most convincing argument, Dora thought, and her hope faded quickly. In all probability, she would be condemned to spending eternity up here among the clouds.

She sneezed and her halo slipped sideways.

After tucking in his six-year-old niece for the night, Tony Falcone returned to the kitchen. His next-door neighbor, Millie Sullivan, put away the last of the freshly-washed supper dishes. Her flushed face, surrounded by a halo of black curls, screwed up in a frown of concentration as she worked to slide the clean casserole dish back into her tote bag.

"Thanks for the lasagna, Millie. It wasn't necessary, you know. I can take care of feeding Penny and myself."

Millie shook her head and waved a dismissing hand. "I had to cook for two anyway. What's two more? Besides," she added, throwing him a mildly reprimanding look, "that child's told me about the meals you fix for her." She made a *tsking* sound and shook her head. "Poor baby. Hot dogs and beans, cereal, chili dogs, pizza. What nutritional value can she get from all that junk food? Your sister . . . God rest her soul," she made the sign of the cross on her chest, "would turn over in her grave if she could see it."

Millie had been his sister's neighbor for five years. From the time Rosalie and her husband had found their house and bought it, Millie had been a good friend and neighbor, part of what Rosalie had always viewed as the miracle that surrounded the purchase of this house.

When Rosalie and Matt had inquired about the house, they'd been told that, despite the *For Sale* sign on the front lawn, it had already been purchased by another couple, and the real estate agent had forgotten to remove the sign. Oddly enough, two days later without warning or reason, the couple had withdrawn their down payment and moved cross-country. Rosalie had always believed that, knowing how much she wanted this particular house, Heavenly intervention had made it all possible. Tony, on the other hand, had attributed it to being at the right place at the right time.

After the car crash that had killed the little girl's parents, Tony had moved in to care for his niece. That was when Millie had shown up and, feeling it her duty, had taken on the task of caring for Tony and Penny. Though Tony was grateful, Millie sometimes got on his nerves with her well-meaning advice. He didn't need to be reminded of what a lousy job he was doing taking care of Penny, not when he already realized it every day. But he usually smiled and said nothing.

Millie meant well. She loved kids, and if she had any regrets about her life with her husband, they could all be boiled down into one thing: Millie was barren and, as a result, she and Preston had never been able to have any children of their own. Tony believed the world had become Millie's child to care for, guide, and feed well.

Still, her good-hearted prodding sometimes got under Tony's skin.

Tony was trying his level best to do what was right for Penny, but having no previous experience with children made it tough. What made it even tougher was that Penny never complained, so Tony constantly entertained doubts as to whether or not he was doing the right thing. He'd tried to do what he thought Rosalie would have wanted, but without his sister to guide him . . .

Determinedly he pushed aside thoughts of Rosalie. It had been a little less than a year since her death, and she would never give him advice again. Dwelling on it still hurt too much.

Tony enveloped his neighbor's slight shoulders in a hug. "You worry too much. Penny loves the meals I prepare for her, and I make sure she takes her vitamins every morning just in case. We're fine."

But were they really fine? Oh, maybe Penny was. A quiet, obedient child who enjoyed playing alone in her room, she seemed to be adjusting much better than Tony to the loss of her parents. Millie's words right after the funeral—*Children heal fast; thank God, they forget much easier than we do, and they have little trouble getting on with their lives*—had been prophetic.

Though Penny still had moments when the loss of her parents crept up on her—and Tony could see those moments by the sadness in her eyes—such incidents were becoming more and more rare, even if she wasn't able to talk about them. That had to be a good sign.

Tony was another matter. When he'd lost his sister, he'd lost his best friend, his mentor, and his surrogate mother.

He'd been told that Penny needed to live in familiar surroundings. So he'd sold his condo and his business, packed up his life, and left Georgia to come back to upstate New York and move into Rosalie's eight-room, rambling, colonial house. He'd accepted that. What had come as part of the package, he was finding harder to accept.

Until Rosalie's death, he'd never expected to be responsible for raising his niece. There were so many things about the responsibilities entailed in caring for a little girl that were beyond the comprehension of a confirmed bachelor. There were little challenges he hadn't counted on and simply could not seem to get the hang of. Bottom line was, he was just no good at coping with the needs of this little girl.

Maybe, if Penny had been a boy . . .

Hell, who was he trying to kid? The sex of the child wouldn't have mattered at all. Truth was, boy or girl, he'd never expected to be responsible for raising *any* child. Aside from Millie, he was on his own, and she had a sick husband to tend to, so relying on her too much was out of the question. Aside from Penny's invalid paternal grandparents, Tony was the only other relative Penny had left, so taking care of her had fallen to him. Of course, there was Lisa, Matt's sister. But no one in the family had seen or heard from her since she'd walked out of rehab after only a week, and that was years ago.

Having to be Penny's caregiver hadn't seemed like a big thing at the time of the accident. After all Penny's was Rosalie's blood, and he owed his sister that much. She'd raised him, taken on the task of being a mother after theirs passed away, and gave up her life to work two jobs to send him through college.

Not until he'd actually arrived here and realized the enormity of the task he'd taken on, did it fully hit him how totally unprepared he was to look after his niece. That had been a little less than a year ago, and things had not gotten better. If anything, they'd gotten measurably worse.

In his defense, kids and marriage had never been high on his list of must-dos. He'd enjoyed the freedom of his bachelor lifestyle. No one to report to. No one to worry about. No one to—

"Have you done any Christmas shopping?" Millie's voice cut into his thoughts. "Penny'll be expecting a visit from Santa, you know. You only have four weeks. And what about a tree? She'll definitely expect a tree." Tony could almost hear her brain ticking off the items on her mental to-do list. "Aren't Rosalie's decorations in the attic?"

Christmas? Presents? A tree?

Damn! With everything else going on in his life, he'd forgotten all about the upcoming holiday. Tony ran his fingers through his hair. Just what he needed, one more problem to add to the growing list.

What did he buy a six-year-old for Christmas? He'd never had a problem with one birthday present or one Christmas present for Penny. Now, he'd have to make sure that on Christmas morning more than one gift was under the tree, not to mention stuffing a stocking, planning a Christmas dinner and cooking it, and putting on a holiday face. The mountain of problems he was facing just seemed to keep getting higher and higher. But there was one that he didn't have to add to the list.

"I brought my aluminum tree with me when I moved here. Rosalie's in-laws gave it to me when they moved out West."

"Aluminum?" Millie's disapproving frown spoke volumes. She clicked her tongue disparagingly. "I haven't seen one of them for almost fifty years. I thought they died along with the hippies and the Beat Generation." She shook her head. "No. Trust me, Tony, the child needs a *real* tree, one that makes the house smell like Christmas. Not a decorated replica of the Tin Man from *The Wizard of Oz*."

Tony sighed. "The aluminum tree will be fine. Besides, trees and Christmas presents are the least of my worries. What Penny needs more than a real tree is a woman's touch. Now that she's started school, she needs someone who knows how to handle a little girl, someone who can pick out her clothes and comb her hair."

He dropped into the closest kitchen chair and recalled his disastrous attempt at braiding Penny's long, copper curls the previous morning. It had taken hours to untangle her hair, and the whole incident had upset her so much, she'd ended up missing school that day. Which meant he'd had to stay home with her and have his foreman oversee the work at the Falcone Builders' construction site, something that had been happening all too frequently lately.

He leaned back and emptied his cup of coffee in one long swallow.

"You know you can call on me whenever you need help."

Tony patted Millie's hand. "I know. You've been a big help and for that you have my undying gratitude, but you have your own burdens to see to. Besides, I need someone who will live here all the time so I don't have to worry about Penny. I've been leaving a lot of my construction business in my foreman's hands. I'm lucky Jake's a good man. But I can't keep doing that."

Millie sighed, untied her flowered apron, and folded it neatly before sliding it into the tote bag with the casserole dish. Then she sat across from him. "Have you thought about getting a full-time, live-in nanny to see to Penny?"

Tony went to the side counter, removed the glass carafe from the coffeemaker, and refilled his cup. He sipped the lukewarm liquid, made a face, then set the mug aside. "Yes, I have. In fact, Jake's sister gave me the name of an agency." He reached into his back pocket and extracted his wallet. Opening it, he fumbled through it until he found a slightly dog-eared business card. He studied it for a moment, then tossed the card on the table and sighed. "I don't know what to do. These people are strangers. Besides, I'm not sure I can afford to pay a nanny."

"You can't always put a dollar sign on things. Sometimes we can't look at how much it will cost to do something, but rather how much it will cost *not* to do it." Millie picked up the card, read it, and then beamed. "Ah, *Angel Guardians*. How bad can they be with a name like that? I've got a good feeling right here about this, Tony." She placed a hand over her heart, her signal that her *feeling* came with some phantom, absolute approval. Most probably the angels she put such stock in. "You need to call them tomorrow."

A slow smile spread across his lips. His trusting neighbor believed devoutly in angels. Her house bore witness to it with the many ceramic statues of the celestial beings that occupied shelves and tables. She swore that each human had an angel in the wings to help when things got rough. He laughed to himself. His personal angel must have been napping for the last few years. She hadn't been helping him, that's for sure.

Well, his Guardian Angel might be sleeping on the job, but Tony knew if he didn't agree to call, Millie would nag him into eternity about it. Then again, the company *had* come highly recommended by his foreman's sister. As much as Tony hated to admit it, his neighbor's wise words about cost-versus-need hit the nail right on the head. Penny needed a woman in her life, and he needed to get back to his business full-time. If he had to tighten his belt to do it, then he would. He'd just have to find a way to pay for it.

"All right, I'll call them in the morning."

Only moments passed before Calvin reappeared out of the cosmos. Dora's wings trembled in nervous anticipation of his answer. When he remained silent for what seemed like forever, she could wait no longer. "Well?"

Calvin stroked his strong, square jaw. His wings' feathers, which had been in total chaos, slowly rearranged themselves, but even then, some remained protruding, a sure sign that what he had to tell her troubled him. Her stomach dropped below the cloud cover. She feared the news was bad and that the Council had turned down her request.

Finally, Calvin cleared his throat and said, "You can become a mortal."

Dora felt happy tears gathering in her eyes. She couldn't recall the last time she'd felt so elated. The tears began to flow in earnest. When she saw the alarmed expression spreading over Calvin's face, she blinked them back.

"Now, wait. It isn't all good news. The Heavenly Council said you can go down below—"

Dora didn't care if there was bad news, too. Right now, all she could concentrate on was that her dream was about to come true. She was going down to live among the mortals. No longer able to contain her happiness, she let out a whoop of joy that vibrated through the sky, displacing several clouds and tossing off the angels inhabiting them. At first they looked angry, but when they saw it was only Dora, they merely shook their heads.

"Sorry," she called sheepishly.

They sent her an understanding smile and then fluttered off to another cloud, one safely beyond the reach of her emotional reactions.

Calvin scowled at her. "If I might finish . . ."

"Of course." She sat down on the fluffy cloud, then folded her hands in her lap and tried not to fidget.

"They said you may go below, but only until Christmas Eve. At the stroke of midnight, you will return here with no arguments." He paused. "Agreed?"

Four Earth weeks hardly seemed time enough to do all she wanted to do, see all she wanted to see, but she nodded, taking what she could get.

"Very well. While you're there, since you may need some of them, your . . . uh . . . special angelic talents will be limited." He paced in front of her, making the cloud wobble precariously. Dora clutched the edge to keep from toppling off. "I will be your contact, and Grace will stand in for me if I'm not available, just in case you need me for anything and to make sure all . . . goes smoothly." He frowned at her, and then glanced around, as though checking to make sure he would not be overheard, and turned back to her.

"This part is very important. While you are there, you will have a limited history of a life on Earth, last name, social security number, driver's license, birth certificate, and such. We've found sending angels down there in human form without all our ducks in a row can cause innumerable problems. Humans are so inquisitive, and so set on living through forms and documents. I've heard one can't do anything down there without the proper related papers." He clucked his tongue and shook his head. "If they spent half as much time worrying about their fellow human beings as they do about whether their driver's license is current—" He stopped and dismissed the rest of his thought with a sharp wave of his hand. "That's not my department."

Dora could hold back her excitement no longer. She shot to her feet. "When do I leave?" The cloud tipped and swayed. Calvin extended his arms and swung them like an airplane propeller to keep his balance.

When he was sure he wouldn't topple off, he continued with his instructions. "You'll leave immediately after your briefing. While you're there, you will work with a family who is sorely in need of guidance." He took Dora's shoulders in his large hands. "There are two things you must remember. If you're successful in this, there's a good chance there will be a promotion to Guardian Angel in it for you."

The thought of a promotion to Guardian Angel didn't come close to exciting her a fraction as much as going to Earth. Dora grinned and started to pull away, anxious to get started. Calvin's grip tightened.

"This is the most important thing you have to

remember. You're young, impressionable, and inexperienced. Mortals have a way about them that . . . Well, suffice to say, take care in your dealings with them. Do not, I repeat, *do not* get emotionally attached to any humans, and under no circumstances are they to know that you're an angel."

Half-listening, Dora nodded vigorously, while she danced in place, waiting for a sign that Calvin was done with his list of conditions. He wasn't.

"I cannot emphasize this enough. If you violate any of the terms of your transition to mortal form, Dora, when you return here, there will be dire repercussions. *Dire.*"

A tiny chill of foreboding chased down her spine, but she ignored it. Before Calvin could find more reasons to detain her, she raced off to report for her briefing and then the final preparations for her long-awaited transformation to mortal form.

❖ ❖ ❖

Tony answered the doorbell and found a woman standing there. Could this be the first candidate for the nanny position? He checked his watch. The agency said she should arrive around this time.

He blinked. With the sun behind her, she was totally surrounded by a glowing bright light. He couldn't see her face, but he could see the delightful outline of her body in silhouette, and delightful it was in every way. He took a deep breath and knew that his reaction had nothing to do with Penny's neglected needs and more to do with his own.

A distant rumble of thunder broke the silence, and just then a large dark cloud seemed to appear from nowhere to cover the sun.

The woman extended her hand and smiled up at him with eyes the color of a velvety night. "Hi, I'm Dora DeAngelo."

That smile and her voice did things to his insides that made his head light and his heart thump loudly in his ears. The thunder rolled again, this time closer. Tony glanced at the one dark cloud hanging almost directly above them. *A thunderstorm in the dead of winter?* He shrugged. *Crazy weather.*

"I'm here to apply for the nanny job." Another rumble of thunder pounded overhead.

"Hi. Thanks for coming so quickly." Another ominous rumble came from above. He glanced heavenward again. "You'd better come in. I think the sky's about to open up."

He shoved the door wider and stepped aside to allow her passage. Before she slid past him, she looked questioningly at the sky and then frowned. As she moved through the doorway, he inhaled a fragrance he'd never smelled before, one that made him think of summers at the lake with Rosalie mixed with the perfume of those large, pink flowers she cut from her garden every spring and put in the middle of the dining room table.

He shook his head and pulled back from the memories, both physically and mentally. This was ridiculous. He had to keep his mind on Penny and get himself under control before he scared Dora away in the interview.

Dora walked into what she expected to be a disheveled living room cluttered with a child's toys and games. To her surprise, the room was immaculate, not a thing out of place, not a speck of dirt or dust to be found. *Unlived in* came to mind. Where were the signs that a six-year-old lived here . . . for that matter, that *anyone* lived here?

She tucked that thought away for the moment and looked around her, fascinated by finally being inside one of the houses she'd been seeing for so long in the Earth Pool. Tentatively, she touched the dark green fabric of a wingback chair. So solid, so strong. Nothing like the insubstantial, ethereal clouds she was used to. She looked up to find the man watching her, a faint smile barely curving his full lips.

"Your home is lovely," she said in explanation of her inspection.

"Thanks." He glanced around as though to confirm

her assessment of the house. "I can't take the credit, I'm afraid. My sister always had a good eye for decorating. She did all of this." He waved his hand to encompass the room.

For the first time, Dora concentrated on him. A tingle tripped up her spine. She'd heard some of the angels telling stories about the Greek and Roman gods, and she was sure this man was what they meant by *handsome*. His dark, wavy hair framed his face and brought into prominence his deep-chocolate brown eyes. Sad eyes. Eyes that seemed to carry no life in their depths. But she saw one other thing . . . fear. Why fear and of what?

Then she remembered what she'd been told in her briefing. He had lost his sister and had been left to raise his niece on his own. He had no previous experience with children. Perhaps the fear stemmed from the idea of having to raise this child by himself? Then again, maybe he just feared life.

He moved closer and, when confronted by his physical appearance, her troubled thoughts vanished. Instead, her attention centered on the man.

His blue work shirt's sleeves bulged with the muscles hidden beneath the material, and his square jaw announced his strength of will and determination. Why then did he look so . . . defeated? He smiled, but there was no joy in the expression. Nevertheless, it had the power to send a new and unfamiliar warmth coursing through Dora's body.

Outside the thunder grew louder. She glanced out the window. Calvin. How was she to do her job if he kept reminding her that she was just an angel? If she was to blend in with these mortals and help them, then she had to behave as they would. She ignored the following rumble from the sky.

"Please, sit down so we can talk." The man gestured to the sofa, and Dora took a seat. She gave a little bounce, enjoying the firmness of the furniture beneath her. She leaned sideways, testing to see if it would tip and throw her off as the clouds often did. To her delight, no matter how much she moved, the furniture remained stationary.

The man sat across from her in the wingback chair. Leaning forward, he rested his arms on his thighs. "We might as well get right to it. I'm sure the agency already told you that I'm Tony Falcone. I need a nanny to look after my niece, Penny. It'll be a live-in job, and I'll expect you to cook and clean as well as take care of the laundry." He paused as if waiting for her to object.

"That's fine," she said.

He seemed surprised. "You'll dress Penny, do her hair, feed her breakfast and drive her to school each morning, and pick her up at the end of the day."

Dora nodded and smiled, although the word *drive*

caused a shiver of apprehension to shimmer up her spine. Then she recalled that Calvin promised she would have every skill she had to have when the need arose. Still, the idea of actually getting behind the wheel of one of those cars filled her with dread.

"Unfortunately, I can't afford to pay you much," he went on, rousing Dora from her troubled thoughts.

"I have little need for a lot of money, Mr. Falcone. Whatever you can pay will be adequate."

He released a sigh and leaned back in the chair looking relieved. "I'm not much on formalities. Please, call me Tony." He went silent for a moment, his brows furrowed in thought. "I guess all that's left is for me to see your references?"

References?

Calvin hadn't said anything about references. She didn't even know what this reference thing was. She must have been staring blankly at Tony.

"Could that be it?" He smiled and pointed to the sofa cushion beside her.

She gazed down and found a black purse at her side with a white envelope protruding from it. As she pulled the envelope out, she read *References* written across the front in a black scrawl.

Calvin's words rang through her mind. *I've heard one can't do anything down there without the proper papers.*

With an apologetic smile, she removed the envelope and passed it to Tony. As he opened it and scanned through the sheets, she watched his face for a reaction. He studied the words with a concentration that might have been compared to a government official studying a peace treaty with a warring power. His strong hands deftly turned each page and tucked it behind the others as he read. A wave of midnight-black hair fell forward on his brow. An unexpected itch to push it back, to see if it was as silky as it looked, jarred her with its intensity.

Outside, the thunder rumbled angrily. Again, she ignored it.

At one point he glanced up at her, and she could see an easing of the worry lines etched across his handsome face. But she knew it would take more than a few words on paper to completely erase them and the darkened circles beneath his eyes. Her heart twisted in her chest, and a deep longing to ease his pain raced through her.

After a few minutes had passed, he refolded the sheets, stuck them back in the envelope, and handed it to her. "Your references are excellent. If you want the job, Ms. DeAngelo, it's yours. When can you start?"

"Right now," she said, happy that he looked a bit more at ease. "And I'm not much for formalities, either. Please, call me Dora."

"But don't you need to get your things, Dora?"

"I brought everything I'll need with me. My things are right out there." She indicated the front door.

He rose, walked to the door, and opened it. There, right beside the welcome mat, were two brown suitcases. Tony tried to recall seeing them when he'd first opened the door to her. He replayed her arrival in his mind and then decided that the sun had been so bright behind her, and he'd been so preoccupied with his sensual reaction to her, that he must not have noticed the bags.

Grabbing the suitcases, he pulled them inside the foyer. A warm awareness spread down his left side, and he realized she had come to stand beside him. He moved away from her magnetic beauty. Right then he decided that making a pass at her, no matter how enticing he found her to be, could mean disaster. He needed her to look after Penny, and he couldn't take the chance of losing her simply because his testosterone had risen to a new and alarming level.

An hour later, Dora was settled into a charming bedroom at the top of the stairs, complete with a canopied bed covered with a colorful patchwork quilt and a washstand with a blue and white Delft bowl and pitcher. The filmy, white tiebacks framing the two large windows reminded her of clouds, except, when they moved, they didn't throw off little wisps of vapor.

A tall mirror with an ornate frame hung on the wall. She was able to see herself from head to toe in it, and she took great delight in examining this unfamiliar attire that she'd been given before she left. Jeans hugged her slim hips and a bright yellow sweater clung to her upper torso, accentuating pert breasts. White running shoes encased her feet. She turned to get a full perspective and found she rather liked what she saw. Her angel robe's shapelessness hid the woman beneath. Not so the mortal attire. With these clothes, no one would ever guess her true identity. That was one of Calvin's cautions she wouldn't have to worry about.

Since Tony had hurried off to pick Penny up at school, a chore that would fall to her after today, she unpacked and stowed her suitcases in the closet and her clothing in the dresser, and decided to explore.

Back downstairs, Dora walked through the room in which Tony had interviewed her and into a homey, immaculate dining room, complete with a lovely, honey pine table, six chairs, and a hutch showcasing snowy, milk glass dinnerware. The kitchen, located at the back of the house, was much like the living room and dining room had been—immaculate and overly tidy.

No dirty dishes filled the sink and no fingerprints

marred the glow of the countertop's matted shine or the fronts of the glowing appliances. No child's drawings were secured on the refrigerator with colorful magnets as Dora had seen in other houses while gazing into the Earth Pool. The kitchen, designed like one that had been used in colonial days, held all the modern appliances mortals relied on to get through a day of providing three meals for a family. Each appliance was carefully concealed behind pine doors with black, strap, wrought-iron hinges.

From observing the mortals in the Earth Pool, she already knew the function of most of the appliances. The toaster took pieces of white bread and made them brown and hot enough to melt butter. The refrigerator kept food fresh and cold. The stove cooked the food, and the dishwasher cleaned the dishes when the meal was done.

But she didn't recognize the machine holding a large, glass cylinder with a handle on its side and a lid on top. The cylinder sat atop a base that had an array of buttons across the front. Experimenting, she pushed one of the buttons. The machine came to life with a deafening roar. It vibrated and shook while a silver thing spun madly in the bottom. Frantically, Dora sought for a way to silence the machine. She pushed another button. The machine only grew louder and more aggressive.

It's called a blender, Calvin's familiar voice whispered in her mind. *Press the button marked* OFF.

Obediently and with a large measure of relief, she pushed the last button and the machine went silent. Though she appreciated the help, a small part of her resented Calvin's interference. Was he going to watch every move she made? She certainly hoped not. This was her mission, and, sink or swim, she wanted to do it alone.

Nevertheless, she thought, *Thank you, Calvin.*

Heaving a sigh of relief, she decided that she would push no more buttons until she became better acquainted with what the result would be.

Slowly, she strolled out of the kitchen and into the hall that provided passage from the front door to the rooms at the back of the house. Halfway down the hall, a small side table stood beside a large mirror exactly like the one in her room. She stopped to run her fingertips over the surface of the table, enjoying the solid feel of the dark wood beneath her touch. It was nothing like the ethereal clouds, more like the firmness she had imagined could be found in the muscles that pressed against the material of Tony's shirt.

Thunder rumbled outside. Dora rolled her eyes at the ceiling and shook her head.

Ready to move on to do more exploring, she glanced in the mirror and came to a screeching halt. She looked down at herself to confirm she still wore the yellow sweater, sneakers, and jeans Calvin had assured her were age-appropriate for a young woman on Earth.

Hesitantly, she raised her gaze to her reflection in the mirror. Gone were her Earth clothes, the dark tresses, and the brown eyes the Angel of Transition had given her. Dora the angel looked back at her, complete with white-blond hair, blue eyes, halo, wings, and robe.

CHAPTER 2

"Disaster. I knew it," Calvin mumbled into the Earth Pool as the roar of the blender in the Falcone kitchen subsided into silence.

"What disaster?"

He turned to find Dora's best friend, Grace, standing at his elbow and peering over his shoulder. Wringing his hands, his wing feathers protruding every which way, he shook his head and paced the cloud.

"You need to ask? Dora, of course. She's so preoccupied with the . . . material things that she's given little or no thought to the emotional problems facing Tony and little Penny. This is going to be another of Dora's disasters. Only instead of looking for a place to happen, she's found it."

The Head of Celestial Maintenance ran his hands through his mop of snowy hair. His halo tilted and slid off, slicing through the cloud and disappearing from sight. Grace launched herself over the edge, wings flapping confidently, and reappeared moments later with the lost halo clutched in her hand.

"Thank you." Calvin set it back in place, then resumed his pacing, stirring up large puffs of cloud as he turned and headed back to retrace his steps. "I just knew I would regret this. Her antics will have me consigned for eternity to—"

"Calvin." Grace laid a calming hand on his arm, bringing his movements to a sudden halt. "You're working yourself into a lather unnecessarily. She's only been down there for a few hours. Give her time to acclimate. She's really a bright girl. She'll do fine."

Calvin huffed. "You always stick up for her. To tell you the truth, Grace, I'm surprised you can say that after what happened with your wing feathers."

Grace shook her head, sending her blond ringlets into a bizarre dance around her cherubic face. "It was a small mistake."

"Small? Mistake?" The benevolent attitude of Grace in respect to Dora's *small mistakes,* as she called them, baffled Calvin, especially when Grace had been on the receiving end.

His wings' feathers popped out around him like buds opening on a warm, sunny spring day. Calvin frowned.

"I wish I had your confidence."

"Dora has a good heart and an extraordinary understanding of humans and their needs that has helped more than one Guardian Angel out of a tough spot. Just last Valentine's Day she helped Faith bring that lovely Anderson couple back together." She smiled gently. "Give her a chance to prove herself." When the frown between his eyes remained, she added, "If the Heavenly Council had enough confidence in her to agree to this, then you should, too." She smiled gently, patted his arm once more, and fluttered off into the cosmos, leaving Calvin with his misgivings and visions of his uncertain future.

He hadn't told Grace or Dora, but the Heavenly Council had been waiting for Dora's request, and despite what he'd intimated to Dora, they'd been eager to allow her to take this trip to Earth. They hadn't shared with him why, but he had his suspicions.

It was because of him, Calvin, Head of Celestial Maintenance . . . for now. They had gotten word of Dora's disastrous past performances, and they were going to judge him by how well Dora carried out her assigned task below. If she did well, perhaps she wouldn't be the only one moving up the celestial promotion ladder. However, if she failed, he could already hear the deafening rumble of the thunderclouds he'd be tending and the sharp edge of the lightning bolts he'd be polishing for the rest of eternity. He sighed. How had his entire heavenly career ended up in the hands of one inept angel?

He would simply have to keep a wary eye on Dora and hope he could head off trouble before it started.

At that very moment, Dora's thoughts wafted heavenward.

Would his hair feel as smooth as this wood? Would his muscles be as firm as the wood beneath my fingertips? Would—?

Calvin snatched up the thoughts and squeezed them in his fist until they disintegrated into nothing more than a wispy *poof*. The last thing he needed was Dora's wayward thoughts drifting helter-skelter around the heavenly cosmos. More importantly, he didn't need them to reach the Hall of Prayers and the ears of the Heavenly Council. He sighed. Even in heaven's abbreviated time frame, this was going to be a very long four weeks.

Setting his face in a stern expression, he leaned over the edge of the Earth Pool.

Dora blinked and looked into the hall mirror again. A white ball of light appeared over her right shoulder and grew, until it took the form of Calvin, his normally smooth features compressed into a disapproving frown, his wing feathers a total mess.

"I'm going to remind you once more . . . do *not* get attached to the mortals."

His scolding tone brought the hackles on Dora's neck to attention. "I am not getting attached." She glared mutinously at his reflection in the mirror.

"What do you call speculating about Mr. Falcone's . . . physical attributes?" Calvin crossed his arms over his chest and arched one pale eyebrow in challenge. She knew if she could see his foot, it would be tapping the cloud aggressively.

Dora frowned. He was reading a great deal into some innocent musings. "I call it familiarizing myself with my charges."

"Hmm. Just be certain you don't *overfamiliarize* yourself."

She huffed impatiently. "Honestly, Calvin, if you're going to monitor everything I do and think, how am I supposed to do what needs doing?"

His arched eyebrow straightened, then dipped in unison with the other into a no-nonsense scowl. "Need I remind you of your past performances?"

Pouting her lips, she shook her head. "No, you don't. But, please, it's very important to me that I do this on my own."

For a moment, he considered her request. "Very well. I'll step back . . . just a little, mind you. If you need me, call, and if it's something we need to discuss at length, come to this mirror." He started to shimmer out, but stopped mid-shimmer. "You might want to look into this mirror from time to time, just as a reminder of who you are and why you're there, but be careful the mortals aren't around. We don't want them to see you as an angel."

"Will this," she waved her hand at their images, "happen whenever I see my reflection in anything?"

Calvin shook his head. "No, just in this mirror."

If he was so concerned that no one saw her as an angel, why had he picked a mirror positioned in the center of the downstairs of the house with so much traffic, rather than its twin, which hung in the privacy of her bedroom? She started to ask just that, but the front door opened, and Calvin shimmered out of sight.

Dora turned to find Tony and a small girl standing in the hallway. Hiding partially behind Tony's leg, the child stared at her with large, green, frightened eyes. The color of her bright red coat collided with the copper-colored hair peeking from beneath her white knit hat. The coat gaped open to reveal a white blouse half in and half out of the band of a green and navy blue, plaid skirt. An overstuffed, heavy-looking backpack with fluffy, gray elephant ears dug deeply into her slim shoulders.

"Hello, you must be Penny," Dora said quietly.

Squatting to the child's eye level, she held out her hand. "I'm Dora."

Penny turned her big green eyes to the man towering above her, silently asking permission to accept Dora's greeting. Dora followed the child's gaze.

"Say hello, Penny. Dora is your nanny, and she'll be in charge of things while I'm at work." While not stern or mean in any way, Tony's tone was hardly what Dora would have expected from a loving uncle to a hesitant, obviously nervous six-year-old. More like one that he'd use to address a business associate.

Penny turned back to Dora. "Hello," she said, barely above a whisper. Cautiously, she let Dora enfold her small hand.

The child's touch brought an array of emotions surging through Dora: apprehension, confusion, and the strongest ones of all—loneliness, and oddly enough . . . guilt.

"Why don't you take that heavy backpack off and put it over there so it'll be ready for you to take with you tomorrow morning?" Dora smiled, and pointed to a spot on the floor beside the hall table.

"That would just clutter up the hallway. Besides, I have homework to do in my room." Penny twisted her hand free.

Dora wondered how such adult words could come from such a small child. There would be time enough to speculate on that later. Right now she wanted to spend some time with her new charge. "Why don't you bring it out to the kitchen table? I can make you a snack, and you can keep me company while I make supper."

Supper? She hadn't thought about that. Did she know how to cook?

I told you, you'll have what skills you need when you need them, Calvin reassured her.

She sighed in relief and turned her attention back to the child.

As she started toward the stairs, Penny's step hesitated. "A snack?" She glanced at her uncle again, longing evident in her eyes.

Tony removed his coat and hung it in the hall closet before speaking. "Penny doesn't have snacks before meals. It ruins her appetite." He turned to his niece. "Take your things upstairs and get started on your homework."

"Yes, Uncle Tony."

Dora stepped forward. "May I come with you? I haven't seen your room yet." When Penny nodded silently, Dora followed her up the stairs.

Tony watched the pair ascend. He fought the urge to call them back and tell them that he wanted to go into the kitchen and have that snack with them, to sit around the table like he and Rosalie used to do and share their day's events, to become a real family again, but he couldn't. He'd been a family with Rosalie and lost her, then ended up experiencing more pain than he ever dreamed he could bear and still live. He just couldn't open himself to that kind of agony again, not even for his beloved niece.

Besides, she had Dora now. Dora would be good for Penny, and for more than just having a woman around to fix her hair and pick out her clothes and all the other *girl* things Penny needed. She'd be someone for Penny to talk to about her parents. Something Tony found impossible to do.

He glanced at the spot on the staircase where they had disappeared from sight. His mind played over the image of Dora's swaying hips and dark, silky hair. Then he shook away the vision. He really needed to get himself under control. He couldn't afford to lose Dora and he would if he kept drooling over her and scared her away. Penny needed her. He needed her, and his infant construction business needed his attention. He could no longer divide himself between Penny and his job and hope to be successful at either.

Starting up a fledgling business in a new area hadn't been easy. That he'd gotten this project at all had been a stroke of good luck. Completing it meant the difference between success and failure. As such, the Jefferson project had to come in on time. If it did, he could sit back and relax a bit. His business would be on solid footing at last, and he would be able to look forward to more such lucrative projects.

Upstairs, Dora entered Penny's bedroom. Penny set her backpack on a chair in front of a neatly arranged desk. She took off her coat and hung it in the closet. Dora looked around. As with the rooms downstairs, Penny's was clean and tidy.

A four-poster, white bed stood against the far wall, its flower-bedecked coverlet neatly pulled over the pillows and tucked under. A brown teddy bear, a lavender bunny, and a green stuffed turtle sat propped against the pillows. A spotless, white rug covered the polished pine floor. The room looked like something in a furniture showroom. Certainly not like a room a six-year-old girl lived and played in.

"Your room is lovely," Dora said in an attempt to get Penny to talk to her. She walked to a series of shelves hanging above the dresser that held about a dozen dolls. "Are all these yours?" She picked up one with a yellow dress and long black curls.

Penny removed it from her hand and replaced it. "Thank you." Returning to her desk, she pulled a book from her backpack and then a notebook. "I have to do my homework," she said and sat down, flipped open the book, and picked a pencil from the holder on the desk.

Though Penny's tone had not been in the least rude, Dora felt as if she'd been summarily dismissed from the room. "Of course you do. I have to go start supper."

She let herself out, closed the door, and stood in the hall for a while. To her mental to-do list she added, *Teach Penny to be a child.*

Thoughts of his business had driven Tony to the wall phone in the kitchen. He picked up the receiver and dialed a number from memory. The phone rang twice before his foreman, Jake Armstrong, snapped, "Falcone Builders."

Tony cringed. "Jake, what's up?"

A deep sigh came through the wires. "The lumber was just delivered."

"And?" Tony held his breath and waited.

"The boards are all *checked.*"

A load of split wood. Damn, just what they didn't need.

"We'll have to send the whole load back. It's gonna really screw with the schedule." A background voice called Jake's name. Jake barked an order, and then a door slammed. "Damn. I can't even get two minutes for a phone call without someone needing something."

Guilt swamped Tony. Jake should not be carrying this extra load. He had enough to do supervising the laborers, and Jake was right, waiting for another delivery of lumber would put the project behind. As it was, with this change in the weather, making the building's completion date would be close, too close. They already had two feet of snow on the ground, and the weatherman had promised more that night. If anything else went wrong . . .

"I'll be right there."

"Great." Relief echoed from Jake's voice, but concern replaced it quickly. "What about Penny?"

"I hired a nanny today from that company your sister recommended. This woman is heaven-sent. I think she's going to solve my problems. I'll be able to spend much more time at the site. But this new twist with the lumber is the last thing we needed." Tony ran an agitated hand through his hair. "If we have to wait for another delivery, we'll need a miracle to make that deadline."

"Tell me about it." Jake paused. "Tony, this new nanny . . . is she a likely prospect?" A hint of teasing colored his voice.

A heavy, exasperated sigh escaped Tony. Jake's determination to get him hitched was wearing thin. "The nanny's a knockout, but that's all I'm saying. Now, get your mind back on business, and I'll see you in a little while."

Tony hung up the phone and turned to find Dora standing in the doorway. Her dark, velvety gaze held his. Damn, a man could crawl into those eyes and forget his troubles in their inky depths. She blinked, and he could feel his nerves loosen. Then he felt a surge of warmth. He flinched. He'd never met a woman who could send such sensations coursing through his entire being without touching him. He suddenly wanted to forget she was Penny's nanny and just sit down and talk with her. Since Rosalie's death, he hadn't *really* talked to anyone, not even Millie.

"Problem?" she asked.

He immediately jolted from his daydreams. For a split second, he thought she'd read his mind. But that was crazy. No one could read minds. She must have overheard his conversation with Jake. But how much had she heard? Had she been there when he'd called her a knockout?

Embarrassed at the idea, he averted his gaze and rubbed at an imaginary smudge on the spotless countertop. "I . . . uh . . . I have to get over to the building site. We had a bad lumber delivery." He raised his gaze to hers.

"Checked," Dora said. He raised an eyebrow. "I heard." She knew nothing of lumber and building. She smiled and licked her lips. "Why is that a problem?"

At first he tensed. Then his shoulders loosened. "Checked . . . split lumber is weak and will result in an unsafe building."

"Ah. And it will put you behind if you have to order more, and then you won't be able to be here with us . . . with Penny."

He nodded. She really wished he wouldn't do that. Every time he did, a thick wave of his hair fell over his forehead, and she had to fight down the urge to brush it back in place. She crammed her hands into her jeans pockets. "Well, then, you'd better be going."

Relief flooded his face. "Don't wait supper for me." He hurried past her, grabbed his coat, and disappeared out the front door.

Dora stared at the door for a long time, thinking about Tony's conversation with Jake and his need for a miracle. She hesitated for only a moment, glanced at the ceiling, then back to the closed front door. Grinning, she lifted her hand and waved it through the air.

"See you for supper, Mr. Falcone," she said, brushed her palms together, and then opened the refrigerator, wondering what a *knockout* was and if it was a good thing to be.

❖ ❖ ❖

As he stepped outside the construction shack, Tony slapped a yellow hard hat on his head. A cold wind blew off the river, biting painfully at his exposed face and hands. He turned up his collar and stuffed his hands into the pockets of his down-filled work jacket. Bending his head against the buffeting blast of icy air blowing off the frozen river just beyond the hills surrounding the work site, he followed Jake. Snow crunched under their feet, and the brittle crust made it a challenge to stay upright.

"Here it is," Jake said, pointing to the stack of new lumber. "Every last one has a split running anywhere from three to six inches."

Tony leaned down and picked up one of the boards. He turned it in his hand, closely inspecting the wood. "This one isn't split, Jake." He picked up another board. "Neither is this one."

Board after board proved to be in perfect shape. In fact, they had never received such a superior load of wood. Tony turned to find a questioning frown pleating his foreman's brow.

Jake stepped around Tony and removed a board from the pile, running his experienced fingers over the wood, searching for the splits. "This is nuts. These boards were split. Hank saw them, too." He stood and looked around for his second-in-command. Seeing him near the construction shack, he called to him. "Hank, come over here."

Hank ambled over. "Did you show Tony that crap the lumber company sent us?"

Without another word, Jake turned back to Tony. "Need I say more?"

When Tony pulled into his driveway in plenty of time for the supper he'd told Dora he'd miss, he still couldn't figure out what had happened to the lumber. Not for one moment did Tony doubt that Jake saw what he'd reported. So what was the explanation?

He, Jake, and Hank had discussed it at length, inspecting every board in the shipment, and none of them could come up with a reasonable explanation for why lumber that had been defective had suddenly become perfect.

They'd finally all agreed that no matter the reason, it meant the project, barring any other problems, would come in on time, and they would all be home for supper. That should please Dora, who hadn't seemed particularly happy about him missing the meal with her and Penny.

Dora. He quickly climbed out of the truck and headed for the house, suddenly very eager to see Penny's nanny.

The sound of Tony's truck pulling into the driveway brought a smile to Dora's lips. When the front door closed and he strode into the kitchen, she reminded herself to look surprised to see him.

She swung around to face him. "I thought you were going to miss supper," she said innocently.

"Things weren't as bad as I thought at the site," he said, obviously not about to try to explain the mix-up with the lumber. Dora knew he couldn't explain it to himself. How was he going to explain it to someone whom he presumed knew nothing about it? He smiled, and her stomach felt bottomless, just like it always did when Lucas, the Storm Angel, threw a rainbow across the heavens after a torrential summer rain.

Weak-kneed, Dora searched for something to hang on to. With her hand braced against the counter in front of her, she forced her lips to return his smile.

"Penny will be pleased. She seemed disappointed that you weren't coming home to eat with her."

He grabbed a can of soda from the refrigerator, flopped into a chair, popped the top, and stared at her. "Disappointed? I didn't think she'd even notice."

Shocked at his words, Dora stared back. "Didn't you know? Penny notices everything about you."

This seemed to surprise Tony. "Really? And having been here for just a matter of hours, you know this how?"

Uh-oh. This bit of information had been part of the briefing Calvin had given Dora before she came down to Earth.

She shrugged. "Just an educated hunch I've developed from working with children."

Hunch. She liked that word and had heard many humans use it as an evasion tactic. It seemed to work. Tony sipped his soda and let the subject drop. Either that or he just didn't want to discuss Penny with her.

Tony finished his drink, crushed the can in his strong fingers, and threw it in the recycling bin beside the trash basket. He paused next to the stove and sniffed the aromas coming from the oven. "Smells delicious. How long before dinner? I want to take a shower."

Dora stared at him. She'd found a recipe in one of the books for the chicken and cheese casserole, but had never checked to see how long it would take to bake.

Thirty minutes. The voice came from inside her head.

Thank you, Calvin.

You really need to start acting more like a mortal if you're to complete this assignment successfully, he scolded.

"I will," Dora said in exasperation.

"Will what?" Tony was staring at her as if she'd grown an extra head.

"Uh . . . I will . . . let you know. It'll be about thirty minutes."

He nodded, stared at her for a few seconds longer, and then left the room.

She waited until she heard the bathroom door close behind him. Determinedly, Dora strode into the hall. After checking to make certain the coast was clear, she stepped in front of the mirror. As before, her image as an angel peered back at her. She waited a respectable few seconds for Calvin to appear. When he didn't, she called to him in a forceful whisper.

"Calvin!"

In the mirror's sleek surface, a shiny light shimmered over her right shoulder and slowly took the form of her boss. "Yes?"

"You have to stop hovering."

"Hovering?" He frowned indignantly. "I beg your pardon. I have never hovered in all my years as an angel. Guided, instructed, educated, but never hovered."

She frowned, and her halo slid sideways. She quickly righted it. "You hovered, and you have to stop it. I have to do this on my own. Otherwise, I can't prove anything about my worth to the Heavenly Council."

For a long moment, he just stood there, arms crossed over his chest, brows knitted in a thoughtful frown. Then he straightened. "Very well, as of this moment, you are on your own." He shimmered out of sight.

Dora stared at the mirror where his image had been.

Suddenly doubts buffeted her. Had she done the right thing by asking Calvin not to interfere, or had she guaranteed her own failure?

"Did you mean that, Calvin?"

Calvin jumped. "You have to stop sneaking up on me, Grace," he said sternly to the angel standing right behind him.

"Sorry." She stepped forward into his line of vision. "Well, did you mean that?"

"What?"

"That you'd leave Dora alone to make her own decisions down there?"

He avoided her eyes. "Of course." His discomfort growing due to his blatant lie, he turned to her. "Aren't you supposed to be cleaning robes for the Christmas choir?"

For a long time, Grace stared at him. Finally, she shook her head and flew off.

He hated having to lie to Grace, but he couldn't take the chance that she'd contact Dora and tell her he would still be watching her every move and, if necessary, intervening. And with Dora, intervening had become a way of life for Calvin.

CHAPTER 3

At first, Dora concentrated her full attention on savoring her first supper as a mortal. The creamy cheese and spicy chicken caressed her palette the way the bland, celestial ambrosia never had.

If she did say so herself, she'd done an excellent job cooking her first mortal meal. Calvin had lived up to his word that whenever she needed a skill, she would have it. To her complete astonishment, cooking seemed to be one of those skills at which she excelled.

She's nearly finished her second portion of casserole, when she realized that, other than the clank of silverware against china, there had not been another sound in the cozy kitchen. The entire meal had been eaten in absolute silence. The family dinner conversations she'd listened in on at the Earth Pool, and had so looked forward to taking part in, had not happened.

Dora eased back in her chair and looked at her dinner companions. Tony, head bowed, shoveled food into his mouth like a starving man, but said nothing. Calvin had told Dora during her briefing that Tony had opted for hot dogs and pizza as the main staples of his and Penny's limited diet. On occasion, Mrs. Sullivan from next door brought over homemade pasta and sauce, but that happened only when her ailing husband felt well enough not to demand her undivided attention.

Penny, too, ate with relish, and, like her uncle, she did it in complete silence. The little girl exhibited none of the behaviors that Dora had seen from other children during the many hours she'd gazed into the Earth Pool: no talking with her mouth full, no chattering about her day at school, no filling them in on what she'd done with her friends.

Since Dora had detected Penny's deep loneliness, she'd thought the child would be delighted to have her uncle there, but if she was, she showed no sign of it. They could have been two total strangers sharing a meal.

Maybe they just needed a kick start.

"Aren't you excited that Christmas is only a few weeks away, Penny?" Dora asked.

Penny's fork paused midway to her mouth. "I guess so." She went back to eating.

Strike one.

"What do you want Santa to bring you this year?"

Penny took a sip of milk, and then said, "I haven't made my list yet."

Strike two.

"If you'd like, I can help you make out your list, and then we can take it to the mailbox together." Dora smiled at the child.

Penny shrugged. "I can do it."

Strike three.

Okay, maybe a different approach. "I noticed you don't have a tree yet. When will we be going to buy one?" she asked Tony.

He stopped eating, raised his gaze to meet hers, and then mumbled, "We won't be buying a tree. I have one already, and we'll put it up as soon as I find time to drag it down from the attic."

"The attic?" Dora was confused. She could have sworn people went to those little roped-off lots on Main Street where they sold fresh-cut fir trees. "You mean you're not getting a real tree?"

She glanced at Penny and caught the glimmer of hope that shone from her green eyes.

Tony nodded. "I don't see any sense in getting a real tree. We have a perfectly good one in the attic. It's stored in a box up there with the ornaments."

"In a box?" Dora didn't try to cover the shock in

her voice.

"It's 'lunium," Penny added. "Uncle Tony says 'lunium trees don't drop needles all over the rug. They're also flame re . . . retar . . ." She glanced at Tony for help.

"Retardant," he supplied.

"Right. That means it won't catch fire." Penny nodded sagely. "In the long run, it's much safer and cleaner. Just a wise choice all around." Then she returned to eating.

Once more, the adult-sounding words coming from the six-year-old stunned Dora. Only one thing would explain them. Penny was parroting Tony.

Despite that, Dora couldn't believe her ears. Penny seemed to accept the fact that they would not have a real tree.

An aluminum tree? Good grief, she hadn't seen any of them being used by the humans she'd watched in the Earth Pool since the fifties. Penny obviously would prefer a real tree. She deserved a fresh-cut tree, one that would fill the house with fragrances that would forever remind her of happy Christmases. She deserved a tree that would be the perfect backdrop for lights, homemade paper chains, popcorn strings, and candy canes.

Before Dora said something that would cause Calvin to send a lightning bolt crashing down on her, she bit her tongue. Fuming inwardly at the idea of having a tree made out of something in which a turkey should be cooked, she stood, gathered the dirty dishes, and stacked them in the dishwasher.

Behind her, Penny spoke softly. "I need to finish my homework. Can I be excused?"

"Yes, you *may*," Tony said. Dora heard Penny leave the room. Then she heard the sound of Tony's chair scraping across the floor. He came to stand behind her. "Great dinner, Dora."

"Thank you," she said stiffly, and moved away from him. "If you want some, the coffee is ready."

For a time, silence hung in the air. Out of the corner of her eye, she saw Tony frown and lean against the cabinet. "Is something wrong?"

Dora filled the encrusted casserole dish with liquid soap and warm water to soak, never questioning how she knew to do it. Once more she'd tapped into knowledge that waited right at her fingertips. Too bad she couldn't simply tap into a way to show Tony what he was doing to Penny.

Dora tried with every ounce of her strength to hold back the words she wanted to say, but she lost the battle. Calvin would probably bring all the fire and brimstone he could muster down on her head, but this had to be said for Penny's sake. She gathered her courage, swallowed her anger, and spoke from the heart.

Dora faced him, her gaze steady, her tone even and

clear. "I could say nothing's wrong, but that would be dishonest. Much like allowing a child to accept an aluminum tree because she's afraid to argue for what she actually wants, a real tree." She held her breath and waited for him to fire her for interfering.

Instead, he just stared at her for the longest time. "Afraid? Penny's not afraid of me."

"No, she's not afraid of you. She's afraid of *your disapproval*." Dora walked past him and out of the room.

Tony stood in the kitchen for a long time after Dora left, digesting what she'd said. Penny afraid of his disapproval? Nonsense.

Dora had to be wrong. Penny simply didn't want to share her Christmas list with a stranger, that was all. She would have to get to know Dora better before she'd confide in her. But Dora hadn't been talking about Penny's Christmas list. She'd referenced the aluminum tree. Did Penny really want a live tree?

As his sister, Rosalie, had done with him, Tony had always encouraged Penny to speak her mind and let her wants be known. So why couldn't he recall one incident when Penny had had an opinion on anything? Was she really afraid of him? If so, why?

Not once, since he'd come to live in his sister's house, had he laid a hand on the child. Like Rosalie, he didn't believe in physical punishment. Maybe, on a rare occasion, he raised his voice, but it certainly wasn't a common occurrence.

Could it just be that Penny had been a quiet, well-behaved child from day one? Perhaps it wasn't in her nature to be argumentative.

Or had she been afraid to risk his disapproval? Was Dora right?

He poured a cup of coffee and carried it to the table. Cupping the earthenware mug in his hands and inhaling the rich aroma, he stared down at the design in the plaid place mat.

Tony had to admit that when he'd come here to live, he hadn't been thrilled with the idea of raising a child, despite the fact that he loved his niece very much. Hell, he hadn't even thought about marriage, much less kids. But he'd done the best he could with the limited knowledge he had of children. But had that been a mistake? Should he have found someone in the family better equipped to raise Penny? Had he done her a disservice by taking child rearing on when he knew so little about children?

For perhaps the hundredth time, he mentally reviewed the options that had been available.

His only remaining parent had passed away when

Tony was only a little kid, which was why Rosalie, his much-older sister, had raised him, and which accounted for their closeness and his heartache at her death.

Penny's paternal grandparents had raised their son, and although they were probably much better equipped to raise Penny, Matt had been a late-in-life child and his parents lived in California. Aside from that, neither of them were in good enough health to contend with a six-year-old. And since no one knew where she was, Matt's good-for-nothing sister, Lisa, wasn't even a consideration. No, there had been no alternative decision to make. He'd done the right thing by taking on Penny's care. But had he really taken on Penny's care or had he merely moved into her home?

With the tip of his finger he traced the navy line in the place mat's plaid design and thought about the months that had passed since he'd moved into his sister's home. Friends had warned him to make as few alterations as possible to Penny's world to help her get through the loss. So he'd tried very hard not to change one aspect of the colonial house she'd known all her life as home.

He'd even tried to cook meals he thought Rosalie would have cooked. However, his culinary skills left a lot to be desired. But Penny had eaten the food put before her without a complaint.

Tony sipped his coffee, and then suddenly straightened. Why? Why hadn't she complained? Any other kid would have yelled at the top of her lungs about the burnt toast and the overcooked pasta, maybe even re- fused to eat it. Was Penny afraid he'd get angry if she voiced her disapproval?

Dora's words rang through his head.

She's not afraid of you. She's afraid of your disapproval.

The more he thought about it, the more he conceded that Dora might be right. Standing, he went to the sink, poured the remaining contents of his cup down the drain, then rinsed the mug and turned it upside down in the dish rack.

As he climbed the stairs, his mind swam with ideas to change the way his niece perceived him.

The next morning, Dora came downstairs and peered out the window in the front door for the morning news- paper. The sight that met her eyes made her gasp in surprise. The world Dora had come into yesterday had been transformed in a fairy-tale landscape.

It had stormed during the night and a new blan- ket of white covered last week's snow, which had turned gray and ugly. The wet snow blanketed the limbs of the trees, and the bushes sagged under the added weight.

The plows had already been through, and the sides of the street were piled with hills of sparkling white.

Her first snow.

With excitement filling her mind to the exclusion of all else, she turned the knob and threw the door open. Disregarding the fact that she was in her pajamas, robe, and slippers, she dashed out into the yard and scooped up a handful of the cold, white stuff.

Squeezing it in her hands, when she opened her fingers, she was surprised to find her palm wet and empty. The snow had melted. Disappointment washed over her. She'd forgotten that snow was so insubstantial, as insubstantial as the new life she'd stepped into. A wave of sadness swept over her.

"Are you trying to catch pneumonia?"

Startled, she turned sharply toward the sound of Tony's voice. He must have just showered because his hair still glistened with wetness. Leaning against the door frame, he'd crossed his arms over his chest, hooked one leg in front of the other, and flashed that grin that made Dora fight for breath. She gasped at the way her heart fluttered.

"No," she said hastily, dragging her attention away from Tony. She wiped her wet hands on her robe, and then eased past him into the house. "I was just enjoying the snow. It's so beautiful and so renewing."

He straightened. "Beautiful and renewing it may be, but every time a new layer of snow falls, it makes my job more difficult. It's hard enough building in the cold without having my men slipping and sliding and risking injury."

Work.

Why must he think of everything in relation to his business? Why wasn't he looking at the snow as an opportunity to spend time with Penny building a snowman? "There are some happy aspects to snow: snowmen, snowball fights, sleigh riding . . ."

He laughed and the sound vibrated through her. Her fingertips tingled and her mouth went dry.

"I guess so, but I tend to look at it from a practical perspective. If I owned a ski lodge, I'd be celebrating right along with you." He took her shoulders and steered her down the hall. "Now, how about breakfast? Penny should be coming down any minute."

Dora was so preoccupied with his touch and the way it made her skin come alive, that she never thought about the mirror until they were almost in front of it. She couldn't risk passing in front of the mirror with Tony so close. Slipping from his grasp, she twisted back the way they had come.

"I forgot to grab the morning paper," she said, heading for the door.

Tony grinned again. "Okay, you get the paper, and

I'll start the coffee."

Half an hour later, Penny, Tony, and Dora were finishing up their breakfast of eggs, bacon, and juice. Tony and Dora lingered over coffee while Penny ate the last of her eggs.

It hadn't escaped Dora's notice that when asked how Penny wanted her eggs cooked, that she had chosen over easy . . . the same way Tony had his. From the frown on his face, it hadn't gotten past Tony, either. Dora hoped it was because her words from last night had sunk in.

"Don't cook supper tonight," Tony announced out of nowhere.

Penny stopped eating and stared at him.

"Why?" Dora asked.

"You'll see. Just be ready to go out when I get here." He stood, waved at Penny, and then smiled secretively at Dora. Whistling, he gathered his dishes and deposited them on the counter by the dishwasher. "See you both around six o'clock."

By six thirty, all three were sandwiched in the cab of Tony's black pickup truck and driving to an unknown destination. A small paper fir tree that swung from the rearview mirror saturated the warm air inside the truck with the sickening smell of artificial pine.

Dora curled her nose and absorbed the brilliance of the colored lights strung across the porches and eaves of the homes they passed. In one yard, deer outlined in tiny white lights bowed their heads as if grazing on the snow. In another, a tall, pine tree bathed in colored lights towered against the night sky. In yet another, strings of white lights dripped from the eaves of the house like sparkling icicles.

Excitement bubbled up in her. How she wished she could be here for Christmas morning to watch Penny and Tony open their gifts. Her excitement dimmed a bit, but was soon reborn when they turned down Main Street and she saw the decorations the city fathers had strung across the streets.

Bright green and red lights crisscrossed the thoroughfare, their colors reflected in the snow. Illuminated wreaths, reindeer, and snowmen hung from each streetlight. On the sidewalks people bearing gaily wrapped packages chattered happily to each other as they hurried along. Kids threw snowballs at one another. It was like a picture on the cards Dora had seen the mortals exchange each year at this time.

But Penny didn't seem to notice any of it.

"I wonder where we're going," Dora whispered to Penny. The stoic child shrugged and continued to stare out the windshield. "Aren't you even curious?" Penny shook her head and burrowed deeper into her baby blue ski jacket.

Dora and Tony exchanged a glance above the child's head.

"We're almost there," he announced, his excitement sounding forced.

A moment later, he pulled the truck to the curb behind a small car, nearly hidden under the large pine tree tied to its roof. When Dora glanced to the side, she saw the Christmas tree lot. She turned back to Tony. He grinned, and her heartbeat nearly deafened her.

Penny glanced up and for the first time that night, she became animated. "Are we getting a real tree, Uncle Tony?"

He grinned down at her. "We sure are. And guess what? You get to pick it out."

Penny's eyes grew wide. "Me?"

"Yup. You." He opened his door, stepped into the street, then reached for his niece. She stood on the seat, held out her arms, then slid into his embrace. Carrying Penny, Tony came around to Dora's side of the truck and opened the door for her. "Come on, Dora. You have to come, too. After all, this was your idea." Though the last words could have been accusatory, his soft tone and ready smile made them sound more like a thank-you.

Dora didn't need a second invitation. She sprang from the truck to the sidewalk. As her feet hit the ground, they slipped out from under her on the ice, and she would have gone down if Tony had not been there to slide an arm around her waist and catch her while he balanced Penny on his hip. He held Dora against his side. The warmth of his big body seeped through her layers of clothing and sent a chill rushing over her that had nothing to do with the winter weather.

"Thanks," she mumbled, caught in his gaze. He stared silently down at her for a long time before he nodded, then released his hold on her.

When Dora had regained her composure and her footing, she looked at the other people milling around the lot. Laughing adults wandered among the variety of trees, and the excited chatter of children filled the air. Piped in from some unseen location came the strains of "Santa Claus Is Coming to Town."

They could have been one of those "normal" families out getting their Christmas tree. But they weren't. Forgetting that would be a foolish thing to do. But Dora refused to let anything ruin the night. She pushed aside thoughts of her imminent return to Celestial Maintenance, and absorbed every bit of her surroundings, stuffing it into her memory to play back when she could no longer experience it firsthand.

Tony set Penny on her feet. "Well, you better get going. Find us a tree."

With a smile glued to her lips, Penny scampered off obediently, leaving Dora and Tony to weather the awkward silence left by the child's absence. Pulling her coat closer around her, Dora turned her attention to a blue spruce.

"Look at how beautifully this is shaped," she said to fill the tense void.

Tony took the end of one of the limbs in his hand, and then broke one of the tiny fragile needles. The smell of fresh pine seeped into the cold night air. Dora breathed deeply, storing the fragrance with the rest of the memories.

Tony watched her. "If I didn't know better, I'd think this was your first Christmas."

Dora froze. She couldn't very well admit that it *was* her first Christmas, or at the very least her first on Earth. "I feel like every Christmas is my first," she said quickly. "I just love this season of the year."

He grinned again.

Dora almost wished he wouldn't do that. Every time he smiled she felt as if her insides were that ball of snow that had melted in her hand that morning. Not good.

The streetlights blinked on and off several times. Dora glanced around her and found, from the other people's complete disregard for anything but selecting a tree, that she'd been the only one to witness the blinking lights. Evidently, Calvin didn't approve of her musings.

"We'd better find Penny," she told Tony, then sidled past him and into the clump of trees into which Penny had disappeared moments earlier.

Once inside the thick barrier of trees, Dora became instantly disoriented. Looking around her, she tried to decide where she'd come from, but every direction looked the same, a wall of impenetrable pine trees. She turned to retrace her steps and ran headlong into Tony's wide chest. When she again lost her footing on the slick snow, his arms automatically encircled her.

Raising her face to thank him, she lost all sense of time and place. He was staring down at her. His eyes held warmth and, for the first time since she'd come into Tony Falcone's home, a faint glimmer of life. Mesmerized, she held her breath and waited. For what, she had no idea. She only knew that something momentous was about to happen to her. Something that would change her life forever.

Very slowly, Tony lowered his head and gently touched her lips with his. His mouth was cool at first, then turned warm and sweet and oh, so inviting. She curled her arms around Tony's neck and hung on, never wanting to let the moment end. Never wanting to—

Out of the corner of her eye, Dora could see every

light in town blinking madly. Instantly, she pulled free of Tony's embrace.

"Dora?"

"We can't let this happen again," she said, her voice choked with regret.

Tony stared at her, but before he could ask the questions she knew hovered on his lips, a scream came from the other side of the lot.

Penny.

CHAPTER 4

WHEN TONY AND DORA REACHED THE SPOT where Penny stood unharmed, they stopped dead in their tracks. Penny was jumping up and down next to the most pitiful-looking tree Dora had ever seen, a brilliant smile transforming her usually solemn face.

Both heaved a deep sigh of relief. Penny had screamed with excitement and not in distress as they had feared. Dora couldn't recall being that frightened ever before.

Out of the corner of her eye, she saw Tony open his mouth to scold Penny for scaring them. But Dora nudged him and shook her head. He closed his mouth.

"Well, what do you think?" The little girl turned sideways and surveyed her find with adoring eyes. "Isn't it special?"

Special was one way to describe it. The tree couldn't have been more than five feet tall and the branches, though heavily covered in healthy needles, were sparse and fragile looking. Dora wasn't sure they could even support the weight of the ornaments. The top curled decidedly to the left on the end of an equally crooked trunk.

Tony cleared his throat. "Are you sure this is the one you want? Did you look at some of the others?" He grabbed a tall tree at random from the group beside him. "How about this one?"

Penny's smile wilted. The indecision in her face made Dora want to cry. Obviously, Penny wanted to please Tony, but she also wanted the tree she'd picked. Finally she said, "You said I could pick the tree."

"That's right," Dora said, going to stand beside Penny. She looped her arm around the girl's slim shoulders. "You did say that."

Tony replaced the tree he'd selected and stared at them.

"Uncle Tony, this isn't the most beautifulest tree, but if we don't buy it, it'll have to spend Christmas all alone. Nobody else will want it." Tears glistened in Penny's eyes. "It's not the tree's fault that it's not perfect."

Dora could see the hesitation still filling the girl's face. This was a big step for the child. Not only was she transferring her own loneliness to the tree, but she was also weighing the result of her disagreement with her uncle.

Silently Dora pleaded with Penny to stick with her

decision to buy that particular tree. It was time the child realized that if she didn't agree with her uncle it would not harm their relationship, that if she didn't want another tree, Tony wouldn't stop loving her. How could Dora get that across to Penny without coming right out and saying so?

Of course. A democratic decision. Wasn't that how most mortals solved disputes? Perhaps, if she sided with Penny, it might give the little girl the courage to stand by her tree selection.

"Let's take a vote," Dora suggested. "I think we should take this tree," she said, raising her hand. She turned to Penny. "What's your vote?" Slowly and with a lot of obvious trepidation, but perhaps feeling bolstered by Dora's willingness to take sides with her against her uncle, Penny raised her hand, too.

Tony looked from one to the other, and then grinned broadly. "I vote we buy it, too." Penny whooped with joy, then ran to her uncle and hugged his legs.

Looking awkward and uncomfortable with the show of affection, Tony appeared to be searching for a way to react. Finally, he simply patted Penny's shoulder. As if she sensed his discomfort, Penny pulled away and moved back to Dora's side.

Well, at least Penny got her tree. That was something. Dora breathed a sigh of relief and looked heavenward.

She made an imaginary line in the air with her finger. *One for the angel.* The streetlights blinked once, then burned steadily. Calvin evidently approved.

"It will be so pretty when we get all the ornaments on it, you'll see," Penny told Tony, her excitement fired up again. They dragged the tree to the cash register balanced on the tailgate of a pickup truck.

"We want this one," Penny announced to the salesman.

He glanced at the tree and shook his head. "It'll take a little work," the man said, quickly taking Tony's money before he could change his mind.

That he was relieved to have gotten rid of the tree was quite obvious, and he was doing nothing to cover it and spare a little girl's feelings. He probably would have been a lot more polite if they'd bought one of the perfectly shaped, more expensive trees.

"It's a bit pitiful now, but when you add a few balls, some lights, and a little tinsel, it'll be passable." He counted out Tony's change.

For the first time that Dora could ever remember, she actually wanted to slap someone. Couldn't this man see he was hurting Penny's feelings? Then again, maybe he simply didn't care. He had his money, and he'd gotten rid of a tree that he hadn't had any hope of selling, so what difference did it make if he walked over the feelings of a little girl?

As Tony carried the tree to the truck and secured it in the back, Dora glanced over her shoulder at the salesman, smiled, and then fluttered her fingertips. The cash register drawer flew open, spilling money all over the snow. *Calvin was right; these mortals put value in all the wrong things*, she thought as she watched the man scramble to collect the coins and bills fluttering in the sudden winter breeze.

"That's the last of them," Tony announced, placing a big cardboard box bulging at the seams with ornaments on the living room floor. He straightened and massaged his lower back.

The room hadn't been in this kind of disorder since he'd moved in. Pine needles littered the rug, along with discarded ornament boxes and strings of colored lights draped over the sofa arm. In the corner, secure in the stand, was the tree. If possible, it looked more forlorn than it had in the lot.

He had some serious doubts as to whether it could support the four boxes of ornaments he'd dragged out of the attic and that Dora and Penny planned to hang on it. Even if it did manage to withstand the strain of being bedecked in dozens of shiny balls and several strings of glittering lights, the tree was hopeless. But he didn't say anything.

On the floor in front of the coffee table, Dora and Penny were busy removing all the balls from their boxes and fastening a hook on each one. The glow in Dora's eyes and the animation in his niece's face confirmed his decision to get the real tree and to keep his opinions of it to himself. The two of them were having the time of their lives. He just wished he could feel the joy they were experiencing.

Unfortunately, the whole scenario merely served as a painful reminder of the one person who wasn't there to join in the fun—his sister. Until she'd gotten married, he and Rosalie had always decorated their tree together, just the two of them. It had been a special time filled with laughter and celebration. She would have made hot chocolate with those tiny marshmallows and set out a plate of assorted homemade Christmas sugar cookies to snack on while they worked. The old stereo would have blared Christmas carols, and they would have sung along in their off-key voices, laughing hysterically when one of them screeched out a sour high note.

"Uncle Tony?"

He roused himself from his thoughts to see that Penny was holding up the tree topper, an angel dressed in white flowing robes with a sparkling halo and majestic, golden wings. Rosalie's tree topper.

"Yes, Penny?"

"I found the angel. Can you lift me up to put her on top like Daddy used to?"

Tony felt as if someone had sucker punched him. All the air had left his lungs. A memory of his sister lifting him to place the tree topper on when he was a little boy flashed through his mind. His stomach turned over. A sharp pain pierced his heart. He glanced at Dora.

Dora stared at the angel in Penny's hands. It reminded her of the stories the other angels had told her about Michael, one of the Archangels on the Heavenly Council. Dora wasn't sure Michael wouldn't like the notion of him wearing a flowing robe or being referred to as a *her*. To Dora's knowledge, the only female on the Heavenly Council was Gabriel, and ofttimes, even the mortal theologians and scholars argued about that.

"Will you?" Penny asked again.

Roused by Penny's question, Dora turned to look at Tony, who had neither moved nor spoken.

"Uncle Tony?"

Still Tony didn't move. His face had turned unusually pale. It occurred to her what must be rushing through his head; other people, other Christmases. She got up and went to him. Placing her hand on his arm, she felt his anguished thoughts rushing through him, and they confirmed her own conclusions.

"Treasure the old memories and keep them close, but make room for the new ones," she said quietly so Penny couldn't hear.

Tony stared down at her for a long moment and then shook his head. "I'm sorry. I just can't," he blurted, and rushed from the room.

"Did I do something wrong?" Penny asked, her voice cracking on a sob.

Dora hurried to her side and hugged her close. "No, sweetie. You didn't do anything wrong. Uncle Tony isn't feeling well." She held her at arm's length. "Now, I think you and I need to get this tree dressed for Christmas." Leaving the tree topper on the coffee table, she handed Penny a bright red ball. "I think this one might look really good right in the front, don't you?"

Penny took the ball, glanced at the treetop, and nodded. "Maybe tomorrow, when Uncle Tony feels better, we can put the tree topper on."

Dora smiled and nodded. "Yes, maybe tomorrow." But she imagined it would take longer than one day for Uncle Tony to face that tree topper and overcome the memories in which it was wrapped.

Early the next morning, Dora returned from driving Penny to school, a harrowing trip to say the least, but one she was sure she'd get used to in the days to come. Unlike her cooking skills, driving didn't seem to be something she would be doing with any degree of proficiency in the near future. So far not one appliance had tried to cut her off on the way to the refrigerator, nor had any of them made rude hand gestures at her.

Certain that, given a few moments, her hands would stop shaking and her knees wouldn't feel quite so rubbery, she hung up her coat and grabbed the empty coffeepot. The coffeemaker had just belched its last when the back door opened, and a woman's singsong call disturbed the silence of the house.

"Yoo-hoo!"

Standing just inside the back door was a rosy-cheeked woman in her late fifties, smiling at Dora, tight salt-and-pepper curls framing her face, and a bright, flowered apron encircling her slightly ample girth. Cradled in the woman's hands was a blue cake plate, on which sat a chocolate confection dripping in gooey, white icing dotted with plump, red strawberries.

As Dora dried her hands on a paper towel and smiled back, her salivary glands kicked in, flooding her mouth with moisture. She was developing a real fondness for mortal cuisine, especially the sweet desserts, and this one looked especially scrumptious.

Dora dragged her gaze from the cake, swallowed the new accumulation of moisture her salivary glands had flushed into her mouth, and grinned. Calling on the details the Angel of Transition had told her, Dora decided this had to be Millie Sullivan. "Hello."

"Hello, dear. I waited until you'd gotten back from taking Penny to school." The woman extended the cake. "I thought we could have a bite of cake and some get-acquainted coffee. I'm Millie Sullivan. I live next door."

Before her trip down here, Dora had been filled in on a few of the facts about the bighearted woman who had deemed it her job to watch over Penny and Tony. As a result of her deep belief in and abiding love for the celestial residents, Millie had gained quite a following *up there*. Oddly, her limited knowledge about Millie aside, Dora felt an instant affection for the woman.

"I'm Dora DeAngelo, and I'd love some of that luscious-looking cake. I have fresh coffee just waiting to be shared." She got out two cups and saucers, cream and sugar, forks, and cake plates. Handing Millie the cake knife, she said, "You cut the cake, and I'll pour the coffee."

Moments later, they were settled at the table, each with a large slab of chocolate bundt cake and a cup of steaming, fragrant coffee in front of them.

"I am so glad Tony decided to bring someone in to

see to Penny. It's been such a strain on him, and although he means well, he's been feeding the poor child all kinds of unhealthy food." Millie tilted her head in Dora's direction, a conspiratorial look in her sparkling blue eyes. "Between you and me, the man couldn't cook his way out of a brown paper bag." She laughed, and the sound flooded over Dora like sunshine. Then Millie went suddenly serious. "You can cook, can't you, dear?"

"Oh, yes. And I must say I'm pretty good at it," Dora said, finding Millie's laughter infectious.

"Probably something you inherited from your mother. I always believed that a talent for good cooking runs in a family."

Dora refrained from replying.

"I can see you and I are going to get along very well. I have more cookbooks than the local Barnes & Noble. Preston, he's my husband, says that one day he'll have to build an extra room just to hold them all." She took a sip of her coffee. "And if you need any help with Tony and Penny, dear, you just yell. Lord knows, I've tried to help them all I can, but Tony is so pigheaded and seems so determined to do this alone." Millie stopped talking long enough to shovel a bit of cake in her mouth and then follow it up with a another sip of coffee. "I sometimes think he's trying to prove something to his dead sister." She made a *tsk-tsk* sound with her tongue.

"How long has it been . . . since the accident?" Calvin had told her about the day that had changed Tony and Penny's life, but she wanted to hear Millie's take on it. Dora picked up a particularly fat strawberry and popped it in her mouth, savoring the sweet juice that flowed over her taste buds and then prolonged the pleasure by licking the chocolate from her fingertips.

Millie furrowed her brow. "I think it's a little over a year now. Yes, it was September, shortly after the school year started." She shook her head. "So sad. Rosalie was so young, so full of life. She and Matt were so in love, and both of them adored that little girl. Tony—" She put her hands together and looked heavenward. "Tony thought Rosalie was the be-all and end-all. He loved her dearly." She brushed some cake crumbs from the table into her palm and deposited them on her empty plate. "Rosalie and Matt were on their way to get pizza after they'd picked Penny up at school, when a car ran a red light and smashed into them. The driver was so drunk he didn't even realize he'd been in an accident until the police showed up, gave him a sobriety test, and issued him a ticket, then carted him off to jail. Rosalie and Matt died instantly, thank the Lord. Penny was fortunate enough to go unhurt." She made a derisive sound with her tongue. "There was no one else to care for little Penny, so Tony sold his condo and moved here from Georgia." Millie covered Dora's hand with hers. "I can tell you, I wasn't sure that man would ever recover from his sister's death."

Dora wanted to say that he hadn't recovered, but she held her tongue. She hadn't been around long enough to make that type of observation without causing a shower of questions.

Obviously feeling quite at home, Millie got up and retrieved the coffeepot. She filled both their cups and returned the pot to the base. Dora smiled inwardly. She had a feeling that Millie was what they classified *up there* as a *Giver*, someone who gleaned all their life's joys from doing for others.

"Do you have children, Millie?" Dora asked on an impulse.

The joy faded from Millie's eyes. Moisture gathered immediately in their blue depths, and Dora regretted her question. She should have remembered that Calvin had told her Millie was barren. Dora could have bitten off her tongue. The last thing she wanted was to cause this sweet lady any distress.

"Oh, Millie, I am so very sorry. I shouldn't have pried."

"It's all right, dear. The Lord never blessed us with children." She bowed her head. "I used to mourn the fact that I would never have a baby of my own to hold. But I've become resigned over the years. I'm sure He had a good reason."

"I'm so sorry," Dora said again, the words coming from the deepest part of her heart. Though she professed otherwise, Dora wasn't so sure Millie had ever become completely resigned to her fate.

Millie sniffed, dabbed at her eyes with the corner of her flowered apron, and smiled. "Water under the bridge, Dora. Water under the bridge." She laid her hand on Dora's again.

For a moment, Dora was so stunned by the amount of love pouring into her from Millie, that she almost snatched her hand away. Never had she felt a love like this before. It embodied everything she'd always imagined of love: strength, warmth, comfort, understanding, forgiveness, and genuine affection for those for whom she cared deeply. It was the kind of unconditional love a mother gave a child. How sad no child would ever know it.

When Millie stood and removed her hand, severing the connection, Dora almost cried out at the loss.

"Well, I've bothered you long enough. Besides, Pres may be up from his nap."

"Pres?"

"Preston. He has a heart condition, and he naps every morning and afternoon." She shook her head as she headed toward the door. "Personally, I think a bit of exercise would be more beneficial than a nap, but . . ." She shrugged and extended her hands in a helpless gesture. "In all our years together, he's never listened to me, so why should he start now?" She gave a little resigned laugh.

Dora made a mental note to speak to Calvin about Preston. He could check the Book of Lifetimes and see where Preston's name fell in the Time Continuum. Of course, she wouldn't be able to pass anything she learned on to Millie, and she wasn't sure exactly why she wanted to know, but she felt an urgent need to find out if Preston was scheduled to leave Millie any time soon.

"When she gets home from school, you make sure Penny gets a piece of that cake," Millie said as she opened the back door and pointed at what was left of the bundt cake.

Cold air rushed into the warm kitchen. Dora shivered but followed Millie onto the porch. "Tony discourages Penny from having snacks, especially sweets, before dinner. He says it'll ruin her appetite."

Millie stopped on the back porch and swung quickly around. "What? That poor baby has such a small tummy; she needs something between lunch and supper." She shook her finger at Dora and continued in a no-nonsense tone. "You give it to her anyway, and tell Tony if he has a problem with that, he can talk to me." She stepped off the porch and hurried through the snow to her back door, mumbling as she went.

"I'll tell him what you said." Wrapping her arms around herself to ward off the cold air, Dora ducked back inside, closed the door, and headed for the hall mirror. Positioning herself in front of it, she squared her shoulders and called out, "Calvin."

Silence.

Louder. "Calvin!"

More silence.

Frustration began to swell inside her. She had told him to stop hovering, but she'd hoped he'd still be available for special consultations.

"Calvin!" This time, her volume made the mirror tremble on its hook.

A ball of light appeared in the center and slowly began to enlarge. "You called?" Calvin asked, when he finished shimmering into view. His pale brows were drawn together in a straight line, a definite sign of his impatience with this interruption of his duties.

"Yes. I have a favor to ask of you."

"What is it?" He smiled, and she knew he was hoping she was, as the mortals said, crying uncle.

"I want you to check the Book of Lifetimes, and find Preston Sullivan listed in there. Then look to see when his time will come to an end."

Dead silence again. He crossed his arms over his chest and slanted a look of distrust at her. "And just why would that concern you?"

How could she give him a reason when she wasn't sure herself why she wanted to know? Dora blew out a frustrated breath. "Does there have to be a reason for everything, Calvin?"'

"There does when this is none of your business, when it's not the reason you were sent down there."

"Please, Calvin. This is important."

He shook his head. "Not a chance. You should not be butting in where you have no business. Gladys and Ezekiel are assigned to watch over the Sullivans. Leave this to them."

She stomped her foot. Her halo slid sideways. She ignored it. "How do you know that it's not my business? How do you know Gladys and Ezekiel don't need assistance? It wouldn't be the first time an angel found she had more than one assignment or that one assignment overflowed into other areas."

"Not this time," he said firmly, obviously not about to budge. "Trust me. I know. You will leave this to the Sullivans' Guardian Angels and keep out of it. Are we clear?"

Her mouth set in a defiant line, Dora nodded.

"Good. Now, I suggest you forget this foolishness

and concentrate on what you're there for—helping the Falcones." He started to shimmer out and then stopped.

"By the way, that little thing," he fluttered his fingertips, "you did at with the salesman at the tree lot and with the shipment of lumber at Tony's construction site? Frowned on, Dora. Strongly frowned on. Someone could have seen you at the tree lot, and the child might have walked in on you at the house. Oh, and I might add that I'm not pleased with this stubborn streak you've adopted since going below. It's not becoming. It would appear that I'm going to have to keep a very close eye on you, Dora." Instead of fading slowly, as was his custom, the ball of light popped loudly, and Calvin was gone.

Dora was about to turn away when she heard a loud *pssst* coming from the mirror. She looked back and found her best friend's reflection. "Gracie!"

"Shh," Grace said, her voice a mere whisper. She glanced around her, and then turned back to Dora, her face a study in concern. "We don't have much time. I know an angel over in the Time/Life Department. I'll see if I can get the information you asked Calvin for."

Dora grinned. "Thanks, Gracie. I owe you one."

"Wait here. I'll be right back." Grace circled her thumb and forefinger and then vanished.

While Dora waited, she thought about Calvin's attitude, and the longer she dwelled on it, the angrier she got. How dare he tell her she couldn't help anyone but her assigned mortals? She liked Millie and if she could help her, she darned well would. And she knew just how to keep Calvin from harassing her anymore.

"Dora."

Her friend's husky whisper yanked her from her thoughts, "Yes, Grace. Did you find anything out?"

Grace smiled. "My friend Jonathan looked through the next twenty years, and Preston's name appears every year in the Book of Lifetimes, and there is no termination code next to it." She started and looked over her shoulder. "Uh-oh. Here comes Calvin. Gotta fly." She dissolved into a vibrant ball of light and instantly zoomed out of sight.

"Bye, Gracie, and thanks." Dora heaved a sigh of relief. Preston still had a good many years ahead of him with Millie. What she'd do with that information still eluded Dora, but she was happy about it.

Now, to deal with Calvin. She lifted the heavy mirror from its hook and looked around. Then she carried it upstairs to her room, took down the twin mirror, and hung the hall mirror in its place. From the linen closet, she took a sheet and draped it over the mirror, then carried the other mirror downstairs and hung it in the hall. They were exact in appearance so no one would notice the switch. If they did, she'd make some excuse for exchanging them.

"There," she said, brushing her hands off with a great deal of satisfaction. "So much for you, Mr. Nosey Head of Celestial Maintenance."

"Did she just do what I think she did?" Calvin asked, his voice reflecting his incredulity as he stared fixedly into the Earth Pool at a wall of white.

"Yup, she sure did," Grace said, her smile lighting up the heavens. "I think she cut you off, Calvin."

"I . . . I . . ." He sputtered for a good fraction of an eon before he finally got his anger under control, cleared his throat, and fluffed his disheveled wings. "This is unacceptable. Totally unacceptable. What if she does something that will cause trouble, and I'm not there to intervene? What if she . . . ?" He put a hand to his forehead. "Oh, dear, this is not good. Not good at all." He paced the cloud, sending up wisps of mist.

Grace giggled. "Easy Calvin. You're popping wing feathers." Grace leaned down and picked up two or three feathers that had fallen from Calvin's wings. Carefully, she reinserted them and smoothed them down. "Dora will be fine. You have to start putting some faith in her judgment."

He stopped, having worn a rut so deep in the cloud

that he had to look up at Grace. "Faith? The only faith I have in Dora is that she will be instrumental in getting me assigned to polishing lightning bolts in my retirement. The only certain thing with that angel is that she *will* mess up again."

Grace laid a hand on his shoulder. "Trust her. She'll do fine. She may not be able to repair angel wings, but she has an inborn sense for understanding the heart of these mortals, more than any angel I know." She patted his shoulder and then fluttered off into the cosmos.

"Inborn sense, my halo," Calvin mumbled. "She's a disaster looking for a place to happen is what she is, and it's not going to be on my watch." He glanced into the Earth Pool, but all he could see was the expanse of white sheet covering the mirror on the other side. With an exasperated sigh, he shimmered out.

❖ ❖ ❖

"Look!" Penny yelled as they pulled into the driveway. She bolted from the car and made a dash for the front porch, leaving her elephant backpack behind for Dora to bring into the house.

When Dora got close enough to see what had so excited the child, who had, until then, stared stoically out the windshield, she caught her breath. Sitting on the porch right in front of the door was a pitiful-looking, large, dirty white, shaggy dog.

Penny was on her knees with her arms wrapped around the dog's neck. "Can we keep him, Dora?"

There was more life in Penny's eyes than Dora had seen since she'd arrived. How she'd love to say yes, but she knew she didn't have the authority to make this decision. "We'll have to ask your uncle, sweetie."

Penny's smile melted.

CHAPTER 5

"PLEASE, CAN WE KEEP HIM? PLEASE? I'LL TAKE care of him. I promise." Penny looked down at the pitiful animal she had enfolded in her arms. "He looks so sad and so lonely."

Dora's heart ached for Penny. She could understand Penny's empathy for the dog and would have loved nothing better than to have been able to tell the child she could keep him, but in her heart, she sincerely doubted Tony would go for it. After all, the man was Mr. Neatness himself and seemed to be intolerant of anything that left a mess in the house. Dogs were notorious, or so she'd been told by some of the Guardian Angels whose job it was to watch over the animals of the mortals, for chewing on various objects that didn't belong to them, and for not always understanding the need to go outside for . . . certain things.

Besides, the dog was filthy. His fur was a tangled, matted mess, and he smelled of wet dog. On top of that, she thought, as she watched him lift a hind leg to scratch vigorously behind his ear, he was probably playing host to an infestation of fleas. Dora didn't have the heart to tell Penny that she was fighting a losing battle. Tony would most definitely not want this animal in the house.

She opened her mouth to tell Penny the dog would have to go, but the child looked at her with big, sad eyes glistening with moisture, and Dora's heart twisted.

Unable to stand the pleading in those enormous green orbs, Dora made a decision she knew would entail a lot of explaining to Tony. "Tell you what. We'll bring him inside where it's warm and give him something to eat, but don't get too attached to him because your uncle might say the dog has to go." In her heart, Dora knew the warning had already come way too late. If the sappy look on Penny's face meant what Dora thought it did, the poor child had already fallen in love with the disreputable beast. "He'll have to stay in the laundry room until your uncle comes home."

Dora opened the front door and stood to the side to allow both child and dog to enter. Since the dog had no collar, Penny grabbed a handful of its neck fur and pulled the animal into the house. As they slid past Dora, the dog raised his dark-eyed gaze to her, and she could have sworn it reflected smug satisfaction. She followed the two down the hall and frowned at the wet, dirty paw prints the dog left in his wake on the shiny pine floor.

Penny obediently guided him straight to the laundry room and grabbed one of the snowy towels stacked on the washer. Before Dora could stop her, she began drying the dog. The white towel quickly became spotted with large globs of mud and dog hair and, in Dora's mind, instantly became the dog's personal property.

Penny sat back to assess her work. "There. That's much better, isn't it, Dora?"

Dora didn't have the heart to tell the child the improvement in the dog's appearance was miniscule. He still reeked of damp doggy odor and God only knew what else, and, if possible, the rubdown he'd received had matted his hair even more. But for Penny's sake, she fibbed.

"Uh . . . yes. He's very . . . uh . . . beautiful."

"Dora!" Penny said, shaking her head. "Boys aren't beautiful. Boys are handsome."

An image of Tony flashed through Dora's mind. On that she had to disagree with Penny. Tony Falcone, from the top of his dark hair, to the muscles that rippled down his arms, to the tips of his toes, was beautiful. As beautiful as any Roman god.

The dog raised his shaggy head and emitted a low growl. The sound drew Dora's attention away from her thoughts. There was so much belly hair hanging down that it was impossible to tell what sex he was just by looking at him. For now, they'd play it by ear and assume. However, given his snarky attitude, *he* was probably correct.

"I think you insulted him," Penny said, looping her arm around his neck. "It's okay, Jack. Dora only meant that you look good. She doesn't know boys get upset when you say they're beautiful."

Oh, goodness. She's named him.

Immediately, Dora regretted her decision to allow Penny to bring the animal in the house. In a few short minutes, the attachment had progressed way too far. If Dora allowed it to go any further, when Tony declared the animal had to leave, which she knew he inevitably would, she'd never be able to separate Penny from the dog without breaking the child's heart.

Dora pulled an old blanket from a shelf above the dryer and spread it on the floor. "He can use this as a bed for now." She looked at Jack and in a stern voice commanded, "Lie down."

Jack looked at her, then stepped onto the blanket, turned in a circle several times, and finally flopped down. Well, at least he was obedient.

"I'm home! Where is everybody?"

Tony's voice rang through the house. His heavy footsteps were heading for the kitchen. Dora grabbed

Penny, hauled her outside the laundry room, and closed the door on their secret guest. The two of them stood like soldiers on review when Tony entered the kitchen.

"What's up?" he asked, looking from one to the other.

"Nothing," they said in unison.

Dora muffled a groan. Even if they'd tried, she knew they couldn't have looked or acted guiltier. From behind them a muffled, low whine slipped from beneath the laundry room door.

"What was that?" Tony asked, stretching to look around them.

Instinctively, they moved closer together. "What?" they again asked in unison.

The whine came again, this time a bit louder.

You're blowing it, Jack. If you want a full belly and a warm bed for tonight, you'd better be quiet.

"That," Tony said, his dark brow arching in silent question.

"I didn't hear anything, did you, Dora?" Penny raised her cherubic face to Dora, the innocence in her eyes as false as a Halloween mask.

Dora forced a smile. She pushed Penny forward. "Why don't you show your uncle that paper you did at school today, and I'll start—"

Her next word was drowned out by a sharp, high-pitched bark. She and Penny froze in place. They turned guilty faces toward Tony. Penny slipped her small hand into Dora's and pressed against her leg.

Woof! Woof! Woof!

Well, there was no covering it up.

Way to go, Jack.

"Is there a dog in there?" Tony pointed at the closed door. He took a step forward, but Dora held up her hand to stop him.

She considered saying no, but with another *Woof! Woof! Woof!* coming through the door, she calculated that her chances of convincing Tony were growing more distant with each bark. She took a deep breath and swallowed hard.

"Yes. We found him on the porch when we came home from school. Penny would like to keep him."

There. It was out.

Penny's grip on Dora's hand tightened.

Aside from the three of them breathing, not a sound could be heard in the kitchen. Silently, Dora begged Tony not to send the dog away. Until they'd found that dog, she hadn't seen Penny this excited about anything. But when she'd spotted the animal, she'd let loose of that stoic front so unnatural on a child. Dora watched the expression on Tony's face closely for a sign he'd allow the mutt to stay.

Tony studied the two guilty faces staring at him as

though they stood before a jury waiting to be charged with some heinous crime. *A dog. Great.* The last thing he needed around here was something else to be responsible for. He opened his mouth to tell them the dog had to go, but when he saw the look on his niece's face, the words froze on his lips.

Even though her brow was creased in a pleading expression, for the first time since the accident Penny's eyes sparkled with life, and her cheeks were pink with excitement. Even getting the Christmas tree hadn't provoked this kind of animation. Could he, in all good conscience, make her get rid of the dog when it had already brought her such happiness—something he had failed to do?

Woof! Woof! Woof!

Tony sighed. "Okay. Let's see him," he finally said, but, when Penny let out a *whoop* of joy, he added, "That doesn't mean he's staying. A dog is a big responsibility. He has to be fed, bathed, walked, and brushed. And, if he makes a mess inside, you'll have to clean it up."

Penny grabbed his hand and began tugging him toward the laundry room. "I will, Uncle Tony. I'll do all those things. I promise."

"There's one more thing to consider." He stopped her forward motion, and then squatted down to her eye level. "Penny, he might belong to someone and, if he does, we can't keep him, no matter what I say. We'll have to put an ad in the newspaper so his real family knows we found him, and they can come get him. Do you understand?"

Penny nodded and some of the light went out of her eyes. "Yes, I understand." But her brows furrowed. "But if he has a real family, why didn't they take care of him? He's so sad, Uncle Tony. He has no one to hug him and talk to him. If we keep him, I can be his friend and hug him any time he wants to be hugged."

Over Penny's head, Dora stared down at them. Tony had the distinct impression Penny was not only referring to the dog, and the look on Dora's face told him he was right.

"Well, we'll see. Now, let's take a look at this dog."

"Jack, Uncle Tony. His name's Jack."

"Okay. Let's take a look at Jack."

Penny opened the laundry room door to reveal the most pathetic excuse for a dog Tony had ever laid eyes on. She flopped down beside the mutt and encircled his neck with her arms.

She looked at Jack as though he were the latest Hollywood hunk. "Isn't he handsome, Uncle Tony?" Then she cupped her hand around her mouth and whispered, "Don't say *beautiful*. He gets insulted."

"Insulted?" Tony glanced at Dora, who raised her eyebrows and gave a tiny nod of her head, silently warning him not to say anything disparaging about Jack. "He sure is handsome all right." He waited for a bolt of lightning to strike the house in retribution for his blatant lie. He curled his nose at the smell emanating from Jack. Wet manure came to mind. "But you know what? He'd be even more handsome if he had a nice bath."

As if on cue, the dog backed away from him. Evidently bathing wasn't high on the mutt's list of priorities.

"Great idea," Dora said brightly. "You and Penny can bathe him while I get supper started."

Tony stifled a moan and turned to glare at Dora. "Okay, but we'll do it in here in the laundry room sink." He pointed to a very large, deep stainless-steel sink where Rosalie had done hand-washables or soaked stains out of clothes before they went into the washer.

"Well, I'll leave you two to it," Dora announced, backing away. "I'll be in the kitchen."

"Thanks," Tony ground out and cast another you'll-pay-for-this glare at Dora.

Forcing back a grin, Dora left them to their unsavory task and went into the kitchen. As she pulled the makings for stew from the refrigerator, she could hear Tony giving Penny instructions for the bathing of Jack. While his tone was friendly and patient, to Dora's ears it lacked something. Warmth? That special tenor one uses when talking to a cherished child. Dora didn't for one minute doubt Tony's love for his niece; she only wished he could show it.

"Pull the stool over by the sink so you can reach it." A pause followed and then she heard the sound of the scraping of metal legs across the floor as Penny obeyed her uncle's wishes. "That's it. Put the plug in the bottom so the water doesn't run out. Now, turn on the water and add a little soap. That's enough. Good job! Let the hot water run until it's hot, then turn on the cold water until it's warm." Next came the gush of water hitting the metal sink and then the shuffling of feet. "I'll put Jack in the sink and show you how to wash him. Come here, Jack." More shuffling of feet followed by a loud grunt and a bark.

"Jack, please be good and let Uncle Tony put you in the sink. Let's face it, you're handsome, but you smell like poop." Dora stifled a chuckle. She could picture Penny's pert little nose curling up.

More shuffling, another bark, and then a muffled curse and a splash came from the room off the kitchen. Dora assumed Jack had at last made it into his bath.

About an hour later, a large pot of fragrant, beef stew was bubbling on the stove and the table was set. Dora hadn't heard any noise from the laundry room for about fifteen minutes. Suddenly, the door opened and out bounded Jack, snowy white and smelling like spring sunshine. Following him were Tony and Penny, looking like they'd emerged from a swim in the local swamp.

Dirty water dripped from both of them and puddled at their feet. Dog hair clung in clusters to their clothes and skin. Their cheeks were pink with a combination of the heat from Jack's bathwater and the exertion of bathing him. Penny's school uniform was past ruined. Tony's white T-shirt no longer resembled anything close to the crisp, clean garment he'd put on that morning.

Penny sported a satisfied smile, while Tony glared at Dora, the threat of retribution written clearly on his features.

"Isn't he just the handsomest dog ever, Dora?"

Dora wouldn't go that far, but he certainly was a vast improvement over the disreputable mutt that had been standing on the front porch a few hours ago. Now that the tangles had been brushed out, his fur laid smoothly over his back and head and the fringe on his tail reminded her of the feathers in an angel's wings. Dora squatted down and looked Jack over. She couldn't believe how white he was. If she'd had to venture a guess as to whether or not he would have ever cleaned up, it would have been that the filth and matting were going to be part of Jack for eternity.

"He certainly looks much better." Dora patted his damp head. "And he smells a lot better."

"All he needed was a bath and a few hugs," Penny said, dropping to the floor and embracing the dog.

Jack seemed to enjoy the hugs for a while, and then he pulled from her grasp and fairly strutted around the kitchen as though showing off his newly washed, snow-white fur.

"He looks so . . . so self-confident now," Dora said to no one in particular.

"That's 'cause he knows I love him," Penny said. "Everybody always feels better when they know somebody loves them." She stood and grabbed a handful of Jack's neck hair and led him back into the laundry room. "Come on, you need to be brushed some more."

Penny's words hit a raw note of awareness in Dora. Though the child had been talking about her dog, Dora knew that the truth behind the words came from some unfulfilled need deep inside.

Dora glanced at Tony, who was preoccupied picking gobs of wet dog hair off his jeans. She couldn't say for sure, but her guess was that he had totally missed what Penny had said. Would she ever get through to him that his niece needed his love to thrive as much as a flower needed water to flourish and grow? How would she go about breaking through the protective wall he'd built around his heart?

CHAPTER 6

TONY HUNG UP THE WALL PHONE NEXT TO THE refrigerator and turned to Dora, who was finishing up the supper dishes. "The *Tribune* will run the ad tomorrow. Because it's a lost pet, they'll run the ad free of charge. If the owner comes forward, we should know in a few days. Where's he now?"

"Penny took him upstairs." She waited for Tony to object, but he didn't.

Instead, he placed the pad on which he'd written the newspaper's classified division phone number on the counter and leaned his hip against the Formica edge. "The stew was great, Dora. Where did you learn to cook like that?"

Dora froze in the process of drying a plate. What was she supposed to say? *The Angel of Transition made sure I had the skill when I came down here?* She fumbled for an explanation and snatched the first one that drifted through her mind. "It . . . uh . . . just comes to me out of the blue." Her answer teetered precariously on the edge between truth and lie. She recalled Millie's belief that cooking talents were passed down through the family and added, "Sort of an inherited talent."

For the most part, pretending to be mortal was easy, but every once in a while, she hit a snag like this one. So far, she'd been able to make it past them. Hopefully, she could continue to do so without making Tony suspicious. Of course, he'd never guess she was an angel in disguise, but there were a myriad of other, less than savory possibilities he could choose from.

"Well, wherever you picked it up, you did a good job." Tony shuffled his feet nervously, as though he wanted to say more, but couldn't find the words.

An uncomfortable silence hung heavy in the kitchen. Then Tony looked directly at her, his dark gaze sending ripples of strange, unaccustomed pleasure racing down her spine.

The dish towel dropped from her numb fingers. Dragging her gaze from his, she bent to retrieve the towel, just as Tony reached for it. As her hand closed over the material, Tony's hand enveloped hers. Tiny tingles of awareness skittered over her skin. Together, they straightened, neither of them relinquishing their grip.

Cautiously, Dora raised her gaze to meet Tony's. She tried to read the look in his eyes, but failed. That expression was as foreign to her as anything she'd run into so far on Earth, and she had a feeling she would get no Heavenly help deciphering it.

Then she felt the tug. Not on her hand. The pull came from deep inside her, as though some unseen force was urging her to step forward into Tony's arms. She could tell by the intensifying of his strange expression that he felt it, too.

A memory of being in Tony's arms at the Christmas tree lot flashed through her mind. She could never recall a time when she'd felt happier, more content, or so totally in tune with everything in Heaven and Earth. It had been as if that was where she belonged, as if she'd come home.

The pull grew stronger by the minute, until Dora had to grit her teeth to keep from giving in and falling into Tony's arms.

Although every ounce of her being said *do it*, she knew in her heart that Calvin would never approve. He'd been emphatic about not getting emotionally involved with the mortals and the dire consequences that would result.

Then a small voice inside her head whispered, *If Calvin doesn't know, it can't hurt him.*

But would Calvin know? Since Calvin's last visit to

the mirror, Dora had had no contact with the angel. No blinking lights, no whispers in her subconscious, nothing. Perhaps he'd taken to heart her plea to let her fulfill her mission on her own. Perhaps he had no idea what was happening here. She took a tentative step toward Tony.

Out of nowhere a white streak zoomed by in her peripheral vision. It seemed to fly across the kitchen and straight at Tony. He had to release her hand to catch it before it ended up in the sink.

To everyone's surprise, Jack nestled securely in Tony's arms. Dora's mouth fell open partially in surprise and partially with dread at what Tony would say. Penny, who had followed Jack into the kitchen, stood in the doorway, her apprehensive gaze fixed on her uncle.

"Damned dog," Tony mumbled under his breath, thankfully too low for Penny to hear. He set Jack on the floor.

Now that the mesmerizing spell between her and Tony had been broken, warm embarrassment seeped into her cheeks. Thank goodness for the interruption. If Jack hadn't shown up when he did, Dora wasn't sure what would have happened, but she knew that whatever it might have been, Calvin would look dimly on it, and she would be the recipient of another reprimand from her boss.

Dora avoided looking at Tony and busied herself by

putting away the dried dishes. From the corner of her eye, she watched for Penny's reaction.

"Wow, Jack, that was some jump!" The child's grin lit up the room. "Guess he likes you, Uncle Tony," Penny said brightly, unaware of what she and Jack had interrupted. She grinned up at her uncle and patted Jack's shaggy head. "Come on, Jack, let's go outside." She darted from the room with Jack at her heels.

"Put on your hat and mittens," Dora called after them.

Tony started for the door, and then paused. "Dora, I—"

Before he could finish, a high-pitched voice broke in from the back porch. "Yoo-hoo? Is anyone home?" Millie.

"Yes. We're home. Come on in, Millie," Dora called in answer, happy for the second interruption. Something told her it was infinitely better that she never got to hear whatever it was Tony had been about to say. When she turned back, Tony had left the room.

Millie came in, her face pink from the cold. She stomped the snow off her boots on the rug in front of the door, slipped the boots off, and padded into the kitchen in her socks. Clutched in her hands was a plate of Christmas cookies.

Dora took the plate and set it on the cleared table. "You don't have to bring food every time you visit," she told the older woman.

Millie patted her hand. "Dear, I love doing it, and since Preston doesn't eat sweets, and I don't have any little ones of my own, I'm afraid your little family is my only outlet." She laughed and patted her ample middle. "Besides, I refuse to get fat alone."

The words *your little family* hit Dora in the heart. Tony and Penny were never going to be her little family no matter how much she wished it otherwise. Though it would break her heart, she was resigned to the fact that when Christmas Eve came, she'd be gone, never to return to the Falcone household—or Tony.

Millie took her customary seat at the table while Dora poured coffee for them and tried not to think about leaving Tony and Penny.

"Did I hear a dog barking over here?" Millie asked with undisguised curiosity.

Dora smiled. In the short time she'd been living at the Falcones', she'd learned there was little that went on in their household of which Millie was not aware. "Yes. Penny found a stray, and Tony's letting her keep it until the owners claim it."

Millie frowned. "Is that wise? I mean the child will get attached, then the owners will come, and she'll have to give it up. It'll break her heart." She made a *tsk-tsk* sound. "She's had so much heartache already, poor little thing."

After setting two steaming cups of coffee on the

table and adding a bowl of sugar and a small pitcher of cream, Dora took her seat. "I worried about that, too, but there was just no separating her from that dog. She was head over heels in love with the mutt, and before we made it from the porch to the kitchen, she'd even named him Jack."

"*Jack*?" Millie sucked in a breath. Her blue eyes filled with alarm. "Oh, dear."

Dora looked at their neighbor's suddenly pale face. "What is it, Millie?"

Millie took a deep breath and shook her head. "I'm probably just being foolish."

Something about the dog's name had really upset Millie, and Dora couldn't let it drop. "Nonsense. Tell me what's bothering you."

The woman took another deep breath, then asked, "What color is the dog?"

"Considering how dirty he was, it took a long, hot, fragrant bath to discover he's white," Dora said, taking a bite of a delicious sugar cookie bell decorated with red and green sprinkles and trying to act unconcerned so as not to add to Millie's upset. "Why?"

Millie sighed and leaned her elbows on the table. She glanced at the door through which Tony had vanished earlier. In a subdued voice, she leaned closer to Dora and said, "When Penny was born, her dad gave her a toy dog. She never went anywhere without it." Tears gathered in Millie's eyes. "The day of the accident, the dog was destroyed. We told Penny that it was lost. She was heartbroken." Millie laid her warm hand on Dora's arm. "The dog was white, and she'd named him—"

"Jack," Dora finished for her with a sinking heart. Millie nodded.

This complicated everything. However, it totally explained Penny's change in personality and her instant attachment to the stray, but it made having to give the dog back to its owners, should they come to claim him, severely problematic. In her child's mind, Penny no doubt thought that not only had Jack come home to her, but that he'd done so as a real dog.

❖ ❖ ❖

After Millie left, Dora went in search of Tony to talk to him about the dog and its significance to his niece. He had to know that if the owners ever showed up, he should be ready for what giving it up would do to Penny.

However, when Dora found him in the living room, sitting on the couch and looking downcast, she hesitated. Cradled in his big hands was the angel that had never been added to the tree. He looked tortured, as if his soul was bleeding, and her insides twisted in pain for him.

Silently, she sat beside him, all thought of the dog and Penny pushed from her mind.

Tony turned the angel over and over, staring blankly at it. He probably wasn't even seeing the white silk dress, richly embroidered with gold threads; the snow-white, gold-trimmed marabou-feathered wings; or the sparkling halo resting on the angel's golden curls. Dora was certain that what he did see were past Christmases playing like a movie in his mind.

"Putting the angel on the tree," he said in a soft voice, "was always a big deal for my sister, the final touch. It was as if, until that moment, Christmas wasn't really official. When I was little, Rosalie would lift me up so I could do it. As a teenager, she held the ladder while I put the angel in place." He chuckled softly. "When I got taller than her, I told her I'd lift her up so she could put it up there, but she was always afraid I'd drop her into the tree, so I'd end up doing—"

His voice broke, and he stopped talking. Instead, he blinked repeatedly and glanced at the ceiling as if sending up an unspoken plea for help in understanding why his beloved sister had been snatched from him.

Aside from the overused, useless platitudes about destiny, it being Rosalie's time and such, Dora could think of nothing to say that would bring him the peace he so desperately sought. The pain for him that sliced through her almost made her cry out. At a loss for anything else, she took his hand and squeezed it in silent assurance that she was there for him, and she understood.

"Maybe it's time to start a new tradition," she said softly.

Tony turned to her.

"Maybe it's time for you to lift Penny up there to do the honors." She smiled. "You know, passing on the duty to the next in line. Don't you think her mother would like that?"

Tony shrugged and continued to rotate the tree topper in his hands. "Maybe," he finally conceded grudgingly.

He stood and moved next to the tree. For a long moment he stared at the topmost limb, then moved away. He threw Dora a look that said *I can't*, then he placed the angel gently on the coffee table and strode from the room.

Dora watched him go in silence, knowing he couldn't bring himself to relinquish this one last tie to his sister. Allowing anyone else to put the angel on the tree would be like acknowledging that Rosalie was truly gone forever. How could she make him see that as long as Penny was here, Rosalie would never be truly gone? That every time he looked at that child, his sister's face shown back at him?

Suddenly, Dora felt grave doubts about the success of her task. Was it one of futility? Would she ever be able to bring this family back together and establish a loving, close-knit bond between uncle and niece, or were they too badly damaged to ever allow true love back into their hearts?

CHAPTER 7

TONY SAT ALONE IN THE CONSTRUCTION SHACK, staring down at the blueprints for the houses his company was building that lay on the table before him. A sense of intense pride flowed through him. These were the kind of houses Tony had always dreamed of building—affordable housing for the common man.

They weren't fancy houses, just small, square dwellings that consisted of a kitchen, bath, living room, and two bedrooms. Each structure was devoid of the deluxe accoutrements some of the homes his contemporaries constructed. When completed, the landscaping would also be minimal: two trees, a lawn, and a few bushes. When the houses were finished, they would provide homes for some of the poorer residents of the town.

Then his gaze wandered to a bit of pencil scratching on the corner of the paper, shaped oddly like a smiling face. Next to it was scribbled a name—*Dora*. As if on cue, the blueprints blurred and another image took their place. Tony blinked, trying to dispel the image, but it persisted.

He wasn't surprised. This was how it had been every day since Dora had come into his life. He'd be concentrating on something and the smallest thing would send his thoughts spiraling off in her direction. And he didn't seem to be able to stop it. Like right now when, instead of the blueprints filling his vision, Dora's face shimmered in front of him. Her face appeared as it had been last night when she'd found him holding the tree topper. A face filled with compassion and understanding.

But how could she understand? How could anyone understand what he was going through? Rosalie, the woman who had been both mother and father to him for most of his life, was gone, and nothing or no one could ever fill the void left behind.

He rubbed his tired, burning eyes with his forefinger and thumb. Would this wretched, aching loneliness ever go away?

Then it dawned on him that last night had been one of the few times he'd missed Rosalie since Dora had come to live with them. He'd been so busy forcing himself not to think about Dora as more than Penny's babysitter and straining to keep his distance from his enticing employee that he hadn't had time to think much about his dead sister. Or was he just getting used to her being gone?

Keeping the visions of Dora at bay hadn't been easy. At the most inopportune moments, she'd pop into his head: Dora bustling about the kitchen, laughing brightly, gossiping over coffee with Millie, or patiently talking to Penny. But mostly, he recalled how she looked and felt in his arms in the tree lot: clinging tightly to his neck, her warm lips pressed to his, responding as no woman had ever responded to him before.

Then the vision would be shattered by her words. *We can't let this happen again.* Deep down, he knew she was right. If they let the relationship, or whatever label could be put on what was happening between them, develop into something more, he could well lose the one person whom Penny had begun opening up to since the accident. But even worse, *he* could lose Dora. That thought seared through his heart like a hot knife, causing as much pain as the memories of Rosalie. Yet he had to keep Dora at arm's length for Penny's sake.

He groaned and combed his fingers through his hair while frustration ate at him with its hungry jaws.

The door to the shack flew open. His foreman, Jake, stuck his head in. "One of the framers just fell off the scaffolding. I think his leg's broken. Better call 911."

Tony placed the call, then, grabbing his hard hat, dashed out the door.

Dora finished making Tony's bed, then sat on it and ran her fingers over the pillow where his head had lain the night before. She didn't understand what was happening to her. Each time she got near Tony or touched something that reminded her of him, her insides turned as soft as the honey confections she'd eaten in Heaven. At the same time, her skin tingled pleasurably with a strange heat, and her heartbeat raced uncontrollably.

If she were a true mortal, she would have thought she had contracted some illness. Since angels were immune to Earthly afflictions, that couldn't be it. If not an illness, then there was only one other explanation, one she really didn't want to even consider, but consider it she must.

Love.

If that were the case, then she was in major trouble. Calvin would have her wings, her halo, and her hide. She'd be assigned the very worst job in the cosmos, coloring the thunderclouds for eternity.

Woof!

Jack came bounding into the room, his hair in terrible disarray. He jumped on the bed and began licking Dora's face. With her hands raised to ward him off, she tried to push him away. "Jack! Get down. You know you're not supposed to be on the furniture. Down, Jack!"

But the dog ignored her and put his paws on either shoulder, pushing her backward into the bedding, and continued to lick her face. Finally, she turned onto her stomach and slipped off the bed. She glared down at Jack.

"Look, I know you miss Penny, but I don't have time to play with you." She pointed at the floor and in her most commanding voice said, "Get down, now!"

Jack bounded to the floor, his hair still in wild disarray. He barked again, then trotted from the room.

One thing Jack's unannounced arrival had done was to remove her thoughts from her boss, but now that Jack was gone, her tortured, confused musings returned with a vengeance. Dora rubbed her hand across her forehead. What was she to do about this . . . whatever it was that was happening to her? How could she help Tony and Penny if her own doubts kept pummeling her? What if it was the worst-case scenario . . . love? How did she stop it?

Gracie. Maybe Gracie would know.

Dora hurried off to her room and swept the sheet from the mirror. Barely acknowledging her angel reflection, she called, "Gracie." She waited, her gaze trained on the mirror. When Gracie didn't appear, she called again, this time louder. "Gracie!" Still her angel friend did not appear, nor did Calvin, who must have heard her call.

They were obviously taking her at her word. She was on her own.

Dora slumped onto the edge of her bed. If she couldn't talk to Gracie, she had no idea to whom she could confide her fears. Tears gathered in her eyes, blurring the image of the forlorn angel in the mirror. She was going to fail to complete her mission, and all because she had let her emotions get in the way, the very thing Calvin had cautioned her against.

But she couldn't fail. Penny and Tony's happiness were in her hands. She had to find a way to stop these feelings she had for Tony. She racked her brain for an answer, but none came. This was all so . . . so mortal, and she had no idea how to control it. How did mortals stop this involuntary flow of emotions toward another person?

The sound of a slamming door at the Sullivans' house broke through her troubled thoughts. Instantly, Dora knew to whom she could talk. Tony was picking Penny up at school after their parent/teacher conference, so she didn't have to worry about that. Dora had the rest of the afternoon to try to solve her troubling problem.

Millie opened the door at Dora's knock and ushered her into her warm, cozy kitchen. "I need to talk to you. Do you have a few minutes?"

"Of course. I always have time for you, Dora. Have a seat, dear. I just made Preston some coffee. Let me take him a cup, and then you and I can visit."

The older woman poured rich, dark coffee into a heavy earthenware mug, then added two teaspoons of sugar and a dollop of Half & Half. After stirring it thoroughly, she placed it on a tray with a plate of cheese and crackers and carried it from the room.

While she was gone, Dora took in the homey kitchen. The odor of something baking in the oven filled the room. Dora's taste buds came to life. So far, she'd been able to avoid picking up on some of the vices the mortals had, but their food was something she just couldn't find it in herself to resist. Millie's food in particular tempted her beyond control.

Pushing the smell of whatever Millie was baking from her mind, Dora concentrated on her surroundings. Everything, from the ceramic angels lining the windowsill over the sink, to the flower print place mats on the table and the small braided rug in front of the sink screamed *Millie*. Her loving touch was everywhere, and it made the room feel like—home.

Dora couldn't help but wonder what it would have

been like for a child to have been raised in this kind of atmosphere, surrounded by angel statues and loved and pampered by a woman who was as close to an angel herself as any mortal could get. The fact that Millie and Preston had never had a child seemed so heartbreakingly unfair. If only they were younger, Dora would have tried to intercede for them with the Angel of Destiny.

Millie came back into the kitchen wiping her hands on her pristine, white ruffled apron. "Preston's watching *Jeopardy*, and that'll keep him busy while we have a cup of coffee and indulge ourselves in some girl talk." Once the coffee was poured and Millie had supplied a plate of her sugar cookies, she took a seat across from Dora. "Now, what is it you wanted to talk to me about?"

For a moment, all Dora could do was play with her spoon. Now that she was facing Millie, she felt foolish. In comparison to the challenges Millie faced daily in her life, the feelings she was having for Tony seemed trivial.

A warm hand slid over hers. "Dora, there's nothing you can't talk to me about."

So many times Dora had heard Earth mothers tell their daughters that very same thing. It warmed her and removed all hesitation. Still, she hedged, not from embarrassment or because she felt it trivial, but because she simply hated admitting her ignorance about such a basic emotion.

"There's this girl I know. A friend of mine. She's falling

in love with this man, a man who is totally wrong for her in every way. She knows it's impossible for her to ever have a relationship with him, but . . ." She cleared her throat. "Well, she wants to know how to stop loving him."

Millie stared at her for a long moment, her expression puzzled. Then she chuckled softly and patted Dora's hand. "Honey, I'm afraid your . . . uh . . . friend is stuck. You see, you can't stop love."

Dora's heart dropped. "You can't?"

"Nope." Millie shook her head vigorously. Her salt-and-pepper curls bobbed merrily around her face. "Once old Cupid fires his arrow into you, that's it."

Dora didn't correct Millie's reference to the legendary bowman. She knew that the Archangel Michael had created Cupid as a practical joke on Raphael. Michael had taken perverse pleasure in circulating a rumor that Cupid, not Raphael, oversaw love in a diaper with a bow and a quiver of arrows strapped to his tiny back. The Archangel had stomped around Heaven for eons protesting, but by then the rumor had taken on a life of its own and now it was impossible to deny.

Putting aside the Cupid reference, Dora protested. "But my friend is all wrong for this man. They come from different places and lead totally different lives."

Millie shook her head again. "Doesn't matter. Love is the only emotion the good Lord gave us that can't be controlled and that's blind to everything but the heart's longings." She bit into a cookie and chewed thoughtfully, then swallowed. "Take Preston and me. No two people were ever more mismatched. He loves those darn game shows, and I'd rather be out in the sunshine digging in my flower bed or curled up with a good book. I like a good shoot 'em up movie, and he favors the old-time musicals. Seems in all the years we've been together, we never agreed on anything . . . except wanting children." Her eyes teared up. "But when we found out I was barren, I couldn't have asked for a more understanding, loving man. If it hadn't been for his love and his strength, I don't think I'd have gotten through that time."

"But—"

Millie's squeezed Dora's hand. "Honey, if you love someone, nothing can change that, nothing on this Earth or in Heaven."

Dora sighed in defeat. Maybe not on Earth, but she knew one angel who would do everything in his considerable power to change it in Heaven.

Millie munched thoughtfully on a Christmas tree cookie. Finally, she put it on her saucer and looked directly into Dora's eyes. "It's Tony, isn't it?"

"Excuse me?"

"Tony. You're in love with him, aren't you?" Before Dora could answer, Millie rushed on. "Oh, I saw it in your eyes that first day. And I couldn't be happier. You and Tony will make such a wonderful couple and a terrific family for little Penny."

Dora's heart dropped to her feet. The chances of that happening were zero to none. Worse, if she hadn't been able to keep the truth from Millie, how would she ever keep it from Tony? "Okay. You're right. I was talking about myself. I do love Tony. But since I hardly know him, I don't understand how that could happen."

Millie shook her head. "Time has nothing to do with anything. One day or one million days, when love hits, it hits. Take my Preston and me. We knew the minute we saw each other that we'd spend the rest of our lives together." She placed her hand over her heart. "You know in here. For some people, it has to sprout, then come to bud and grow, but for others it's there immediately, like an open rose drinking in the sunshine. But no matter which way it hits you, it's there, and the right kind, the strong kind, lives forever."

Dora remembered how her heart had fluttered that first day. Was Millie right? Had she fallen in love with Tony that first day? It was a question she wasn't ready to answer, so she changed the subject. Millie just smiled and allowed their conversation to be led in another direction.

For the next hour they drank more coffee, scarfed down more cookies, and talked about cooking and the pros and cons of ham or turkey for Christmas dinner.

"I'm thinking turkey. It's traditional."

"No," Millie said, shaking her head. "I always liked to do a Virginia-baked ham. There's always such chaos in the house on Christmas and preparing a turkey takes you away from the center of the action. I do so enjoy watching everyone open presents, and I'd miss that if I was stuck in the kitchen shoving dressing into a turkey. With the ham, you glaze it, baste it occasionally, and the rest of the time is yours."

Millie's argument made a lot of sense. Dora finally agreed that a ham was the way to go. But after all, when it came right down to it, it didn't matter one way or the other. She wouldn't even be there for Christmas dinner.

"Dora!"

Tony's raised voice coming from outside the back door pierced the stillness that had settled over the kitchen. Both women jumped and dashed to the door. Outside, Tony stood at the bottom of Millie's back porch steps, fists jammed on his hips, his face raging red, and his eyes fairly shooting fire.

"Where the hell is my niece?"

Dora cringed at the angry man before her. She'd never seen Tony like this, so infuriated. Dread chased up and down her body. Fear stole coherent thought from her head. She fought for words to answer his question, but her mind wouldn't work. "I . . . uh . . . I—"

Millie stepped in front of Dora as though to shield her. "Lower your voice. How dare you use that tone on this child? Who do you think you're talking to?"

Evidently, Millie's stern reprimand hit home. Tony lowered not only his voice, but also his fists from his hips. "Where is Penny?" he repeated in a much more controlled, but nevertheless clipped tone.

"That's better." Millie stepped to the side and turned to Dora. "Where's Penny, dear?"

With a lot of effort, Dora forced her brain to process the question. She glanced at Millie, then turned to Tony. "You were supposed to bring her home with you after your parent/teacher meeting this afternoon."

Instantly, the crimson rage that had colored Tony's face moments before drained away, leaving him shocked and pale. "Oh, my God, there was an accident at work with one of my men, and I forgot all about the meeting," he whispered. He looked at his watch, then met Dora's terrified gaze. "The meeting was over an hour ago."

CHAPTER 8

❖

WITH HIS HEART POUNDING FRANTICALLY, TONY dashed to his truck at a dead run. As he slipped and slid over Millie's snow-covered lawn, he called back instructions to Dora over his shoulder. "You stay here in case Penny calls. I'll go see if I can find her."

Mentally, he beat himself up. How could he have forgotten his niece? No matter what was happening at work, this was inexcusable. Totally inexcusable. He should have remembered and called Dora to pick up Penny. What if something had happened to her? Oh, God! He couldn't even consider it. Not Penny. Not Rosalie's baby girl. Not another person he loved.

Almost before Tony had his door closed, the truck zipped backward down the driveway, slipping and sliding in every direction on the slick cement. He swung the truck around, threw the gearshift into *Drive*, and shot down the street, a prayer on his lips.

As he drove toward her school, he scanned the streets for any sign of the little girl. Time crawled by and still he saw no sign of Penny. As each moment ticked by, his level of apprehension grew. Beads of sweat coated his forehead, despite the cool air in the truck's cab. He gripped the steering wheel with a strength that turned his knuckles a ghostly white. His throbbing heart felt as though it would burst from his chest. He'd never been so scared in all his life.

When he reached the school, he drove up to the front entrance, jumped out, and ran up the walk. He grabbed the door handle. It wouldn't budge. Locked. He looked around, praying for the sight of a small, frightened girl waiting for her tardy uncle to show up, but there was no one anywhere in sight.

The terror inside him grew to alarming proportions. His stomach heaved. If he was this frightened, how must Penny feel thinking she'd been left behind, forgotten, abandoned?

"Penny!" He listened, hoping to hear her answer. Hoping she'd just wandered out of sight of the school. Silence. "Penny!" The absolute, mind-bending fear that consumed him resonated in his voice, making it quaver.

When he got no answer after the third and fourth time he called her name, he raced back to the truck and in seconds was careening down the school's drive onto the street.

Though he drove slowly, the trees and houses he passed were a blur and all he saw clearly were the people moving along the sidewalks. Men, women, kids. None of them his niece. Crazed, impossible scenarios presented themselves in a kaleidoscope of wild imaginings. Each worse than the last. Predators, animals, traffic accidents battered his mind.

Then he turned down a street that ran parallel to the school's and spotted a small girl huddled inside a baby blue ski jacket. He held his breath until he'd drawn up beside her and actually knew it was Penny. He mashed the brake, threw the truck into *Park*, and opened the door. Jumping out, he ran to her.

He wanted to take her in his arms and hold her to make sure she was okay, but he couldn't. Something held him back. The little voice that warned him what happened when he allowed himself to love those around him. He tried to push it aside, knowing Penny needed him to hug her. In the end, however, he could not permit himself that show of emotion. Instead he took refuge in anger.

"Penny, where do you think you're going?"

The child looked at him, then hung her head. "Home," she whispered. "You forgot me, so I was walking home."

As if a hand had reached inside his chest and squeezed his heart, Tony gasped. Guilt, prompted by the truth of her accusation, covered him like a mourning shroud. Still, he could not let go of his emotions and give Penny the physical reassurance that she was safe and loved.

"Get in the truck."

She scooted past him and climbed into the driver's seat, then slid across to the passenger's side. She looked small huddled against the door.

Fear still churned inside him. "Put on your seat belt." The sharp tone of his voice cut deeply into his conscience.

Penny did as he instructed, then cuddled up to the door as if trying to make herself smaller than she was, as though trying to get as far from the angry man beside her as she could. Tony could read the confusion in her face. She had to be asking herself why he was so angry with her when it was he who had forgotten her. Guilt soured his churning stomach.

Almost absently, he patted her shoulder, hoping it would ease her fear but at the same time knowing it was a pitiful gesture to offer a child who had been left in the school yard, left to think she didn't matter. Still, it was all he could allow himself to offer.

The streetlights had come on and now they flashed streaks of light over Penny's pale face. She shivered, probably chilled straight through to the bone. Tony turned up the heat and put the blower on high. Slowly, the interior of the truck grew toasty warm.

It only took minutes for them to reach home. When Tony brought the truck to a stop, Penny jumped out and ran into the house. Tony thought he heard a sob escape her as she ran up the front walk. He loathed himself for causing her more pain, but he just couldn't let the softer side of himself to escape.

What the hell kind of person was he when he couldn't give reassurance to a frightened little girl when she so desperately needed it?

Dora sat in the living room, the phone in her lap. Jack lay curled in a ball on the chair across from her. The message button on the answering machine blinked a bright red. Dora pushed it.

"Dora, I think Uncle Tony forgot me. Can you come pick me up at school?" Penny's voice shook.

She had to be terrified. What had she thought when no one came for her? How long had she stood in the cold waiting for someone who never showed up?

Dora's stomach tightened into a knot. She listened absently while the machine announced that the message had ended, then gave the instruction to delete it.

If only she'd been here and not at Millie's, she would have gotten Penny's message. If only—

Hindsight is twenty-twenty. Now, do you see why I cautioned you not to become emotionally involved with the mortals? You can't afford this kind of distraction.

Great! What a time for him to show up. On top of everything else, this was just what she needed. Calvin and his sanctimonious, I-told-you-so attitude.

"You might show some concern for the missing child, Calvin," she said to the empty room.

Oh, I am, which is why I'm reminding you of your mission. Had you not been next door chatting about love with Millie, you could have prevented this entire problem.

Dora swallowed repeatedly, trying to rid her throat of the lump of guilt Calvin's words had produced. As much as she hated to admit it, Calvin was right. She should have been here instead of next door baring her soul to Millie. This time her screwup had nearly been more disastrous than any that had come before it.

Jack rolled onto his back and cast a sidelong glance at her, as though reprimanding her for disturbing his sleep.

"In my defense, Tony was supposed to be there to pick her up today. And speaking of being there . . . exactly what was Penny's Guardian Angel doing while this was all going on?"

Unlike you, he was doing his job by watching over

Penny so that nothing more terrible happened to her.

Dora sat up straighter. "Does that mean she's all right?"

Silence. Sometimes Calvin could be the most infuriating, the most—

A car door slammed outside.

Dora jumped off the couch and rushed into the hall in time to catch Penny as she hurtled through the door and launched herself into Dora's arms. Tony followed her, but stopped just inside the front door. Dora glanced up at him from where she knelt with Penny enfolded in her embrace, the child's face buried against her shoulder. He stared at them for a long moment, then, turning on his heel, he left the house without a word.

Dora glared at the closed door, then led Penny into the living room and held her on her lap while she cried her heart out. The least he could have done was stick around to reassure his niece that everything was all right, and she was safe.

A long time later, when Penny's sobs had subsided into a few intermittent hiccups, Dora repositioned her in the crook of her arm and settled back on the sofa.

She raised her tear-streaked face to Dora. "Uncle Tony's very mad at me, isn't he?"

Dora plucked a tissue from the box on the side table and wiped the moisture from Penny's cheeks. "No, angel. He's mad at himself because he forgot."

"But why did he forget me, Dora?" A lock of coppery hair fell across her face.

Smoothing the hair back behind her ear, Dora kissed the little girl's forehead. "One of the men who works for your uncle got hurt, and he had to take him to the hospital. I guess in all the excitement, he forgot that he had a meeting with your teacher today." She held Penny away from her and looked her in the eye. "You know he would never do that on purpose, don't you, Penny?"

Penny shrugged. "I guess." Both her tone of voice and her posture said she didn't believe it at all.

"Well, he wouldn't. I promise." She stood Penny on her feet. "Now, let's go have a snack." Penny opened her mouth, to remind her Tony didn't approve of snacks, Dora assumed, but she stopped her. "I think since this is a sort-of special exception that Uncle Tony won't mind."

She led Penny into the kitchen. On the way, Dora became aware of how she had adopted Millie's belief that food could cure anything. In the kitchen, she poured a glass of milk for each of them and got out some of Millie's Christmas cookies. They had just really gotten into seeing who could dunk their cookie for the longest without losing it in the glass of milk when the front door opened.

Penny glanced apprehensively at Dora. The little girl laid her cookie on the plate and stared at her lap. Dora patted her hand and turned toward the door. Seconds later, Tony came in. He stopped in the doorway to the kitchen and surveyed the scene before him.

He smiled. "Is there enough for me?" Penny's head shot up and a half smile curved her lips.

"Sure." Surprised by his request and that he hadn't gotten upset about their snack, Dora jumped up and got him a glass of milk.

He took a seat next to Penny and smiled at her. "I have a present for you." He reached into his pants pocket and pulled out a small, rectangular pink object. Flipping it open, he held it out for Penny to see.

She studied it for a moment. "What is it?"

"It's a cell phone, but not just any cell phone. This one is just for kids. See these?" He pointed at the four buttons on the phone's face. "The one with the picture of the lady is our home number, and the man is my number at work. This one with the red lightbulb is to call the police, and this one with the house on it is for Millie. If you push the one in the middle with the picture of the book on it, you'll find my cell phone number and Dora's. That's in case we're not at the other two numbers." He handed it to her and watched as she fingered the buttons. "Keep this with you all the time, and if you ever need any of us, all you have to do is push the right button and no matter where we are, either Millie or Dora or I will answer."

"But I don't have a cell phone," Dora said, pleased

with the return of the smile to Penny's face.

He reached in his other pocket, pulled out a silver rectangle, and flipped it open to reveal another cell phone. "You do now." He handed the phone to Dora. "I already programmed all the numbers you'll need into your phone and Penny's. I don't ever want Penny not to be able to get in touch with someone when she needs us."

"It's a very thoughtful gift, Tony. Isn't it, Penny?" Penny nodded, still captivated with her cell phone.

Dora smiled, but in her heart she was wondering how much more good it would have done Penny for him to hug her and reassure her from his heart that she was loved. Still, it was a step forward, but Dora didn't have much time left before Christmas Eve, and she wondered how many more steps it would take to get through to him.

She was most certainly going to need the Heavenly Council to extend her time here. Calvin would not be happy about it.

CHAPTER 9

THAT NIGHT DORA WAITED UNTIL EVERYONE IN the house was asleep, then hurried to her room and removed the sheet from the mirror. Used to her reflection appearing as an angel, she gave it scant attention. Instead, she called out for Calvin.

"Calvin?"

No answer.

"Calvin!" This time her voice echoed around the room like a clap of thunder.

Still no answer.

"Ca—" A ball of light shimmered into shape, cutting Dora's next bellow short.

But the shape that appeared was not Calvin. Gracie stood before her.

"Where's Calvin?"

Gracie shrugged, making her wings bob up and down.

"No one's seen him for a day or two." She laid aside a star she'd been polishing and smiled at Dora. "What's up? Can I help?"

For a moment, Dora nearly said no, then she remembered something. Everyone knew the Heavenly Council liked Gracie. When Michael had tripped over a storm cloud and came precariously close to falling into the middle of New York's rush hour traffic, he'd lost his halo. While a group of stunned angels had stood by and watched it spiral into Central Park's lake, Gracie had taken action and retrieved it for him, earning her a special place in the heart of the Archangel. And everyone also knew that Michael's voice held a great deal of sway among the Heavenly Council.

Calvin, on the other hand, held the Council in such awe that he probably would refuse to go before them for her for fear they would lower some terrible retribution on his head.

Taking that into consideration, Dora decided she might be better off having Gracie ask for her time extension.

"Gracie, will you talk to Michael for me?"

The petite angel considered the request for a moment. "What do you want?"

"I need an extension for my time on Earth." She could almost see the refusal hovering on Gracie's lips. Before her friend had a chance to say no, Dora added, "Tony is being very difficult. I can't seem to get through to him, and my time is running out. I need an extension."

For a moment Gracie merely stared at Dora. "Such a request will need more than just Michael's approval. You'll need the unanimous agreement of the entire Council."

"But Michael can persuade them. Please, Gracie."

Gracie finished polishing the star, then spun it off into the sky like a Frisbee. "Is it really concern for your lack of progress or because you don't want to leave him?"

Words failed Dora. Gracie had read her underlying reason for wanting more time. Deep down she knew she wasn't making any headway with Tony, or minimal at best. However, if she wanted to be honest with herself, spending Christmas morning with him and Penny had begun to take up a lot of her dream time. The line between what was most urgent for her had begun to blur.

"That doesn't matter, Gracie. Tony doesn't even know I'm alive."

"Oh, he knows you're alive. Melanie, the Angel of Relationships, told me so. She's heard him thinking about you . . . a lot."

Dora brightened, then fear seeped under her happiness knowing Tony had been thinking about her. "But he can't. I can't. I mean, Calvin made me promise I wouldn't. No. That can't happen." Her fear grew. "If Calvin finds out, he'll bring me back." She couldn't go back. Not now. Not when she hadn't proven herself. Not when she wanted so desperately to spend more time with Penny . . . and Tony.

Gracie frowned. "Calvin made you promise you wouldn't do what?"

"Never mind. He just can't know about what Melanie told you. Promise me, Gracie."

"Easy does it." Gracie laid a hand on the shoulder of Dora's reflection. "Calvin is not going to find out. Melanie promised she'd say nothing to anyone about it."

Dora breathed a sigh of relief. She knew Melanie and Gracie would keep their word. "So will you speak to the Heavenly Council for me?"

Her friend considered the request for a moment, then nodded. "Wait here." Gracie shimmered out of sight.

For what seemed like hours, Dora paced the floor in front of the mirror. Every few seconds, she glanced at the mirror, but only her reflection met her troubled gaze. Then a tiny pinpoint of white light appeared over her reflection's shoulder. Dora held her breath as it grew larger and larger, finally taking the form of Gracie. And Gracie didn't look happy.

"They said no, Dora. I'm sorry."

"But did they give you a reason?"

Gracie shook her head. "They're the Heavenly Council. They don't need a good reason, and even if they did have one, chances are they wouldn't tell me or you."

Dora nodded. "Thanks, Gracie." Without waiting for Gracie to shimmer out, Dora covered the mirror. She didn't want her friend to see her tears.

Feeling terrible for Dora, Gracie stared at the back side of the sheet. "This was not the way things were supposed to go. I'm going to have to look into this and speak to Raphael about arranging to give Mr. Falcone a gentle nudge."

She glanced around her. "As for Calvin, if he doesn't show up soon, he's going to be in major trouble with the Council. I wouldn't be a bit surprised if they sentenced him to counting raindrops during hurricane season."

In the construction office the next afternoon, while Tony worked on a bid for a low-income apartment building to be built downtown, his cell phone rang. Absently, he picked it up and flipped it open. As he did, he glanced at the caller ID. *Penny?* His heart stopped.

"Penny? Are you okay?"

"Yes. I—" Hesitation filled the silence. "I just

wanted to make sure you're there."

For a moment, he considered reprimanding her for using the emergency number for nothing. But a painful twinge in his heart intervened. She just needed the reassurance of knowing he'd keep his word, that he would be there if she needed him. After yesterday, who could blame her?

"Yes, I'm here."

"Good. Bye."

"Bye." He closed the phone and laid it on the desk beside him. He stared at it. The guilt of having forgotten her yesterday came back full force. Understanding how he could have done that still remained a mystery to him. But he'd make damned sure it didn't happen again.

That morning Penny had reverted to the quiet child she'd been before Dora came, and Dora hadn't even been speaking to him when he left. The worst part was, he couldn't blame either of them. He knew he wasn't the best when it came to raising kids, but this went far beyond any of his other shortcomings. This was his niece, his flesh and blood, his responsibility. You didn't just forget those things. No matter what else was going on in your life, you didn't forget the people you loved.

"Tony?"

He jumped. The impatience edging his foreman's voice told Tony Jake had had to call to him more than once. "Sorry. What's up?"

He turned to Jake and stopped dead. Behind him was a light much too bright to be the sun. It seemed to surround him and reminded Tony very much of the light that he'd seen when Dora first came to his house. But as quickly as it had come, it vanished. Tony blinked.

"You okay?" Jake tilted his head to study Tony's face. The sunlight shining through the window glinted off Jake's balding head. That had to be what Tony had seen.

"Uh, yeah. I'm fine. Just thinking."

Jake propped his hip on the corner of Tony's desk and grinned knowingly. "Thinking, huh? About that sexy little number living at your house, I bet."

Tony sighed. Dora had been in his thoughts, but not in the way Jake intimated . . . at least not this time. He'd gotten fairly used to Jake prying into his private life. Correction. Prying into his love life, or lack thereof. But today it hit a very raw nerve.

"No," he snapped.

Showing no sign that Tony's clipped reply had bothered him, Jake adjusted his posterior to a more comfortable position, a definite sign he was not going to let go of his subject. Jake's grin widened. "Well, then, may I suggest you do?"

"No, you may not." Tony rolled up the blueprints he'd been staring at without seeing for over an hour and stowed them in a cardboard tube. "When I need help with my social life, I'll ask you. Until then, stick to playing with your hammer and nails."

Jake shook his head. "It's not your social life I'm interested in. Besides, someone has to interfere. You're certainly not doing much on your own."

Through gritted teeth, Tony snarled, "I can handle my own life. Thank you very much."

"Right, and you've been doing such a sterling job of that lately, haven't you?" Jake swore under his breath and all playfulness disappeared from both his voice and his expression. "Do you realize that by my count, you haven't been out with a woman in over a year?"

He threw Jake an it's-none-of-your-business glare. "I didn't realize you were keeping track of my social life. And did it ever occur to you that my lack of dating might be because I haven't met anyone I'm interested in?"

Jake took the cardboard tube from Tony and stood it in the corner of the work shack, along with several others. Then he returned to continue their conversation.

"That might hold true for the other women you've met, but I saw how you looked when you talked about this Dora. I heard your voice when you told me about her." He shook a finger under Tony's nose. "If that's not interest, I'll eat my hard hat. This one is special, and you'd better get off your ass and do something about it before she gets away."

Heaven save him from matchmaking friends. Still . . .

Tony couldn't argue Jake's point about Dora being special. No matter how much he tried, he couldn't easily dismiss his unprecedented reaction to her from the day he opened the front door and saw her silhouetted against that strange halo of light as she stood on his doorstep, right up to the time they kissed in the Christmas tree lot. To be totally honest, she had rocked his world in a way nothing or no one before her ever had.

From the very first, she'd related to Penny as if she'd known her all her life. She seemed to understand his niece's deepest needs, something he had no hope of ever mastering.

And there lay the crux of his problem.

"There's just one problem with your advice, genius. If I got involved with Dora, and it went south, she'd leave. I can't afford for that to happen. I need her help with Penny. She's good for her, and with her at the house, I can concentrate on this." He waved a hand to encompass the construction shack and the hodgepodge of papers strewn in front of him.

Jake pulled one of the chairs up next to the desk and sat. Leaning his forearms on it, he studied Tony. "So, am I detecting that you'd *like* to get involved, and the only reason you're holding back is Penny?"

Shaking his head vehemently, Tony threw him a glare. "For crying out loud, I didn't say that. Getting involved with her was purely a hypothetical example."

Hitting the desk with his palm, Jake snorted derisively and leaned the chair back on two legs. "Don't give me that shit. I wasn't born yesterday. Penny and this construction site have nothing to do with it. They're excuses. You're just afraid to get involved. You have been ever since your sister's accident."

The carefully hidden wound that cloaked Tony's memories of the accident burned and split open. The conversation had gone far enough. Tony scowled at Jake. "Don't you have work to do?"

"Aha!" Jake dropped the chair back on all four legs. "Hit a sore spot, did I?"

Jake had no idea how sore that particular spot was. Riffling through a stack of work orders on his desk, Tony ignored Jake. The more he argued with him, the more Jake would pry into his personal life. "Did you come in here for any reason or just to antagonize me?" His short, crisp tone must have warned Jake he'd gone too far.

Jake looked abashed. His entire demeanor made an abrupt change, and he cleared his throat. "Oh, yeah. That new kid you hired to replace Jim is good. I think you should consider keeping him on permanently."

Although he could punch holes as big as the Grand

Canyon in his foreman's assessment of his love life, Tony had never doubted Jake's assessment of the men he hired. "If you say so, it's okay with me."

Jake snorted. "I wish it was that easy to talk you into everything." He started toward the door and stopped. He looked at Tony, his expression that of a concerned friend. "I only want to see you happy. You know that, don't you?"

A grin slipped across Tony's lips. His anger of a few minutes before drained away. He nodded. "Yeah. I know. Now, get out of here."

After Jake left, Tony stared at the closed door. Did his foreman really think he was unhappy? A better question was . . . was he? He shook his head. More important problems needed his attention than wasting the day worrying about Jake's assessment of his life, and how to avoid Dora and the attraction he had for her. He chastised himself for being a fool. While he was here agonizing over this, Dora was no doubt home, never giving him a second thought.

Dora sat on the edge of her bed. So, that was that. On Christmas Eve she would have to leave Tony and Penny forever. She clutched her chest.

The other angels had been wrong. It wasn't only mortals who could feel the excruciating pain of a breaking heart.

CHAPTER 10

TWO DAYS LATER, PENNY RAN INTO THE HOUSE with Tony trailing behind her. He and Dora had decided that if he picked his niece up for a few days instead of Dora, it would help confirm for Penny that Tony's forgetting her was a onetime fluke and that she could rely on him. That, along with the cell phone Tony had given her, seemed to have bolstered Penny's confidence that she would not be abandoned again. At least she didn't appear to be worrying about the incident repeating itself.

"Dora, Dora!" Penny called as she ran down the hall and into the kitchen waving a paper in her hand. "I have to write a story for a contest at school. The winner gets to read their story at the Winter Carnival show." She handed Dora the sheet of paper she'd been waving around.

"That sounds like fun. Let's see what you have to write about." Dora studied the paper. "Hmm. It says you have to write about the best Christmas present you ever got." She handed the paper back to Penny. "So, what are you going to write about?"

Penny's brow furrowed. "I'm not sure yet. I have to think about it. Teacher says to think real hard before we start writing."

Tony, who had been regaled with the contest details nonstop on the drive home and was only half-listening to the exchange, studied Dora. With her head bent toward Penny, her hair fell forward and hid her face behind a silken, black veil. But he didn't need to see her face to know what it looked like. Etched indelibly on his mind's eye, he'd seen it every night in his dreams and every day in his imagination—an imagination that had become overly active and unbelievably troublesome, especially at work. It still baffled him that she could have such a hold on him after so short a time.

Dora was the most beautiful woman he'd ever seen. But beyond that, she carried that same beauty inside her and showered those around her with its light. In many ways, she reminded him of Rosalie. Though Tony had not spent much time with his niece before Rosalie's death, he'd spent enough time with them to watch his sister interact with her daughter. Dora had the same innate understanding of Penny and her needs that his sister had exhibited over and over. Recalling Rosalie's love of animals, he could easily see her having shown the same compassion for Jack that Dora had shown, and the same—

"Right, Tony?"

Dora's soft voice jolted him back to the here and now. He shook his head and tamped down the embarrassment of being so absorbed in his thoughts that he'd totally missed the conversation between Dora and Penny.

Both Penny and Dora were staring at him expectantly. "Sorry, my mind was wandering."

"I told Penny we would definitely come listen to her read her story when she wins this contest." She held up the school paper.

He didn't miss the positive *when* and not *if* that Dora had used. "Absolutely," he affirmed and smiled at Penny.

"Do you think I can win, Uncle Tony?"

Tony reached toward her and then pulled his hand back. The disappointment in Dora's expression didn't go unnoticed. "Of course, you can."

Unaware of the hesitation in her uncle's gesture, Penny threw him a smile and then scooped up her backpack and slipped it onto her shoulders. "I'd better get started." She stopped abruptly. "If that's okay."

She looked directly at him, waiting for his approval again. Tony hated that, but he didn't seem to be able to do anything that would make her see she didn't need his constant approval for everything she did.

"Tell you what." He removed the backpack from Penny's slim shoulders and laid it on one of the kitchen chairs. "Why don't you sit right here at the table, and Dora will make you a snack? You can start work on your story later. While you have your snack, you can think about what you want to write."

Both Dora and Penny stared openmouthed at him. Neither of them moved, as though waiting for him to take back his suggestion.

Dora was stunned. In recent days Tony had shown slackening of his rigid rule of no snacks before dinner for Penny. It wasn't a big step, but it was another step in the right direction.

"I just took some chocolate chip cookies from the oven." She pointed to a rack of cooling cookies on the counter. "I made them from a recipe Millie gave me. You can have a couple of them with a nice tall glass of cold milk." She grinned at Penny. "Maybe Uncle Tony would like some, too." She sent him a speaking glance.

Tony hesitated for a second, then pulled a chair from under the table and sat down. "Sure. I would never pass up warm chocolate chip cookies." He glanced at Dora. "You'll have some, too, right?"

Dora flushed. "Sure." She took a seat next to Tony and they exchanged warm smiles. Tony's expression touched her as surely as if he'd laid his hand on her heart.

Contentment, sweet and peaceful, swept through her.

Jack, who had come into the room unnoticed, barked. Everyone turned to him. The dog's fur stood on end and pointed in several different directions, as though he'd been scared to death, and in response it had all stood on end.

"Later, you're going to need to give Jack a good brushing," Dora said, still staring at the dog and trying to figure out what had happened to him that had disturbed him so much.

Penny laughed. "Okay, but first you can have a cookie, too, Jack, but I have to find one without too many chips. Chocolate's not good for dogs." She looked at Tony. "My teacher told me that."

"Well, then, let's see if we can find one for him without too many chips. We can't have old Jack getting sick." Tony pulled the plate of cooling cookies toward him.

To Dora's surprise, Tony began searching through the cookies for one they could safely feed Jack. Since they'd taken the mutt in, he'd tolerated Jack and had paid him almost no attention. That he was now concerned for Jack's health came as a shock. Then it occurred to her his worry centered more on Penny than Jack. The dog had become a central part of her life and if anything happened to him . . .

"Here's one." Dora handed Penny a smaller cookie with

no chips showing. "It's one of the last I put on the cookie sheet and most of the chips were already in the others."

For a while, they all watched while Jack gobbled down the cookie as if he hadn't eaten in weeks. As he ate, his hair seemed to smooth itself out. It reminded Dora of how Calvin's wing feathers went bonkers whenever he was upset and how they slowly fell back into place as he—

The thought stopped Dora cold. Could Jack be—? No. That was ridiculous. Still, he had arrived at the same time she'd told Calvin to stop hovering and had subsequently disappeared from contact above, something to which he'd agreed with uncharacteristic speed. Gracie had said no one had seen Calvin in days and didn't know where he'd gone. And, despite their newspaper's classified ad having run for a few days, no one had called to claim the dog.

Silently, she studied Jack. When he'd finished eating his cookie, he sat down and stared at Dora with a look of total innocence lighting his brown eyes. The look did not alleviate Dora's suspicions.

Calvin? Is that you? she asked.

Silence accompanied by that doleful, put-upon look.

Calvin, if that's you, answer me.

More silence.

Eventually, the dog blinked, stood, and sauntered from the room. Dora frowned. Though she admitted it was a stretch, she wasn't totally convinced she'd mis-judged their furry friend. Calvin had already proven he wasn't above deception to keep track of her. He'd do almost anything to prevent incurring the wrath of the Council, even if it meant masquerading as a mutt, eat-ing off the floor, and sleeping on a ragged blanket in the laundry room.

Feeling only a tad foolish, she made a note to herself to have a private chat with Jack after Penny and Tony went to bed.

Not a sound broke the silence in the Falcone house. Penny had been in bed for hours, and Tony had disappeared up the stairs a short time ago, mumbling something about a lot of work to be done at the construction site the next day. Dora had waited until she was sure both were asleep and then tiptoed into the laundry room where Jack lay curled on his makeshift bed of old blankets.

She stared hard at the dog, watching carefully for anything that would give him away. "Calvin?"

The dog blinked sleepily, rolled onto his back, and stretched his paws above him, an open invitation to get his belly scratched. Any other time, she would have obliged, but if Jack was indeed Calvin, the thought of scratching his belly was a bit more than she could stand. Until she knew for sure this mutt was not her boss, their interaction would have limits.

It didn't appear as if he was going to answer her one way or the other.

"Calvin, if that is you, you need to listen to me. Coming here disguised as Penny's stuffed dog in the flesh was completely insensitive on your part." She waited for a response, but Jack, resigned to no belly scratch, rolled to his side, closed his eyes, and went back to sleep. Lowering her voice to a whisper, she poked his side with her finger. "Don't you dare go back to sleep." He opened one eye, yawned, then closed it again. "Okay, ignore me if you want, but you're the one who's going to break that little girl's heart when you have to go, and you know you will have to leave sooner or later. What then, Calvin? Are you prepared to hurt Penny like that? Will you be able to explain that to the Council?"

"Who are you talking to?"

Dora nearly jumped out of her skin. She swung toward the voice. Tony stood just inside the kitchen door. His gray sweatpants were slung low on his hips, revealing a line of dark hair that ran from his navel and disappeared beneath the waistband. His upper torso was naked. A scattering of dark hair peppered his chest. And, oh, good heavens, what a chest it was. Broad, with a lingering summer tan, and rippling with muscles.

Frantically, she sought for her voice, then for the words to explain why he'd caught her talking to Jack, but none would come. All she could see, all she could think about, was the way his broad shoulders tapered down to his trim waist and how the muscles in his arms rippled with each movement of his body and how his smooth, tanned chest called out for her to touch it with each breath he took.

Finally, she snatched at the first thought that came to mind. "I was . . . uh . . . just talking to myself. Getting my plans for tomorrow in order."

He smiled.

Oh, good grief!

Her stomach lurched into a dizzy spin. Then, God help her, he winked. "You know what they say about people who talk to themselves."

Delightful little chills chased up and down her spine. "Uh . . . no, I don't."

Tony walked to the refrigerator, turned back to her, and tapped his temple. "Wacko." Then he winked again.

Her stomach did another crazy somersault. *Oh, for heavens to Betsy, please don't do that.*

She sprang to her feet and began fussing with the place mats, straightening each until they were precisely the same distance from the table's edge. "I thought you went to bed."

He yawned and stretched his arms over his head. The muscles vibrated across his bare chest, sending her senses into a topsy-turvy spin. "I did, but I woke up and my mouth felt as dry as a desert." He reached into the open refrigerator and extracted a can of soda. Dora had just enough time to catch her breath before he turned back to her. "What are you doing up so late . . . besides talking to yourself?" He smiled again. "Join me?" He held up the can.

Darn! I wish he'd stop smiling like that.

"Yes, I could use a drink." Maybe the cold soda would put out the fire growing in the pit of her churning stomach and bring some kind of logic to her tangled thoughts. Certainly, she needed something to calm the foreign sensations coursing through her tingling body.

Tony pulled another can from the fridge, closed it, and sat in the chair closest to hers. He popped the top on one of the cans and handed it to her. His warm fingertips skimmed hers, and the chills running rampant over her body increased. This was not good. Not good at all. Her gaze shifted from the can and locked with Tony's mesmerizing dark eyes. What, in heaven's name, was happening to her? How did this man have the power to throw her entire body into confused chaos?

Alarm bells were going off in Tony's head. He'd

heard those bells almost every time he'd gotten close to Dora. And he'd always heeded the warning. This time, he ignored it. This time, he wanted to follow his emotions and not his head.

Reminders of how sweet she'd tasted that night in the Christmas tree lot raced through his mind. Her lips had been so soft, so innocent, so responsive. More than he wanted his next breath, he wanted to feel that again.

Holding her gaze with his, he leaned close to her. As though in a trance, she remained stone still. He could feel her warm breath on his face, warm and feathery soft. Then he realized it wasn't just her lips he wanted to feel. He needed to feel the entire length of her pressed against him again.

Without releasing her gaze, he took her hands and slowly stood, drawing her to her feet with him. He gazed down into her dark eyes. Her expression accepted his silent invitation. Grasping her shoulders, he pulled her into his arms. Her slight body molded to his without resistance. A deep-throated groan escaped him. He buried his hands in her silky hair and let it sift through his fingers like grains of sand.

Dora peered up at him from eyes as dark and mysterious as the night sky. Then she closed them as if waiting for the kiss she knew was coming. Tony lowered his head until his warm breath mixed with hers and his mouth was a fraction of an inch from hers.

"We shouldn't," she murmured, her eyes still closed, her lips straining toward his.

Gently, Tony stopped her words with a finger on her lips. "Yes, we should."

He removed his finger and replaced it with his lips. She tasted just as he'd remembered: sweet, pure, eager, and oddly innocent. Tenderly, he cupped her face in his hands and rained butterfly kisses on her mouth. She strained to hold him still, to anchor his lips on hers. Then he stopped moving and devoured her mouth in one hungry, demanding kiss.

Dora laced her arms around his neck and hung on, returning his kiss with all the strength she could muster. She felt his hands on her back, smoothing and exploring. Then one slipped around to her front and cupped her breast.

She couldn't breathe. She'd never before felt anything like the sensations buffeting her, and she wanted them to go on forever and ever and ever. As though reading her thoughts, Tony tightened his arms and deepened the kiss. Her heartbeat raced to alarming speeds. Had it not been for his arms, her knees had grown so weak, she would have melted at his feet.

A sharp bark pulled them apart abruptly. Jack stood beside them, his ears back, a ridge of fur standing on end from his head to his behind. He continued to bark loudly until Tony stepped back and released Dora.

"Damn dog," Tony mumbled. "Has no romance in his soul."

Robbed of the ability to speak and the support of Tony's arms, Dora could only grab the back of the chair closest to her to keep from collapsing at Tony's feet. Her head was swimming along with her senses. Her knees felt like jelly, and her hands shook uncontrollably. Her breath came in short gasps.

"I . . ." was all she could say when the power of speech returned.

Tony held up his hand to stop anything more from her. For a very long moment he studied her with an expression of regret and then, as though coming to a decision, shook his head. He picked up his soda and left the kitchen.

Dora peered down at Jack, who had returned to his bed, curled into a ball, and closed his eyes.

"Damn dog," she mumbled, then flicked off the light and headed for her room.

CHAPTER 11

SATURDAY AFTERNOON FOUND DORA, TONY, AND
Penny sitting around the table eating lunch. Rather
than having to meet Tony's gaze, Dora paid undue attention to the arrangement of the sandwich and pickle
on her plate. Out of the corner of her eye, she noted that
Tony also seemed overly absorbed in his food. Only
Penny, unaware of the tension between the two adults,
ate her peanut butter and jelly sandwich with a relaxed
air about her.

To break the tense silence, Dora got up and grabbed
the mail off the counter. She handed some to Tony and
two envelopes to Penny. "Looks like you got mail today,
sweetie."

Eager to open her mail, Penny laid aside her sandwich and took the envelopes. Hastily, she tore the first
one open. It was a Christmas card with reindeer across

the front. The lead deer had a bright red, glowing nose. Penny opened the card and read silently for a moment.

"It's from Grammy and Grampa Stevens. They sent me money." Penny held up the crisp twenty-dollar bill her paternal grandparents had included in the card.

Carefully, she laid it aside and attacked the envelope flap on the other card. This one had a picture of a tiny mouse making a snowman. Once more, Penny read to herself.

"It's from Aunt Lisa." Her forehead furrowed. She passed the card to her uncle. "What's this mean?"

Lisa? Dora recalled all the negative things both Millie and Tony had said about Matt's absentee sister. Why was she suddenly contacting Penny out of the blue? A bad feeling settled like a lump of lead in Dora's stomach.

Tony took the card and read to himself. Stunned surprise registered on his face. "Well," he finally said, handing the card back to her, "it appears as though your aunt will be paying us a visit."

Penny continued to frown. "Why?"

"I'm afraid she didn't say. All she said was, 'See you soon.'"

Her mind busy trying to figure out why Lisa would come to see Penny when she hadn't even acknowledged her existence all this time, Dora hadn't been paying too much heed to the conversation going on between uncle and niece. She did, however, note that Penny didn't seem to be particularly excited about a visit from her aunt.

Totally dismissing the impending visit from an aunt she'd never met, Penny tucked her Christmas money in her jeans pocket. "Dora, can you take me Christmas shopping today? I have money now, and I need to get my teacher a present and one for you and one for Uncle Tony." The child looked at Dora, waiting for an answer.

Distracted by the parade of persistent questions and an unease that she couldn't understand, Dora only half-heard Penny.

"Dora? Are you okay?" This time it was Tony's voice that beckoned to her. She jumped slightly and turned to him. "Penny's talking to you."

"Yes. I'm fine." That was, if anyone could call the state of her forebodings fine. She turned to Penny. "Yes, sweetie, what is it?"

"I need to go Christmas shopping."

Dora smiled. She had never been Christmas shopping. "Sure. If you want, we can go today."

The idea of walking through all the gaily decorated stores lifted her spirits and cleared her mind of Lisa like a brisk wind . . . that was, until she looked at Tony and he smiled and the emotions he had the innate power to produce flooded through her.

This has to stop, she told herself. For the thousandth

time, she reminded herself this was not what she'd been sent there for. In fact, Calvin had explicitly warned her against it. Determined to banish her wayward thoughts, she shook herself mentally.

To occupy herself, she began clearing away the lunch dishes. But abolishing thoughts of her sexy employer was easier said than done, especially when Tony brushed against her when he brought his dishes to the sink, and the tingles raced up her arm and spread through her entire body.

Again she pushed the disturbing sensations aside and faced Tony. Now that she'd cleared her mind of him and could think about what had taken place at the table, she had to ask about Penny's reaction to her aunt coming to see her. "I couldn't help but notice that Penny didn't seem terribly excited about her aunt's impending visit."

He shrugged. "It doesn't surprise me. Lisa has been estranged from her family for years. I was never told why or what started it. All I know is that she's never seen Penny, and she never even came to her brother's funeral." His voice took on a sharp, unforgiving tone. "Given that she has never been here or seen her niece, Penny doesn't know her except through things her parents had told her about her father's sister. Matt always said Lisa was a self-centered brat who would go to any lengths to get what she wanted. Maybe she's finally grown up some and realized that family is something we all need and it's time she made peace with hers."

Dora and Penny hurried through the doors that marked the main entrance to the Crystal River Mall. Warm air gushed at them and removed the chill that had seeped into their bodies as they'd walked from where Dora had to park at the far end of the crowded lot.

This driving stuff was still a little much for her to handle, but parking the car had the power to strike terror in her heart. Slipping something as big as a car into a space cordoned off by two white lines without hitting one of two other parked cars seemed like a cruel thing to ask anyone to do. But over the past few days, she'd made up her mind to conquer her fear and slowly but surely had gotten better at it.

Excited about her very first trip to a mall, Dora gasped at the sight that met her as she passed through the double, automatic glass doors into the busy shopping center. It was like stepping into a Christmas card. As enthralled as a kid in a candy store, Dora tried to drink in everything at once and store it in her memory.

Piped-in Christmas carols warred with the steady hum of the shoppers' voices, the happy chatter of kids waiting to see Santa, and the loudspeakers of some stores offering special holiday promotion sales. Plump garlands of artificial pine hung in long streamers from one wall to the other. Huge, red velvet bows anchored it in place, and white lights sparkled in its depths.

In the center of the main courtyard stood a towering artificial Christmas tree decked out in all its holiday finery with beautifully wrapped packages nestled at its bottom. At the top a gold star sparkled, its points nearly touching the glass ceiling. It reminded Dora of the angel tree topper that still lay on the Falcones' living room coffee table. She pushed the thought away, refusing to let anything dampen this day.

"Look, Dora!" Penny exclaimed, pulling on her hand and guiding her toward the improvised North Pole Village at the foot of the big tree. Santa was holding court with a long line of cherry-cheeked children in every size and shape, who waited eagerly to impart to the jolly old elf what they most wanted for Christmas. An adult or pair of adults who looked as if they were being subjected to the tortures of hell accompanied each child.

As she and Penny watched, each child climbed into Santa's ample lap and whispered their requests for the gift they wanted most to find beneath the tree on Christmas morning. A robust *Ho! Ho! Ho!* followed his promise to deliver.

"Would you like to tell Santa what you want?"

Penny studied the crimson-garbed man for a while. Turning to Dora, her face sad, but serious, she shook her head. "I don't think he can bring me what I want."

Dora didn't bother asking what it was Penny wanted. She thought she knew, and the child was right . . . Santa could not bring her her uncle's love. Only Tony could do that.

They'd been in and out of almost every store in the expansive mall, and Penny had managed to purchase an apple-shaped pin for her teacher and, for her uncle, a new pen with a tiny enamel heart on it. Very telling, in Dora's estimation. However, she sincerely doubted Tony would understand that, to Penny, it was a symbol of her love.

By the time they'd made several trips around the mall, Dora's feet were throbbing. In the last hour, she'd developed an intense longing to sit down in a big soft chair with a tall, very cold drink, and take her shoes off. However, Penny was on a mission to get something for Millie and was not taking no for an answer.

"In here," Penny instructed and, grabbing her hand, hauled Dora into yet another store.

The *Enchanted Forest* was smaller than the other stores they'd been in, and the limited stock consisted of, among other things such as jewelry and beaded handbags, ceramic statues of fairies and angels, calendars made up of reprints of a well-known artist's rendering of fairies, vials of fairy dust, and books about angels and fairies. On the wall hung white, filmy robes; glittery gold halos; and gossamer wings in various sizes. Anything a little girl could want to dress up like either a fairy or an angel.

Penny went straight to the shelf holding the ceramic angels. She reached for a small figurine of an angel with blond hair and blue eyes, wearing a white gown that fell in gentle folds around her slim body. On either side of her, large, white wings stretched above her haloed head.

Penny picked it up gently. "This is the one I want." She peered up at Dora. "It's just like the way you looked in your mirror." Innocence glowed from her face.

Instant panic flooded through Dora. She froze. For a moment, she couldn't speak. How did Penny know about the mirror? Finally, she forced the words through her lips. "How do you know what I look like in my mirror?"

"I saw you the other night," Penny said, more interested in inspecting her choice of Millie's gift than in the fact that Dora was an angel. "When I couldn't sleep. I came into your bedroom to ask you for a glass of water.

You were talking to another angel named Gracie. Is she your friend?" Then she frowned thoughtfully. "It was funny though 'cause I knew it was you, but you didn't look like you. You were all sparkly and shiny, and your hair was a different color, and you didn't have on your jeans in the mirror. Was that angel magic?"

Dora couldn't answer. She was too busy trying to figure out how this could have happened. The only answer was that she must have been so upset, she'd never locked the door, and then she'd been so absorbed in her conversation with Gracie she'd never heard Penny come into the room.

Her stomach dropped to somewhere below the floor. She'd managed to violate another of Calvin's instructions. A mortal had seen her as an angel. It seemed like the harder she tried, the more her mission fell apart. First, she didn't think she was making any significant headway with Tony and, now, Penny knew who she was. More and more she was coming to believe she was no better suited to being a mortal than she was to being an angel.

Frantically, she tamped down her panic and searched for a way to undo the damage. Maybe, if she swore Penny to secrecy, she could prevent this disastrous slipup from going any further.

"Penny, honey, listen to me." She squatted down to be on eye level with the little girl. "You have to promise me you won't tell anyone about this. It can be our special secret." Her voice was harsher than she intended, and seeing Penny's alarmed reaction, she softened her tone of voice. "Okay?"

Tears had gathered in Penny's eyes, and her bottom lip had begun to tremble. "Was I bad to see you? Will you get in trouble?"

No more than I'm in already, she thought but didn't say. Dora hugged Penny close. "No, sweetheart, you were not bad." She released her but ignored the child's other question. "It's just that you weren't supposed to see that. I wasn't supposed to . . . Well, you see, I . . ." She let her voice trail off. How on earth did she explain to a child that her whole life had been one screwup after another and this was just one more? "Sometimes adults don't understand these things and—"

"I know why," Penny exclaimed, brightening some. "Only special people like Millie are allowed to see angels. Millie says she sees angels all the time in her dreams. Millie's special angel is called Mary Elizabeth." As quickly as her face brightened, the smile melted away like ice cream on a hot summer's day. "But you said I'm not appose to see them, so I guess I'm not special, huh?"

Dora's heart twisted in her chest. "Oh, no, sweetheart. I didn't mean that. You're very, very special. Otherwise, even though you came into my room at exactly the right second, you couldn't have seen me. Right?"

To Dora's relief, some of the light came back into Penny's eyes, but she didn't look convinced. "I guess."

Dora took a tissue from her pocket and wiped the tears from Penny's cheeks. "Well, I know. I'm sure you're just like Millie, one of those very special people who get to see angels." She smiled. "But we can't tell anyone. Okay?"

Penny nodded and smiled. She dug into her pocket and extracted a wad of crinkled bills, the change from the twenty-dollar bill her grandparents had sent. "Can I still get the angel for Millie?"

A deep sigh of relief passed Dora's lips. That was easier than she'd expected it to be. "Of course, you can. Now, let's pay for Millie's angel and go home. Your uncle will be looking for his supper."

They walked to the cashier. Penny gave the girl her money, and then turned to Dora. "Can I tell Uncle Tony about you?"

The stark panic returned. Of all the people who could not know, Tony topped the list.

"No," she said a little too loudly and too sharply. Several people looking at the items on the shelves turned in her direction. She shifted to position herself between them and Penny. "That's not a good idea, sweetie," she added more gently. "I'm afraid your uncle is one of those adults who wouldn't understand."

"He's just not special," Penny said, nodding sagely.

Dora couldn't agree with that assessment of Tony. In her eyes, he was more than special. He was perfect.

"Your uncle is very special, but not in the same ways as you and Millie are. He probably doesn't believe in things like angels."

For a moment Penny considered Dora's statement. Then she said, "You're probably right. He doesn't believe in Santa or the Tooth Fairy, either." Then she shook her head and shocked Dora by mumbling, "Men!"

That night, her newest failure having lain heavily on her mind all day, Dora locked her bedroom door and slipped the sheet off the mirror. As the significance of Penny having seen her as an angel had grown more intense with each passing hour, Dora's guilt had magnified until she saw no other alternative but to confess and face the consequences. If only she'd seen Tony's niece enter her room, she could have moved away from the mirror, but she hadn't, and Penny now knew Dora's true identity.

For a long time, she stared at the swirling gray mist in the mirror. She didn't want to do what she knew she must, but she saw no other honorable way out of it. She'd failed on several levels and today was simply the final slipup, the one she could not honestly excuse. If Millie and Gracie were right, falling in love with Tony appeared to be something out of her control, but allowing Penny to see her? That was a whole different matter.

The bottom line was, she'd been negligent about making sure her door had been locked, and now she had to pay the price for her lack of care. Resigning and asking to be brought back was the only way. Then they could send someone who knew what they were doing, who would be able to bring Tony and Penny together into the loving family they should be.

There was no other way out except to take her punishment, which she was sure would be an immediate callback to face the Heavenly Council. Having failed at her mission and having to face the consequences didn't bother her half as much as the thought of leaving Penny and Tony. The mere idea of never seeing them again left her insides raw and her heart bleeding.

Inconsolable, she flopped on the edge of the bed. Tears burned her eyes. She bit her bottom lip to hold them back. Admitting Calvin had been right about his misgivings in sending her to Earth would be bad enough. Letting him see her dissolved in self-pity and showing him just how deeply her failure was affecting her would be more humiliation than she could stand right now.

Despite her efforts, the tears swelled and overflowed

her eyes, running down her cheeks and onto her folded hands.

"Dora?"

Dora jumped to her feet at the sound of Gracie's voice. Quickly, she swiped at the tears and forced a smile to her trembling lips. "Hi, Gracie."

Gracie tilted her head and studied Dora's damp cheeks. "You've been crying. Why?"

She sniffed loudly. "Is Calvin around?"

Gracie shook her head. "No one has seen him for eons. The angels were speculating that he'd been sent off somewhere on a special assignment." She placed her hand on the shoulder of Dora's reflection. It felt warm and comforting. "Can I help?"

Before Dora could stop them, the tears began to flow again, this time in earnest. Backing up blindly, when the bed hit her behind the knees, she dropped on it and buried her face in her hands. "Oh, Gr . . . Gracie," she wailed. "I've . . . f-failed . . . s-so . . . miserably."

"How?" Gracie waited. Dora continued to cry in heart-wrenching sobs.

Finally, when she was sure she didn't have one more ounce of moisture in her body, Dora dried her tears, hiccupped loudly, and then laughed derisively. "How I didn't fail would take less time to relate." Her reflection's halo slipped sideways and threatened to fall off, but Gracie caught it and replaced it. "I guess I'm no better at being a mortal than I was at being an angel."

With a stern look, Gracie shook the shoulder of Dora's reflection. "That's not true. Now, tell me why you think you're a failure. What's happened since the last time we talked?"

Dora stood up, raised her head, and met Gracie's gaze. In a small, hesitant voice, she whispered, "Penny knows I'm an angel. She saw me in the mirror last night when I was talking to you."

Eyes wide with shock, Gracie stared at Dora.

CHAPTER 12

———◆———

DORA GLANCED AT HER AWESTRUCK FRIEND. "No
need to say anything. I know I really messed up this
time. I'll just resign, and they can send someone . . .
someone like you, who can make this right."

Gracie smiled. "Sit down. We need to talk about this."

Dora dropped back to the mattress. Her reflection
collapsed onto the hump of a snowy cloud. "Okay, but
there's really nothing to talk about any more. What's
done is done."

Seating herself beside Dora on the cloud, Gracie
took her hands. "First of all, no one is replacing you,
so you'd better get used to staying where you are. Second, you haven't done anything to warrant coming back
here before Christmas Eve." When Dora would have
protested, Gracie silenced her with a wave of her hand.
"Third, Penny is a child. Many children have seen us

as we are, just as they've seen the spirits of loved ones who have passed into the light and pets that are no longer with them. Their uncluttered, nonjudgmental, open minds allow for all that. It's not until children become adults that they turn skeptical and become nonbelievers in anything they can't explain with logic." Gently, she smoothed Dora's hair away from her tear-streaked face.

"But what if she tells someone? What if she tells Tony?"

A tinkling laugh broke from Gracie. "Haven't I just said that adults don't believe any more? Penny may tell them, but they'll pass it off as a child's vivid imagination."

Dora brightened. "Oh, Gracie, are you absolutely sure? I don't want to come back, especially if I come back as a failure, but mostly because . . ."

Gracie tilted her head, her smile lighting up the room. "Because you don't want to leave Tony and Penny."

Dora nodded shyly. "Not until I absolutely have to."

"Then go back and do your job."

A new wave of sadness washed over Dora. She bit her lip, glanced at Gracie, and decided she might as well make a clean breast of it. "I'm not sure I know how. Nothing I do seems to help. I don't think Tony and Penny are any closer than they were when I arrived."

Gracie *tsk-tsked* at that statement. "How can you say that? Penny is coming out of her shell a bit at a time, and Tony is much more aware of his role as her parent and protector."

"But he still can't tell her he loves her, and I know he does. I can read it in his eyes. He's just got all his love locked up so tight inside him I sometimes think he'll never let it go again."

"It will come. All in good time. These things don't happen overnight, you know. Right now, Tony is terrified of losing someone he loves and he thinks if he holds that back, he can't be hurt again."

Dora had to concede Gracie had a point. Penny had seemed more open lately, and she certainly smiled more. Tony had bought the cell phone so Penny would know he was always just a call away. Maybe Gracie was right. Maybe she was simply expecting too much too soon.

Again, Gracie placed her hand on the reflected Dora's shoulder. "No one said this would be easy. When you're dealing with mortals it never is. You can do this, Dora. I know you can. Sometimes the smallest thing can hold the answers we seek."

Dropping her gaze to her tightly clenched hands, Dora whispered, "I wish I was as sure as you are, Gracie."

Suddenly, Dora recalled how difficult it had been for the Andersons' Guardian Angel, Faith, to bring them back together after their separation. Neither of them had been willing to admit they still loved each other. Faith had been at her wits' end, ready to let another angel take over, but, eventually, she'd managed it and with nothing more than a photo of them on their honeymoon that Dora had noticed lying on their coffee table while gazing into the Earth Pool. That one picture had served to remind them of the love they shared and how happy they'd been. The Andersons had lost their way, gotten so involved with life that they'd forgotten they were living it together and they loved each other very much.

But that didn't help Dora. She had no photos to remind Tony and Penny that they were a family. They'd had no real life together until after Rosalie died. Tony had lived in another city and had limited contact with his niece on birthdays and holiday visits. Then Rosalie had died, and he'd uprooted himself, come here, and started a new business so he could look after Penny. He'd been faced with the daunting task of mourning his beloved sister while simultaneously trying to be both father and mother to a little girl hiding inside her own grief.

Unfortunately, it would take more than an old photo to change things in the Falcone household.

"Dora, very soon Tony and Penny will need you more than ever. You can't leave them now."

"Why?"

When there was no answer, Dora glanced at the mirror. Gracie had vanished. Slipping the sheet over the mirror, Dora decided to go to bed and face all of this in the morning with a clear mind.

Sunday morning dawned with a blanket of brand-new, sparkling white snow covering the ground. Dora took it as a sign things were going to get better, that she would find the way to prove to Tony that love didn't always hurt and to Penny that her uncle cherished her above all things.

By the time she'd made it downstairs, Tony had coffee made and was reading the paper while enjoying a cup at the kitchen table.

He glanced over the top of the paper. "Morning."

"Good morning. Is Penny up yet?" Dora asked as she poured herself a cup of coffee, then slid into a chair opposite Tony.

"Not yet." He kept the newspaper up, blocking her view of his face.

She sipped the hot brew and stared absently at an ad for steel-belted snow tires on the back of the paper.

Was he still feeling uncomfortable about what had happened in the kitchen the other night? Well, even though it would be a hard subject to broach, if she was going to make any headway at all with this mission she'd have to try. "Uh, Tony? About the other night—"

He dropped the paper to the table, then leaned his forearms on it and stared her straight in the eye. "Don't tell me it didn't mean anything, because I won't believe you. And don't tell me it won't happen again, because we both know it will. And don't tell me you're going to quit because of it, because I won't let you. Penny and I will find you and bring you back here." He picked up the newspaper and began reading again.

Dora sat openmouthed, unable to think of a retort.

Behind the paper, Tony waited for Dora to argue. When she didn't, he breathed a sigh of relief. He'd thought about their kiss, and in his heart, he knew it had not been only he who found it earth-shattering. Dora had been with him for every intense, sizzling moment and if that dammed dog hadn't interrupted . . .

No. He wasn't going there. He already had enough to think about with what was happening between them. Hope that Jack's owner would claim him had vanished day by day. It appeared as though Jack would be a permanent fixture in the Falcone house. If he wanted to live here, however—

He stopped short. He refused to think about that furry intruder and add gasoline to an already-raging fire.

Besides, he was tired of walking on eggshells around Dora. It was time he took Jake's advice and see where it went.

"Uncle Tony!"

Tony dropped the paper. Penny raced into the kitchen fully dressed, her face glowing.

"It's snowing outside," she announced to everyone.

He nodded. "I know. We saw it."

"Can we build a snowman?" Penny looked from him to Dora, her face eager.

He glanced at Dora, who shrugged. "Well, I don't know—"

"Please. We got all the stuff we need, Uncle Tony," Penny said. "I'll show you."

She hurried off into the laundry room, where they could hear her rummaging around in the cabinets. A few minutes later, she emerged with a soiled, white cardboard box and plunked it down in front of Tony. Lifting the lid, she showed them what it held.

"Here's his eyes and his buttons," she told them, laying on the table a small, clear sandwich bag containing black plastic objects that resembled coal with pointed sticks protruding from the back side. "And here's his nose." She handed Tony an artificial plastic carrot and then dug into the box again. "And his scarf and his hat. All we need are sticks for his arms."

Tony picked up the flat black hat, and hit it on the table's edge. The center of the hat popped up, turning it into a very handsome silk top hat. The bright red and green wool scarf was one he'd recalled his sister wearing. He fingered the fringe for a moment. His chest began to tighten, signaling the onset of the pain that usually accompanied thoughts of his sister, but this time he refused to acknowledge it. It wouldn't be fair to dampen Penny's happiness with his morose mood.

"Well, then, I guess we're all set. Have some breakfast, and then we'll all go out and build a snowman." He smiled at Penny and glared at Dora.

Dora read his glare loud and clear. Like it or not, she was going to be part of this impromptu adventure. Little did he realize that she wouldn't have missed it for the world.

Inordinately pleased to be included, Dora gave a nod and rose from the table. She took down a bowl and a box of Silly Crunchies Penny had talked her into buying on their last trip to the supermarket, expecting Tony to object to the sugary, marshmallow-littered cereal, but to her surprise, he said nothing.

Setting the bowl of cereal in front of Penny, she poured in the milk and handed Penny her spoon. "Okay, munchkin, eat up. It's gonna take a lot of energy to build a whole man." Tony raised an eyebrow.

Penny took a spoonful of cereal and while she chewed, she muttered, "Mommy used to say that if a lady could build a man, they'd be much smarter."

From the corner of her eye, she saw Tony smirk. Dora's heart did a somersault. It was the very first time Dora had ever seen a smile from this man when his sister's name entered a conversation.

The nippy outside air turned their cheeks cherry red in moments. The sun was hidden by overhanging clouds that spit out a few more snowflakes, as though Lucas, the Angel of Storms, couldn't make up his mind whether to quit or not.

"Come on, Dora," Penny called. She made a snowball, then began rolling it through the wet snow.

Tony watched Penny for a little while, and Dora noticed his face was cloaked in memories. She walked over to him. "You need to make new memories, Tony."

He glanced at her, then Penny. Then he nodded. "I know, but it's hard to let go of the old ones."

She touched his arm. "It'll get easier with time."

He covered her hand and squeezed her fingers. "I hope so." He paused for a moment, then squeezed her hand again. "Thanks."

With her pulse tripping out double-time, all Dora could manage was a weak smile. Then she bent and picked up a handful of snow, which she fashioned into a ball and handed to him. He took it, tossed it in the air, and caught it, and then began rolling it through the snow.

"Let's get this show on the road," he called to Penny. "If this snowman has to be smart as well a handsome one, it's gonna take a lot of work." Penny's giggles filled the cold, turning it a bit warmer.

The look of undiluted happiness the child gave him brought sheer gladness to Dora's heart. Hope rose up to fill her throat. Maybe Gracie had been right. Maybe she could do this after all. Suddenly, as though the gloomy overcast had disappeared, it seemed as bright as any summer day.

❖ ❖ ❖

One very handsome and, as Penny declared, smart snowman later, Tony and Dora stood back and admired their masterpiece while Penny fussed to get the folds of his scarf exactly right.

"There," she finally said and stepped back beside her uncle. "He's wonderful, but he needs a name. Mommy always named our snowmen."

Dora glanced sideways in time to see Tony's muscles tighten. She touched his arm lightly, and he relaxed.

"Well, then, what do you suggest, Miss Penny?" he said, his voice a bit raspy with emotion.

"Hmm. How about Jim?" Dora offered.

Penny shook her head. "Uh-uh. Gym is what I do at school."

Tony laughed. "I don't think Dora meant that kind of gym," Tony said. "How about Tom?"

Again Penny shook her head. "Nope. Tom was our garbage man, and he always spilled stuff on the lawn and made Daddy mad." She thought for moment. "Fred," Penny finally said. "Like that Fred man who danced in the old movies with the lady in the pretty dresses."

Dora looked blankly at Tony and shrugged. Movies had never whet her curiosity and therefore she knew little or nothing of them.

He grinned. "Fred Astaire?"

"Yeah, him." Penny tilted her head. "Don't you think he looks just like him?"

"Oh, definitely," Tony said and then surprised them all by picking Penny up under the arms and swinging her around in a very bad imitation of a dance. She giggled and screamed in delight. Dora's heart swelled.

When Tony set her on her feet, she grabbed his hand. "Come on, Uncle Tony. Make snow angels with me."

Dora froze at the mention of angels. Was Penny going to divulge her secret?

"Come on, Dora. You should be really good at snow angels," the little girl called. Again Dora waited for the words she dreaded hearing from Penny within Tony's earshot.

Tony turned to look at her. The flames of mischievousness burned brightly in his eyes. "Really? And why is that?"

Penny yanked on Tony's jacket hem. "Because—"

"Because I've been doing them for so long," Dora interjected, cutting Penny off before she could say too much. Thank goodness she'd seen children doing this from her vantage point at the Earth Pool.

Then Tony grinned. The mischievousness mixed with a blatant dare. "Well, then, Miss Expert-Snow-Angel-Maker, let's see what you can do."

He took her hand and drew her onto the open part of the lawn. Dora couldn't believe it. She'd never seen this playful side of Tony, and she liked it, very much. His smile was genuinely happy and infectious, and, as a result, her heart felt light and carefree.

"Come on, Dora. Show Uncle Tony how to do it." Penny jumped up and down, clapping her gloved hands in anticipation.

Dora lay down in the snow. Tony and Penny stood to the side watching. Dora extended her arms straight out to either side of her body and spread her legs in a V. Pulling from her memory what she'd seen the mortal children do, Dora began to move her legs back and forth and her arms up and down. Snow seeped under her collar and up her sleeves. The upward motion of her arms sprinkled snow on her face and hair. But the contentment and joy generated by Penny's happiness warmed her through and through.

Then she looked at the expression on Tony's face.

The breath caught in Tony's throat. A woman sprawled in the snow, in a most unbecoming position, should not have been something he found attractive. But, damn, Tony couldn't rip his gaze away from her.

The sight of Dora spread-eagled at his feet had his senses churning like a pot of boiling water. Her dark hair had escaped her blue, knit hat and spread out over the white ground. Snowflakes peppered her bright red cheeks and lips, and then instantly melted, leaving behind tiny crystallike droplets of water. His fingers itched to wipe them away or, better yet, kiss them away.

"See, Uncle Tony?" Penny squealed while continuing to bounce up and down like an out-of-control rubber ball. "I told you she'd be really good at it."

"Yes, she certainly is," he said, his voice sounding strange and seeming to come from miles away.

At the sound of his voice, Dora ceased her movements and met his gaze. The answering desire written clearly in her eyes sent his common sense into a tailspin.

He took a step toward her, his hand extended in invitation. Dora took it, and he drew her to her feet. Their faces were so close the puffs of steam emitted from their mouths mixed together. He searched her gaze to see if he'd read it wrong. He hadn't. The desire was still there, burning just beneath the surface of those dark brown eyes.

Slowly, he lifted his hand to touch her damp skin. Then Jack tore from behind a nearby bush and barked. It broke the spell.

What the hell was I thinking?

Obviously he wasn't thinking at all. Had he lost his mind completely, or had his brain disconnected from his logic? Good grief, they were on the front lawn in plain view of all the neighbors, not to mention Penny stood right there watching their every move.

Hastily, he moved away from Dora and cleared his throat of the need choking off his air. "Uh, we'd better go inside. We're all wet and we need to get into some dry clothing before we all catch pneumonia." He strode rapidly across the lawn to the front door.

Penny grabbed Dora's hand and giggled. "I think my Uncle Tony loves you," she whispered.

CHAPTER 13

AFTER THEY'D GONE INSIDE, TONY HAD CHANGED out of his wet clothes, mumbled something about going Christmas shopping, and then left the house. A bit disappointed by his hurried departure, Dora had suggested that Penny work on her essay while they shared some hot chocolate.

Shortly after they'd settled in at the kitchen table, Millie had joined them, bearing a box of homemade chocolate fudge. While Penny helped herself to the fudge and regaled Millie with nonstop chatter about their shopping trip, school, her essay, and the snowman they'd made, all the things the child should have been eagerly sharing with her uncle, Dora thought about what Penny had said outside.

Did Tony love her? If the look that had settled on his face while she made the snow angel and the intensity of their kiss the other night were anything to go by, she couldn't help but at least give it consideration. Rather than bringing her joy, the idea lay on her heart like a lead weight and caused the panic Dora had recently come to associate with the word *love* to come into full bloom.

Tony couldn't love her. He just couldn't. That would complicate everything. It was bad enough that she had allowed herself to fall in love with him, but if he loved her in return . . . Could his heart withstand another disappointment when she left?

And she had to leave him. There was no question about that.

Would it hurt him as much for her to leave as she knew it would hurt her? That Tony might have to bear more pain than he already had nearly tore Dora's heart from her chest.

You're being foolish. You're taking a kiss, a look, and the romantic musings of a six-year-old as concrete evidence of something that only exists in a child's imagination and your improbable dreams. Tony has said nothing about loving you. Penny is probably wrong. She's only hoping for something that can never be so she has a complete family again. Yes, that's it. That Tony loves you is only a figment of Penny's yearnings and your own vivid, overactive imagination.

Dora uttered a deep sigh of relief. She was twisting herself into knots over nothing.

"Dora?" Millie's gentle voice broke into Dora's thoughts.

Dora looked up from the napkin she'd been pleating and unpleating and was surprised to find that she and Millie were alone in the room. She looked around. "Where's Penny?"

Millie laughed. "She left a few minutes ago. She said she couldn't write with all the noise down here." Her laugh melted into an amused grin. "It never occurred to her, I guess, that she was making most of the noise with her ongoing chatter. I can't believe the change in that child since you came here. She's talkative and lively, just like she was before she lost her parents. I'd say it's nothing short of a miracle." Suddenly, as though a switch had been thrown, Millie stopped talking. Her expression turned serious, and she leaned forward for a better view of Dora's face. "Are you all right, dear?"

"Me? Yes, I'm great."

"Well, from the look of the frown lines in your forehead and that poor, tortured napkin, your thoughts can't be pleasant ones." Millie touched Dora's shoulder. As usual, her touch brought a measure of calm to Dora. "Something you need to talk about?"

For a moment, Dora considered confiding in Millie, but dismissed the idea. Penny had been voicing her dreams, and she'd been reading too much into things, nothing more. There was no foundation to any of it, and, consequently, absolutely no point in discussing it.

"No," Dora said. "It's nothing important. Just wondering what to make for supper." Searching for a change of subject, Dora asked, "Millie, do you know anything about Penny's Aunt Lisa?"

Millie frowned. "That one." A sneer colored her usually friendly voice.

Dora had never heard that tone from the gentle woman who seemed to like everyone she met and never had a bad word to say about anyone. However, if what Tony told her about Lisa not attending her brother's funeral had been right, to someone with Millie's sensibilities about family, Dora could understand how the older woman would find this apparent snub reprehensible and unforgivable.

"That girl's bad news with a capital *B*."

So far, no one appeared to have a good opinion of Lisa Stevens. "Are you basing your opinion of her on the fact she didn't come to Rosalie and Matt's funeral?"

A sharp, derisive laugh issued from Millie. "No, dear. There's more. The funeral is only the tip of the iceberg, Dora. Only the tip." Millie leaned forward, her face grim. "Rosalie told me that girl gave her parents nothing but heartache from the time she could walk. Rosalie even suspected Lisa's behavior had brought on her father's heart attack." She shook her head. "I can't fathom how two wonderful people like Matt had for parents, people who were the cream of God's crop, were cursed with a girl like that.

"Rosalie said that by the time Lisa was thirteen, she was into drugs and booze. She stole her mother's jewelry to pay for it. Bless them, they tried to get her help, but nothing seemed to work. When she was fifteen, she was arrested for stealing a car. She got off with six months in a juvenile delinquents' home on that one, but only because she convinced the judge she was only an accomplice and the boyfriend had committed the actual theft." Millie took a sip of her hot chocolate. "On her eighteenth birthday, she walked out the door, and no one's seen her since. Matt's poor parents went crazy trying to find her." Millie stopped talking and counted out something on her fingers. "She'd be about twenty-five or twenty-six years old. My guess is, she's sitting somewhere in a prison cell by now." She frowned. "Or maybe worse. What brought her up anyway?"

Considering how little Millie thought of Lisa, Dora wondered if she should tell the older woman about the Christmas card Penny had received from Lisa and the specter of an impending visit from the delinquent aunt. Then she realized that if Lisa did come, Millie would undoubtedly find out anyway.

"She's not dead, and she's not in prison. At least it

doesn't appear she's in prison at the moment anyway. She sent Penny a Christmas card and said she'd see her soon."

Millie's mouth formed a surprised *O*. "She's coming here?"

Dora nodded. "She didn't come right out and say so, but that's certainly what her card implied."

Millie sighed and looked at the ceiling. "Lord, help us all. Did she say what she wanted?"

Absently, Dora stirred her hot chocolate. "Tony thinks she might have changed, and that she's trying to reconnect with her family."

"I wouldn't bet the trash at the curb on her changing. That girl never did anything for nothing. If she's coming here, you can bet she wants something. My guess is money." Standing and putting on her coat, Millie gave Dora a look of intense warning. "My mother . . ." Millie bowed her head in respect, and then made the sign of the cross over her chest. "God rest her soul. My mother used to say that the only way a leopard changes its spots is if someone paints them, but the real leopard is still there underneath all the paint." She cast Dora a think-about-that look, then, without another word, she let herself out the back door.

Dora frowned and studied Lisa's Christmas card where Penny had hung it on the refrigerator door next to the one she'd received from her grandparents. If Lisa had as little regard for family as Millie had said, why, out of the clear blue sky, had she suddenly felt compelled to visit her niece? Millie had probably hit the nail square on the head . . . Lisa wanted money.

Tony wandered aimlessly around the mall peering into shop windows. After the episode on the lawn and the surge of sensations he'd had to fight down concerning Dora, he couldn't safely stay in the same house with her. If he had, he couldn't guarantee that he wouldn't have done something stupid, like dragging Dora off to the nearest secluded corner and . . . Escape had been the only option.

As a safe alternative, he'd decided to get his holiday shopping done. But he hated malls and the congestion at this time of year, not to mention the noise. Added to that was the fact that shopping for anything at any time had never been high on his list of favorite pastimes.

However, despite that, he'd managed to fight his way through screaming children, inpatient parents, blinded couples who saw only each other, and find a few things for Penny. The shopping bags whose handles were biting into his hands contained a teddy bear that begged its owner for a hug, a doll that wet itself and cried

"Momma," a nightgown with dogs all over it, and a gold necklace with a tiny heart-shaped locket, inside of which he planned to put pictures of her mom and dad.

But a gift for Dora remained elusive. He'd searched store after store and still hadn't found anything for Dora that was exactly right. He'd looked at silk scarves, perfume, and hat and mittens sets. All but the perfume came across as too impersonal. The perfume had been vetoed because he didn't feel any scent could match the unusual fragrance of spring that surrounded Dora all the time. The gift he finally got for Dora had to straddle the line between too personal and too impersonal. But he wanted it to be meaningful, to capture his gratitude for all she'd done since coming to be Penny's nanny. Unfortunately, he had no clue what that could be, and all the saleswomen he'd asked for help in determining that distinction were irritable, impatient, and looked at him as though he'd grown an extra ear.

He'd just rounded the corner of one of the side mall corridors and inserted himself into the throng pushing and shoving their way down the mall's main thoroughfare when he spotted a huge replica of a winter wonderland in the middle of the aisle. Towering artificial pine trees had been liberally sprayed with fake snow and scattered about the scene. In the center stood a quaint replica of a gingerbread house decked out in equally fake icing at the end of a path bordered with red and white candy canes. In front of the house was a regal-looking empty chair with a sign propped up on the red seat cushion that read: *Santa is feeding his reindeer. He'll be back in 15 minutes.* A few children and parents had already lined up in anticipation of Santa's return.

But the thing that had caught Tony's attention was what stood to the side of the house—an enormous snow man that closely resembled the one sitting on his front lawn. Almost instantly, he knew what he would get Dora. Spirits soaring, he scanned the stores and spotted the one most likely to have it.

When he entered the jewelry store, he headed straight for the case holding an array of necklaces and bracelets. He hurriedly scanned the necklaces for what he wanted, but saw nothing. Then he saw a rotating case on the counter with gold charms. He only had to turn it once before he saw it, a tiny gold snowman with dia mond chips for eyes, onyx buttons, and a ruby mouth.

"I'll take that one," he told the saleslady. "And I'll need a chain for it."

She removed the charm and laid it beside the cash register. "I think I have just the right one."

While she searched for the chain, Tony looked around the store, noting a large display of collectible mouse figurines. He browsed the display and in the middle found one figurine of a little brown mouse making snow angels. Recalling Penny's delight with Dora's snow angel production, Tony grinned, picked it up, and carried it to the cashier.

The saleswoman returned with the chain, and he told her he'd take the figurine, as well. The gifts, the necklace for Dora and the snow angel mouse for Penny, were perfect.

The day had marked a turning point in his relationship with Penny. Although it was far from ideal, he felt closer to the little girl who had become such a large part of his life.

As for Dora . . . It marked the day when he realized just how important she'd become to him and how deeply ingrained she was in his day-to-day existence.

When she saw Tony come home laden with packages, Dora felt better about why he'd rushed from the house. It was a relief to know she hadn't been the cause. He really had gone shopping. Penny had unknowingly planted a fantasy in her mind, and her own tortured imagination had allowed the entire, innocent event to grow way out of proportion.

After Tony reappeared downstairs and asked where

to find ribbon, tags, and wrapping paper, and she had given them to him, he'd vanished upstairs again Dora assumed it was to wrap his purchases. Feeling much better about everything, she started dinner.

An hour and a half later, all three of them were gathered around the table devouring roast chicken breast, mashed potatoes and gravy, and broccoli.

"So how's that essay coming?" Tony asked, taking his second helping of everything.

This kind of dinner chatter was what Dora had loved to see in the Earth Pool. Families catching up on each others' lives. It pleased her that they had finally reached this plateau.

Penny smiled at him. "Great! I'm almost done, and I think I'm gonna win."

"Well, there're a lot of other kids in the contest, so don't pin your hopes on coming in first. Not everyone can win."

Tony's caution set off alarm bells in Dora's head.

She glanced at Penny. The bright smile had melted off the child's lips.

Tony forked potatoes dripping in gravy into his mouth, totally unaware of how his comment had affected his niece.

"That doesn't mean what you wrote isn't good, sweetie, or that you won't win," Dora qualified quickly.

"Your Uncle Tony just doesn't want to see you disappointed if someone else happens to be chosen."

Penny seemed somewhat mollified. But the genuine smile did not return to her lips.

Dora sent Tony a glance that said, *You'd better fix this.*

Laying aside his fork, he frowned and cleared his throat. "Honey, I didn't mean Dora and I don't believe that you'll win. I know your essay is going to be fabulous." He grinned. "How can it not be? You're a very smart little girl."

This time the smile came back full force. "You really think so, Uncle Tony?"

"Absolutely. Not a doubt in my mind. Now, you'd better finish your supper. I've got my eye on that apple pie over there on the counter for dessert, and if I get to it first, there may not be any left for you." He winked at her.

Penny dove into her food with renewed gusto.

Dora had to hold back her grin. This was the first time she'd ever seen Tony so relaxed and playful with Penny. He hadn't even been this at ease with his niece when they'd built the snowman. And the child was soaking it up like a big sponge. In fact, when Dora thought back over the day, she could see some definite cracks in the emotional barrier Tony had set up to hold out the world. With any luck, there was a light at the end of the tunnel she'd begun to believe was never going to be seen.

"I'm done," Penny announced and held up her cleaned plate. "You better hurry up, Uncle Tony, or I'll eat all the pie."

As Dora took her and Penny's plates to the sink, Tony wolfed down the remainder of his chicken and potatoes. "Done," he declared.

He scooted away from the table, deposited his dirty plate on top of theirs, then grabbed pie plates, forks, and the pie knife from Dora and carried them to the table. He was just going back to get the pie when the front doorbell rang.

Damn, he thought. He was really enjoying his time with Dora and Penny and resented the interruption. "I'll get it," he said and hurried down the hall as the doorbell chimed again. "Coming," he called.

When he reached the door, he grabbed the doorknob and swung the door open. All the air sucked from his lungs. He could do nothing but stare. Something sour and unrecognizable churned in the pit of his stomach.

"You must be Tony," the attractive, willowy brunette said and extended her hand. "I'm Matt's sister, Penny's Aunt Lisa."

CHAPTER 14

———✦———

LISA STEVEN'S CONFIRMATION OF WHO SHE WAS did nothing to alleviate Tony's distaste for the woman who had caused his brother-in-law's family so much heartache.

"Yes, I'm Tony," he finally said.

Lisa pulled her expensive-looking, caramel-colored, knee-length coat tightly around her slender form. "May I come in?"

Tony looked the woman over. In her designer clothes and salon hairdo, she didn't look anything like the drug-addicted relative who had been described to him by Rosalie years ago. However, the dark circles around her eyes that makeup couldn't completely hide, the signs of premature aging in a face that should have been fresh and youthful, and the unhealthy pallor of her skin gave away the indulgences of her former life.

An unflattering phrase he'd heard some of the construction workers use, *Rode hard and put away wet*, came to mind.

Without a word, he moved to the side to allow her entry. When he'd closed the door and turned to follow Lisa, he realized that Dora and Penny were watching them from down the hall. Right behind Dora, Penny peered shyly at their visitor while she clung tenaciously to Dora's leg.

Lisa offered him a smile. He did not return it. The smile vanished.

Then she caught sight of Dora and Penny, and once more her face creased in a broad smile. "You must be Penny," she said. She took a step toward the little girl.

Penny shrank back and clung even harder to Dora's leg. "Say hello to your aunt," Dora encouraged.

"Hello," Penny mumbled, much like she had the day she'd first met Dora.

"Dora, while Lisa and I talk in the living room, why don't you take Penny in the kitchen and let her have dessert?" Tony said. Then he smiled gently at his niece. "You better save some of that pie for me."

Dora nodded and guided Penny back through the kitchen door. In the kitchen Dora tried not to show the child her apprehension. She'd known in her gut who the woman was even before she'd told them. Right now, she had a lot of different feelings churning inside her, and none of them were good.

Casting Penny a sidelong glance, Dora cut a piece of pie for her and carried it to the table. All the joy Penny had exhibited before Lisa's arrival had drained away. Once more, she'd reverted to the quiet, stoic child Dora had met what seemed like months ago, but had really only been weeks.

The angels had often said that children have a second sight, an inner instinct about people that adults left behind with their childhood. Had Penny picked up on the negative vibes coming from her aunt?

Once they were gone, Tony turned back to Lisa. "In here." He pointed toward the big room at the front of the house where he'd first interviewed Dora and where Penny's pitiful Christmas tree stood forlornly in the bay windows that overlooked the street.

Lisa walked ahead of him into the living room and took a seat on the sofa. He didn't offer to take her coat. If he had his way, her visit would be brief. Instead, he sat in the wingback chair across from her.

Wasting no time on pleasantries, he got right to the point. "What do you want?"

A saccharin smile curved her full lips. "Can't I come to see my niece?"

This sudden surge of concern for Penny wasn't fooling Tony for a second. "That was never one of your high priorities before. Why now?"

She leaned back, crossed her legs, adjusted her skirt over her knee, and cleared her throat. "Up until the last two years, my life has not been one . . . Well, let's just say I was otherwise occupied. I've changed a lot from the girl I once was, and I regret hurting my family. Now I want to get to know Penny better."

Tony sat straighter, his blood on a slow simmer. "Who the hell are you trying to kid? You ignored your family because you were too busy partying and getting high with your druggie friends. In fact, you didn't care enough to come to your own brother's funeral. Now you expect me to believe you're the salt of the earth. That you've suddenly had an epiphany that drove you to show up filled with love for a little girl who never laid eyes on you until a few minutes ago."

"People do change, Tony."

He made a disparaging sound and shook his head. "If memory serves, from what Matt and Rosalie told me, you needed more than a change. You needed a complete metamorphosis."

Lisa's face transformed before Tony's eyes. The artificially friendly, but austere expression she'd exhibited since he opened the door turned to a venomous glare. "You can't keep me from my niece. Just because I made some mistakes in the past doesn't mean I don't love her."

A harsh laugh broke from Tony. He had serious doubts that Lisa had any conception of what the word *love* meant. "*Some* mistakes? Stealing a car? Getting busted for drugs and booze? Spending six months in a home for juvenile delinquents? Stealing from your own parents to finance your addictions? And those are only the things I know about. You call that *some mistakes?*" He laughed again, even more harshly. Then he added what he'd only been thinking. "Do you even know the meaning of the word *love?*"

Her face grim, Lisa sat up and leaned toward him, challenging him with her posture, if not her words. "That was a long time ago. I've been clean for over three years."

The information only fueled Tony's anger. Three years of sobriety didn't prove anything. His foreman's nephew had had a drug problem, and the doctors had told the kid's parents that the relapse rate was 50 percent for heavy users. The chances of a brief relapse were even higher. Added to that was the fact that, if she were to be believed and he would have to stretch some to make that happen, she'd been drug-free for three years, and only now had decided to come see Penny?

"And what have you been doing for three years?"

"I'm married to a very wealthy Texas businessman. With his help, I was able to turn my life around."

Don't believe her, his logical mind screamed. *These people have lying down to a fine art, and she'd been very good at it for a very long time.*

He had no inclination to argue with her, so he refrained from voicing his opinion of her miraculous rehabilitation and sudden concern for her family. In fact, he didn't even want to talk to her at all. What he did want was to have her out of the house as soon as possible.

"So you're telling me you came all the way from Texas just to pay a Christmas visit to a child you never cared enough about to see before now? Do I have that right?"

She nodded. "But there's no need to make it sound like that."

"Tell me, Lisa, how should I make it sound? If you've been clean for all this time, why did it take you three years to acknowledge this little girl?"

Lisa compressed her lips into a straight line. She stood. "I'm not going to sit here and endure this Inquisition for another minute. I want to see Penny."

"Penny's finishing her supper, then she has to bathe and get ready for bed. She has school tomorrow."

She took a step toward the door. "Surely I can see her for a moment."

Tony grabbed her arm. When she looked down where his fingers encircled her flesh, he let go. "Let's get this straight. Penny's not up for grabs when the whim suits you, Lisa. You can't just pop into her life. I can't take the chance that you'll see her this time, win her affections, and then disappear again. So the answer to your request is no."

Did Lisa really believe he was going to take her at her word that she was straight now? That he would expose his niece to her if there was the faintest possibility that she wasn't? He had no guarantee, other than her word, which had been questionable before, that she had given up drugs and booze.

"Then maybe I can see her tomorrow, after school?"

He shook his head. "No. Penny is my responsibility now. I make all decisions concerning her well-being, and I don't feel that seeing you is in her best interest." He grasped her upper arm and gently urged the woman toward the front door.

Lisa yanked her arm from his grasp. "I have a right to see my niece. After all, I *am* her flesh and blood."

"So am I, and her mother and father left her in my care. I am her legal guardian." He leveled a no-nonsense look at her. "And unless I say so, you have no rights where Penny's concerned."

If looks could kill, Tony would have been prostrate on

the floor preparing to meet his Maker. Lisa flung open the door, then paused to glare at him. "You haven't heard the last of this," she whispered, her voice dripping venom.

"Why doesn't that surprise me?" he threw back, his own voice rife with the same poison. "However, as far as I'm concerned, this is the end of the conversation."

"Don't be so sure," she spat and hurried out the door.

When Dora came downstairs after tucking Penny in for the night, she found Tony sitting at the kitchen table, an untouched cup of coffee clutched in his hands and an uneaten piece of pie in front of him. A troubled frown creased his broad forehead.

She was certain Lisa's visit was on his mind. He hadn't talked about it, and having already witnessed his ability to keep his emotions bottled up, she wasn't sure prodding would get him to do so, but her curiosity got the best of her.

"So, what did Lisa have to say?" She sat down across from him and waited.

He sighed heavily and set the cup down with an angry *thunk*. "She says she's been straight for three years, and now she wants to see Penny, wants to become a part of her life."

An unfinished *but* hung in the air between them. "And?" More than that had to have transpired in the living room.

"And I'm not going to let her."

Opinions of his decision warred inside Dora. On one hand, Lisa was Penny's aunt, one of the only living connections to her father. A child left without her parents needed family . . . all of her family. On the other hand, Lisa's disreputable past and her aptitude for causing trouble within the family presented a huge stumbling block. Could Lisa be trusted?

Because Dora had never known what it was like to have a family, the idea of Penny being deprived of even one of her relatives didn't set well with her. With only that in mind, she would have encouraged Tony to allow aunt and niece to try to establish a relationship.

However, considering Lisa's past history, she could easily see why he'd decided what he had. In the life of an addict, three years was a drop in the bucket of time. Even after three years, it was not unheard of for them to slip off the wagon and return to their old ways. The idea of Penny being anywhere near Lisa if and when that happened made Dora shiver with fear.

But it wasn't her decision, and she was beginning to wonder if it was really Tony's, either.

"Shouldn't you talk this over with Penny?"

Tony's head snapped around. His face had taken on an angry red hue, and his dark eyes bore into her like hot coals. "For God's sake, Dora, Penny is only six. She has no idea what this is all about, what dangers are inherent with allowing Lisa into her life. Why in the name of everything I hold dear would I let her have a choice in this?"

"Penny may be only six, but she's a very smart little girl. I think she already senses something."

He stood so suddenly and with such force that his chair teetered on two legs before dropping back onto all four with a loud *thunk*.

"As long as I have control of whom my niece interacts with, Lisa will not get within a hundred miles of Penny. Period." He strode from the room and stomped up the stairs.

The next morning, the air in the kitchen was thick enough to slice and heavy enough to break the back of a strong man. When Penny skipped into the room and proudly announced that her essay was done and she'd be turning it in to her teacher, it was a wonder the child didn't pick up on the false cheerfulness Dora and Tony injected into the praise they showered on her for her accomplishment. Other than that, neither of them spoke.

Shortly after Penny's arrival at breakfast, Tony left his half-eaten eggs and announced he was going to work. Penny watched him leave with trepidation written all over her face.

"Is Uncle Tony mad at me?"

Dora started. "No, sweetie. Why would you think such a thing?"

Penny shrugged and swirled her spoon through her cereal. "He didn't even say good-bye."

Putting her arm around Penny's shoulders, Dora hugged her and placed a kiss on the child's copper curls. "He's got a lot on his mind. He probably forgot." When Penny didn't seem appeased, Dora forced a chuckle. "If it makes you feel any better, he didn't say good-bye to me, either." From the corner of the kitchen Jack barked. "And he didn't say good-bye to Jack, either."

Jack charged the table, his tail moving back and forth like a leaf caught in a strong wind. He licked Penny's hand.

If Jack *was* Calvin—and Dora had not yet decided one way or the other—he was most assuredly showing his more sensitive side for a change.

She leaned down next to the dog's ear, patted Jack's head, and whispered, "Way to go, Calvin."

Jack ignored her, and, as though he truly were the dog Penny believed him to be, he continued to wag his tail and lick Penny's hand. However, before Dora turned away, she could have sworn the dog winked at her.

"Dora, can angels do magic?"

Penny's out-of-the-blue question caught Dora totally by surprise. "Uh . . . Angels can do special things, but we don't call them magic."

Her brows knitted in concentration. "What do you call it?"

This made Dora think for a minute. "I guess we call them miracles."

For a long time, Penny pondered Dora's explanation. Then she said, "Can you make a miracle thing so Uncle Tony is happy?"

CHAPTER 15

❖

Dᴜʀɪɴɢ ᴛʜᴇ ꜰᴏʟʟᴏᴡɪɴɢ ᴅᴀʏs, ʙᴏᴛʜ Dᴏʀᴀ ᴀɴᴅ Tony waited for Lisa to pay a return visit. When it didn't happen, Dora assumed Lisa had accepted that Tony would not bend on his decision to keep her away from Penny and had returned to Texas. Dora made every attempt to get back to life as usual and focus on her mission.

On the other hand, Tony continued to be as uptight as he'd been right after Lisa's visit, and nothing she or Penny said or did made any difference. His short temper and inattentiveness made it quite clear to Dora that Tony feared they had not heard the last of Lisa and that she would cause some kind of trouble. The type of trouble remained a mystery to Dora . . . but not for long.

Dora had just finished ironing and hanging the freshly laundered curtains when the front door burst open, and Penny raced down the hall and into the kitchen.

"I won! I won!" she cried, jumping up and down and waving a sheet of paper in her hand.

"That's wonderful, but what did you win, sweetie?"

Penny stopped jumping long enough to throw Dora an impatient glance. "The essay contest. I won!" Immediately, she launched into another round of excited jumps.

Behind her Tony beamed like a proud papa. "Mrs. Johnson said Penny's essay was by far the best in the class."

Dora swept Penny into a bear hug and swung her around the kitchen. "Congratulations, Penny. That's fantastic news." She set her back on her feet. "So that means you get to read your essay at the winter show, right?"

"Yup." Penny beamed with pride. Even Jack ran in circles around Penny's legs, looking excited for her.

Tony came forward and sat at the table. "Are you going to tell us what you wrote about?" As he spoke, he reached for the paper Penny was holding.

She snatched it out of his reach. "Nope. It's a surprise." She called Jack and in a hail of giggles, streaked from the room and up the stairs.

Tony shook his head and laughed. "She's guarding that like Fort Knox. Guess we'll just have to wait until showtime to see what she wrote." He stood and went to the refrigerator. After taking out a can of beer, he leaned against the refrigerator door, popped the top, and stared at Dora.

"What?" she asked, his intent study of her sending chills racing up and down her spine.

"Nothing," he said. "Just looking."

Heat rose into her cheeks, and she turned away to fold up the step stool she'd used to reach the curtain rod. He intercepted her.

"Let me do that," he said, taking it from her hands and skimming his fingertips over her skin as he did.

Dora snatched back her hand and rubbed at the skin to get rid of the tingles still dancing over her flesh.

He stood the stool next to the cellar door and turned back to her. "I'll take that down into the basement later."

Dora waited for him to leave so she could catch her breath. Instead, he relaxed against the cellar door, crossed his arms over his chest, and locked his gaze on her. From his eye movement Dora could tell he was taking in her hair, her face, her figure. Instead of the tingles of awareness going away, they intensified with each phantom brush of his gaze over her body. When he took a step in her direction, she knew in her heart that she would not move away because the desire in her matched what she saw glowing in his dark eyes.

Then the front doorbell rang.

Tony whispered a string of curses that included, *If it isn't the damned dog, then it's something else.*

A grin crept across Dora's face as she watched Tony

slam his palm against the kitchen door and disappear down the hall. He had no idea how close she'd come to falling in his arms. The grin immediately vanished.

She hadn't even been thinking about stopping it before it went too far. Instead, she'd simply surrendered her will to him. What made it even more alarming was that each time this unbelievable attraction reared its head, she found it harder and harder to resist, and easier and easier to give in.

Just the thought made her knees go weak. She grabbed the back of a chair to steady herself as Tony came back through the door carrying an envelope. His face was fixed in a deep frown.

"Bad news?" she asked innocently.

"Well, since there's a lawyer's address in the upper left corner of this envelope, and I had to sign for it, I'd say that's a pretty good guess." He threw the letter on the table as though it had burned him.

"Aren't you going to open it?" she asked him. He didn't answer. "Tony?"

He stared at it for a long time. In his gut, he knew it had something to do with Lisa and Penny. Illogically, he didn't want to know what was in it. Logically, he knew he had no choice.

Then again, maybe he was borrowing trouble, and this had nothing to do with either Lisa or Penny. Maybe it had something to do with the construction project. Either way, staring at it would not tell him anything.

Without a word to Dora, he picked up the letter, slid his finger under the flap, and extracted the folded sheet of paper. Pausing for a moment, he opened the stiff paper and read silently. His heart dropped, and his stomach heaved as snatches of the words that glared at him from the white sheet sank into his brain.

. . . *Your presence at a hearing concerning the custody of Penny . . . courthouse conference room . . .* And the name that stood out more than all the other words . . . *Lisa Stevens Randall.*

Lisa was going to try to take custody of Penny from him. "Damn her!" he spat and threw the letter back on the table. "Damn her!"

"What?" He looked up to see Dora's pale face. Fear reflected in her eyes. "What is it?"

"Lisa. I have to meet with her and her attorney on Friday to discuss the custody of Penny."

Dora's mouth dropped open. "Oh, no. What are you going to do?"

"I don't know. I have to think about it, but one thing I do know is that I'll fight her all the way, even if I have to go into debt to pay the attorneys."

Impotent rage rose up to choke him. He swallowed it back. His fists clenched and unclenched at his sides. He wanted to punch something, anything. Anger mixed with terror. He couldn't lose Penny, too. He just couldn't.

"This came too quickly after her visit. I'd stake my life on it that that bitch had this planned long before she showed up here." The words felt like hot coals being torn from his throat. "There's not a lawyer I know of who could have gotten it into the works so fast."

Flinging himself into a chair, Tony buried his face in his hands. No matter how he tried to organize his thoughts, he felt like his mind was going in thirty directions at once. "What am I going to do? When I agreed to be Penny's legal guardian, I never dreamed I'd end up fighting to keep her. What if the judge decides I'm not a good uncle? What if I lose her, Dora?" Pain, deep and cutting, sliced through him.

Dora stood beside him and laid her hand on his shoulder. "You won't lose her. Rosalie knew you'd take care of Penny and love her. Otherwise she never would have left her in your care."

Her touch was like awakening from a long nightmare. As though, with that one simple gesture, she'd swiped away the cobwebs and untangled his thoughts. Suddenly his mind was crystal clear. He couldn't let Penny go, and it had nothing to do with Rosalie or Lisa. He might never be able to give Penny material things, the things Lisa and her rich husband could, but he could give her the one thing that mattered most—love. Letting her walk out of his life without doing everything he could to fight Lisa would kill him. He might not be the best substitute for a dad, but he was by far not the worst.

If Lisa thought for one minute that he'd bend to her will like a tree in the wind and let her take that little girl away from him, she needed a serious reality check. Penny was his and she'd remain his until, when she was of legal age, she left him of her own free will.

Tony picked up the letter and waved it at Dora. "She's been nothing but trouble all her life. She's caused more pain than her selfish, childlike brain can possibly comprehend. Rosalie and Matt didn't have a choice: they had to tolerate her, but I don't. Nothing would make me happier than never having to lay eyes on her again." He stood, his feet planted far apart, his hands on his hips, the light of determination shining brightly from his eyes.

Dora simply smiled.

Dora placed the breaded pork chops on the table and poured milk for Penny. Wiping her hands on the towel, she walked down the hall.

"Penny, Tony, supper's ready."

Tony peeked out of the living room where he'd been watching the news on TV. "Great. I'm starved." After their talk, his mood seemed to have improved a hundred percent.

Dora laughed. "Good, because I'm sure I made way too much food." She looked up the stairs to check for Penny. "Penny?' she called again. "Supper is ready, sweetie." Then, walking ahead of Tony, she led the way to the kitchen.

Tony took his place at the head of the table, and Dora sat to his right. She glanced at the door. "I wonder where Penny is."

Tony got up. "She's probably rehearsing her essay. I'll go get her."

Dora filled Penny's plate with food and had her meat cut by the time the kitchen door opened, and Tony came in. His face was sheet white.

"She's gone," he said.

"Gone? Where?" That was all Dora could force from her throat.

"I don't know. She left this." He held out a piece of pink construction paper. Written across it in purple crayon were words that turned Dora to icy stone.

I'm sorry I was trouble.

Trouble had been scratched out several times before Penny had been satisfied with the spelling of a word that wasn't part of a six-year-old's usual vocabulary.

Dora will take care of you. She's an angel.

"Trouble? How did she get that idea?" Tony paced the kitchen floor. "I never told her she was any trouble. For God's sake, out of everyone in my life, she was the least amount of trouble." He slammed his fist into the palm of his hand. "If that bitch Lisa hadn't come here, none of this would be happening. If anyone is trouble, it's her, with a capital *T*."

Lisa! Instantly, Dora's mind flashed back to their earlier conversation about Lisa. *She's been nothing but trouble all her life.* She tried to think. Where had Penny been during that conversation? Upstairs. But what if she wasn't upstairs? What if she'd come down in time to catch the tail end of Tony's tirade? Dora's heart dropped to her feet.

Tony's pacing jolted to a stop. "My God, do you think she was kidnapped?"

Dora had considered it for a second. She knew there had been such events in the news of late and that each kidnapping had thrown the respective Guardian Angels for each of the victims into turmoil. Sadly, in too many cases, their intervention had come too late. But this didn't seem to fit that scenario.

"I don't think so. She wouldn't have had time to leave the note if she'd been snatched out of her bedroom. Besides, we were right here. We would have heard the door open and someone going upstairs." In her heart she knew Penny had run away because she felt unwanted. She hesitated. Should she tell him what she really thought because of the wording in the note? Should she tell him it was his words that might have driven Penny from the house?

This was no time for worrying about Tony's feelings. They had to start looking for Penny. "Tony, I think Penny might have overheard our conversation about Lisa and thought we were talking about her."

His brow furrowed. "What conversation?"

"The one in which you said nothing would make you happier than to never have to lay eyes on her again."

Tony's face went whiter than the snow covering the ground outside.

CHAPTER 16

❖

TONY IMMEDIATELY CALLED THE POLICE, AND then he and Dora waited in the living room for their arrival. Night had closed in and the outside temperatures had been dropping steadily. The thought of Penny out there, cold, alone, and frightened, gave rise to a desperate helplessness that Dora had never known before. Where would a little girl go?

Right after Tony had called the police, he'd called Millie and woken her up, hoping Penny might have decided to go over there. But Millie said she hadn't seen her since the day before, when Penny and she had had ice cream sundaes together. They were quickly running out of places to check, and it seemed as though the police were taking forever to arrive at the house.

The next calls went out to the homes of Penny's friends, all with the same result. No one had seen the little girl. Their options had been exhausted.

Dora thought about making an excuse to go upstairs and ask Gracie to contact Penny's Guardian Angel, but she didn't want to leave Tony alone. Besides, she knew Penny's Guardian Angel's hands were tied. The fact that she'd left the note told Dora Penny had run away using her free will, and a mortal's free will was the one thing in which angels were forbidden to interfere. A Guardian Angel could only stand by, watch over her charge, hope the choice the mortal made was a good one, and be ready to step in if danger threatened. This thought was the one thing that gave Dora even a small measure of comfort.

Instead, Dora sat on the couch wringing her hands, racking her brain for answers, and watching a distraught Tony pace the length of the room, stopping every few moments to peer out the window for any sign of the police. When the street remained empty, he uttered a string of curses and resumed pacing.

"What the hell's taking them so long?"

"Tony, it's only been twenty minutes since we called them. I'm sure they'll be here as soon as they can." But she might as well have been talking to the chair. Her words bounced right off him.

The explanation was meant to calm Tony. However, even to her it seemed as though hours had passed since Tony had picked up the receiver and dialed 911.

While gazing into the Earth Pool, Dora had seen other parents go through this trauma, but she had never fully comprehended the pain, the agony, or the fear that tore at their insides until now. The helplessness was the worst. The need to be doing something, anything, to find Penny, anything besides sitting and waiting while the child was out there cold and alone, became overwhelming.

Penny was so little, so defenseless. Was she afraid? In danger? Sorry she ran away, but unable to find her way home? The questions tormented Dora until she had to bite her tongue to keep from crying out. Where on earth could the little one be? She drew a blank. Dora hadn't been around long enough to know if Penny had any secret places where she could go to be alone.

In a desperate attempt to distract Tony and herself, she searched her mind for anything that would make him feel he was doing something.

"Tony, try to think about where she may have gone. Does she have any special hiding places where she likes to go and play by herself?"

He stopped pacing and stared at her as though she had grown three extra heads, then his face crumpled. "I have no idea. Isn't that pathetic? I have no idea where my own niece would go to hide."

Dora could have cut out her tongue. Her stupid attempt to ease his pain had only added to it. "No, it's not pathetic. Little girls have secrets, just like big girls do. If she had somewhere that she considered a refuge, a place only she knew about, she wouldn't share it with anyone. That would defeat the whole purpose, wouldn't it?"

For a moment, Tony considered her words, then shrugged. "I suppose." He resumed his pacing.

Knowing he felt less than adequate about caring for his niece, but unable to let it keep her from trying to figure out where she'd gone, Dora pressed him for an answer. "Think, Tony. If she isn't here, where might she go?"

He halted and held his hands out in a hopeless gesture, his eyes hot with impatient anger. "I don't know, Dora! I don't know! If I did, don't you think I'd be there bringing her home?"

Though Dora knew his anger wasn't aimed at her, but came from frustration and worry, she still cringed.

Instantly, remorse washed over his expression. He threw himself on the couch beside her and drew her into his arms.

"I'm sorry. I shouldn't have yelled at you," he whispered into her hair. "I know you're as worried as I am, and you were only trying to help. I had no right to snap at you like that." He pushed her away and stared into her eyes. "Forgive me?"

She nodded, happy to see some of the tension drain

out of his face. "Always," she whispered back. She leaned against him, enjoying the strength of his body next to hers. Somehow, with his arms around her, everything seemed less hopeless, less—

The phone rang. Both of them went rigid. Tony bolted from the couch and snatched up the receiver. Biting down on her lips, Dora leaned forward expectantly and watched his expression for some sign that the phone call was about Penny.

"Yes?" He ran his hand through his already-mussed hair, and then looked at the ceiling. "Thank God." His grim expression melted into one of intense relief. He smiled and nodded at Dora.

The tightness that had gripped Dora's limbs since they'd realized Penny had left the house loosened. She fell back against the couch, too limp to hold herself up.

"Thanks, Millie. We'll be right over." He hung up the phone.

Just as he turned to tell Dora what Millie had said, red lights flashed across the living room walls announcing the arrival of the police. Tony hurried to the front door.

Dora could hear the murmur of voices, but couldn't make out what they were saying. Unable to contain herself any longer, she leapt to her feet and followed Tony. Just as she got to the door, he was closing it behind a uniformed officer.

"Tony?"

He swung around and scooped her into his arms. "Our little girl is all right. She's at Millie's." He kissed Dora's surprised mouth. "Millie couldn't sleep after I called her, and when she went downstairs for a drink, she found Penny curled up on the sofa in the family room. Evidently, she used the key Millie keeps under the back porch mat to let herself in."

Dora was more than delighted that Penny was safe. Joy blossomed inside her. She wanted to jump and scream to the world that Penny was okay. Instead, she hugged Tony close and blinked back tears of gratitude.

"Let's go bring her home." He kissed Dora's nose, then grabbed her hand and ran to the back of the house.

As she followed Tony out the back door, Dora couldn't find words to express how happy she was that Penny was safe and had not been wandering the streets in the icy cold night. However, at the same time, one phrase Tony had used rang through her head and drowned out all other thoughts . . . *our little girl*.

No matter how much she loved Penny, Dora couldn't allow herself to think in those terms. Penny was not *their* little girl. If she had a claim at all on the child, it was tenuous at best, and the time was quickly approaching when she would have to relinquish it. Penny was Tony's.

Tony couldn't believe their good fortune. This could

have turned out badly, but it hadn't. He had to be grateful for that. At the same time, he had to wonder what had prompted Penny to run away.

When Tony entered Millie's kitchen, he and Dora found Penny sitting at the table drinking a cup of hot chocolate piled high with fluffy white whipped cream. As soon as she saw her uncle, she let go of the mug and leaned back, her shoulders hunched forward and her eyes lowered to her lap.

Millie pulled them both to the side and, in a whisper, told them, "She ran away and won't tell me why. When I found her on the couch, she told me she remembered that I kept a key under the back door mat and let herself in. Said she was going to stay here until tomorrow. I have no idea where she planned to go after that. Truth be known, I don't think she had a plan, either." Tony started forward, but Millie stopped him with a hand on his arm. "She wouldn't have done this unless she was really upset about something. Tread lightly." He nodded.

Millie stood to the side and watched Tony, seemingly ready to pounce if he said or did anything to distress Penny further. Dora went to stand beside their neighbor.

For some time, he stood looking down at Penny. How should he approach the situation? Why had she felt she had to run away? Had she, as Dora suspected, heard the conversation he and Dora had been having? Something told him that asking her about it right away would be the wrong approach. Instead, Tony took a deep breath and slid out the chair opposite Penny.

He sat down, folded his hands, and leaned on his forearms. "Hi," he said quietly.

Penny peeked through her lashes at him. "Hi." Her barely audible voice quivered.

So far, so good.

Now, what to say? Nothing came to him. He glanced at the parade of ceramic angels on the window-sill above the sink. This would be a good time for the Guardian Angel Millie professed everyone had to jump in and give him a bit of guidance. But no voice came out of the blue spouting wisdom and feeding him the right words. Evidently, his Guardian Angel had decided he was on his own.

Then out of nowhere and for the first time in his life, he experienced an unsettling wave of what Rosalie used to call déjà vu. A long-forgotten memory of having sat like this before, but with Rosalie, emerged. As though in answer to his plea for Guardian Angel intervention, instantly he knew what to do.

"Millie, I have a craving for some chocolate ice cream."

Obviously perplexed, Millie looked at Dora, then back to Tony. "Uh . . . I think I have some. Let me take a look." She checked the freezer. "All I have is strawberry. Will that be okay?"

Tony grinned at his niece. "Even better. That's Penny's favorite." He winked at the little girl, then turned to Millie. "Would you mind spooning out a dish for each of us?"

"Sure." Her face still showing her puzzlement, she pulled dishes from the cabinet. After scooping the ice cream into two dishes, Millie set them in front of Tony and Penny and gave each of them a spoon, her brow still creased with unanswered questions about his need for ice cream in the middle of a family crisis on a cold winter's night. But she wisely held her tongue and waited.

"Thanks, Millie." He picked up a spoon, scooped out some ice cream, and put it in his mouth. "Mmm." He pointed his spoon at Penny's untouched dish. "Go ahead. Eat up. Everything always looks better after a big bowl of ice cream."

From the corner of his eye, he could see Millie and Dora studying them, puzzled frowns still knitting their foreheads.

"You know, Penny, when I was about nine, my friends and I decided to play a game of catch in the neighbor's yard. Our ball got stuck in a tree, and we couldn't get it down." He took another spoonful of ice cream and savored the icy coolness running down his dry throat before he spoke again. "We decided that if we threw something at it, we could make it fall out of the tree. We tried throwing rocks and boards and other balls, but nothing worked. The darn ball was just plain stuck."

"How did you get it down?" Penny asked timidly.

Silently congratulating himself that Penny had at least started looking at him, he continued. "Well, I found a rock. A really big rock that I was sure would get the ball out. So I gathered all my strength and threw it as hard as I could."

"Did it come out?" Penny picked up the spoon and took a taste of the ice cream.

Millie punched the air and grinned at Dora, then flung her arm around her and gave her shoulders a squeeze.

"Oh, yes, the ball came down. The problem was, the rock bounced off the ball and went right through our neighbor's window."

Penny's mouth opened in a wide, surprised *O*. "What did you do?"

"I ran. So did all my friends. We all met at my house and made a pact that we wouldn't tell who broke the window."

"But that wasn't being honest."

"You're exactly right," Tony said, pointing at Penny with his spoon. "It was not honest. Deep down inside, I knew I should admit what I'd done and pay for the window, but I was afraid of getting in trouble. So I kept quiet. But the problem was, it really, really bothered me, and before long, because I felt so guilty, I got cranky and started losing my temper. I was worried all the time that your mom would guess what I'd done. Pretty soon, I couldn't think about anything else." He leaned closer and whispered, "I even thought about running away, but I was too afraid."

She looked at him, aghast. "You were afraid?"

Getting a jolt of happiness from the fact she didn't think he could be afraid of anything, he nodded. "Scared to death. You're much braver than I was."

Penny lowered her gaze to her dish. "But I only ran next door."

"I didn't even do *that*," Tony said, taking another spoonful of ice cream.

"Did you ever tell?"

Tony nodded. "Your mom guessed that I'd broken the window because of the way I was acting, so she called me inside, sat me down at the table, got us each a bowl of chocolate ice cream, and we talked about it. I had to pay for the window, but because I finally told, I felt so much better."

Penny glanced at Millie and Dora, then at Tony. She laid her spoon down and leaned back.

"Maybe, if you tell me why you ran away, we can fix whatever it was that made you do it. I promise you'll feel better, too."

For a long time, Penny studied her hands. Finally, she looked at Tony. "I heard what you told Dora about me causing trouble and that you didn't want me in your house anymore."

Millie gasped and started to speak, but Dora shook her head and silenced her.

Tony felt as though a ten-ton truck had run full force into his chest. Pain radiated out from his aching heart. His throat filled with emotion.

He couldn't even come close to understanding the feelings of abandonment that must have driven Penny from her warm house into the winter night. Why hadn't he been more careful and kept his voice down?

He rose and walked around the table, reached down, lifted Penny into his arms, and hugged her close. She snaked her little arms around his neck and hid her face against his shoulder. Unable to speak, he stood for the longest time, holding her close, searching for the words to erase her pain. He clenched his teeth against the painful rush of renewed emotions sweeping through him.

Over Penny's head, he caught Dora staring at them

and saw her almost-imperceptible nod.

Tell her, she mouthed.

Tony knew exactly what Dora wanted him to tell Penny, but the words lay trapped in that dark, ugly place deep inside him, hidden from the light of day behind a protective wall. As long as they stayed there, he'd never again have to endure the pain of losing a loved one.

Instead, he set Penny back in her chair and squatted in front of her. Taking her hands, he said, "Honey, I wasn't talking about you. I would never want you to leave our house, to leave me. You're my niece. Why would you think such a thing?"

Once more Penny avoided eye contact. She fidgeted with the hem of her sweater, and then took a deep, ragged breath. "Because you hate me."

CHAPTER 17

FOR A MOMENT, TONY COULDN'T SPEAK. HE HATED her? Surely he had heard wrong. His gut, however, told him he hadn't. For some reason, known only to her, this beautiful little girl thought he hated her.

Speechless, he glanced at Dora and Millie, whose faces told him they were equally taken aback. Before he could form the words to deny it, Penny began to cry in great wrenching, heartbreaking sobs.

"I . . . I'm s . . . so . . . s . . . sorry, Uncle T . . . Tony. I d . . . didn't . . . m . . . mean for it to h . . . happen."

"For what to happen, sweetheart?" He'd never felt so powerless in his life. He could order around a crew of big, tough construction workers, but he couldn't get a little girl to stop crying.

Confused about how to handle the situation, he

looked to Dora for help.

Dora went to him. "Don't ask questions. She's tired, and questioning her will only upset her more. Just pick her up, and we'll take her next door and put her to bed."

He glanced at Millie as though unsure if this was the best course of action, and Millie smiled her approval. "Take her home. The poor baby is exhausted. Tomorrow's soon enough to talk about this."

Tony nodded and picked Penny up. Her sobs slowly subsided to intermittent hiccups. She again put her arms around his neck, buried her face in his shoulder, and finally closed her eyes.

❖ ❖ ❖

"She's asleep," Dora announced as she entered the living room, where Tony sat staring blankly at the Christmas tree. Jack lay curled at his feet, appraising Tony with his expressive dark eyes. "Poor thing was absolutely wiped out. She never even stirred when I took off her clothes." She sat next to Tony on the couch and laced her fingers with his. "You okay?"

As if rousing from a dream, he blinked and turned to her. "I'm lost. Why would she think I hate her? I've gone through everything that's happened since the funeral, and I can't think of anything I've said or done to make her think that."

For someone on the outside looking in, the answer was so simple. But for Tony, who was far too close to the problem, finding the answer was the equivalent of climbing Mount Everest. Perhaps just a nudge. Dora tightened her fingers. "Maybe it's something you *haven't* said or done."

"Well, that's a lot of help, Dora." He wrenched his hand free from hers, stood, and began covering the same stretch of floor from the tree to the door that he'd traveled while they'd waited for the police. "Seeing as how I came into this situation without a clue, I'm sure there's a whole bunch of things I haven't said or done. Could you be a bit more specific?"

Knowing he needed to find it out for himself, Dora remained silent. That Tony loved Penny was perfectly obvious to Dora. However, the loss of the people she loved and who had unconditionally loved her had left Penny on the same rocky ground as Tony. She needed the reinforcement of words.

The question was, would Tony ever realize that on his own? And could Penny wait for him to come around?

Tony felt he was protecting himself by holding back the words that would put Penny's mind at ease. The problem was that Penny needed the reassurance of hearing him say that he loved her.

The seemingly insurmountable dilemma made her head spin. If Dora told him why Penny felt he hated her, perhaps they could get on with the healing process for both of them. However, just mouthing the words wasn't enough. Tony had to open his heart to this insecure little girl.

Just then Jack growled low in his throat, drawing Dora's attention away from Tony's pacing. The dog lying at her feet had his dark, censuring gaze fixed on her.

No longer willing to chalk it up to coincidence that the dog inserted his canine opinions into the conversation, or himself between her and Tony at critical moments, Dora glared at him.

Calvin, is that you?

Silence.

Okay. You're leaving me no choice. I knew you were masquerading as Jack, and I told Gracie. I'll ask her to go to the Heavenly Council and have you recalled. You know Michael is particularly fond of Gracie, so he'll do it. Michael will make sure the Council knows, too. Try explaining your way out of that.

Truth be known, she hadn't actually been positive that Jack was Calvin. It was more of a hunch, but he didn't have to know that, and with any luck, she'd be forgiven the small white lie when she reported back.

Jack jumped to the couch, sat beside her, and poked

her arm with his nose. *You win. It's me. Happy?* His ears perked up. *You have more important things to think about than the fact that I'm a dog. If you're thinking of telling Tony why Penny hates him, don't. It's critical to your success that he figure it out on his own.*

I wasn't going to, and I already realize it's something he has to discover by himself. She cleared her throat. *As for you . . . Jack.* She lowered another dark glare on him. *We'll talk about this later. Count on it. Now, get out of here, and let me concentrate on helping Tony and Penny.*

Calvin's . . . Jack's ears laid back. He barked sharply and jumped down. With a toss of his head, he walked out of the room.

"Could you forget about that mutt for a minute and help me figure out what's wrong with Penny?"

As Jack disappeared up the stairs, Dora swung guiltily toward Tony. "Sorry." She stood. "Why don't I make some coffee? It appears it's going to be a long night." *In more ways than one*, she added silently.

He nodded. That tempting lock of hair fell onto his forehead. Dora curled her fingers against her palm to resist the temptation to brush it back and assure him that everything would be okay.

His lips twisted into a half smile. "How about a stiff drink instead?"

She frowned.

"Okay. Coffee."

As she walked down the hall to the kitchen, the warmth radiating over her back told her Tony had followed close behind.

He slumped into a kitchen chair and rested his elbows on the table. "I've racked my brain, and I can't figure out why she says I hate her."

Dora abruptly stopped pouring water into the coffeepot. "Then maybe you need to ask her. By morning she should be in a better frame of mind to talk about it."

"He's doing what?" Gracie's eyes grew large and her mouth set in straight line of disapproval. As her agitation at the news of Calvin's masquerade grew, her wings beat faster, and the clouds swirled angrily behind her. "The Heavenly Council needs to know about this."

Dora sprang from the edge of the bed toward the mirror. "No, please. Don't say anything. They'll recall him, and then what will Penny do? She'll be heartbroken if Jack leaves, and she's lost too much already. I have to figure out how he can go back and not hurt Penny."

Gracie considered Dora's request for a time. "You have enough on your mind. Leave this to me. I'm sure if I put my head together with some other angels, we can find a solution."

Gratitude washed over Dora. She had no desire to get Calvin in trouble, just to save Penny's heart from more pain. "Thanks, Gracie. I owe you one."

"Keeping an eye on that . . . mutt will be thanks enough." Shaking her head, Gracie shimmered out while mumbling, "What in heaven's name was he thinking?"

Thankful that at least one problem seemed to be on its way to a solution, Dora unlocked her door. If Penny came looking for her during the night, she wanted to be certain she was accessible. Dora flopped back on the bed and heaved a big sigh. It had been a very long day, and all she wanted right at the moment was sleep.

Retrieving her nightgown from the closet, she started for the bathroom. Then her bedroom door hinges creaked. Expecting it to be Penny, Dora was surprised to see Jack/Calvin slip around the door and into the room.

Jumping up on the bed, he turned to her. *I suppose you told Gracie.*

"Yes, but she's promised not to tell the Council. She's going to talk to the other angels and figure out how to get you out of here without hurting Penny." Dora sat beside him. "What were you thinking when you did this, Calvin? You must have known you'd have to go back. Didn't it occur to you that Penny would be heartbroken when her dog disappeared?"

To Dora's utter shock, Jack's ears folded back, and he lowered his head and relaxed his tail. *I'm afraid I wasn't thinking about anything but making sure you didn't . . . uh, make any mistakes.*

Her heart went out to him. He seemed genuinely repentant, but that didn't solve their problem. Gently, she ran her hand over his head. "If I make mistakes, I'm the one who will have to answer for them."

Oh, how I wish that were true. Jack jumped to the floor and sauntered out of the room, defeat written clearly in his slumped posture.

Though Calvin didn't believe it now, Dora would make sure he suffered no backlash for her failures.

❖ ❖ ❖

The next morning found the Falcone household in an uproar. Everyone had overslept, and Penny had to be rushed from the house so she wouldn't be late for school. So, along with a throbbing headache from lack of sleep, Tony had driven to work with his heart laboring under the burden a little girl had unwittingly placed on it.

Once at the office, everything seemed to go wrong. After Tony had spilled coffee on the floor and then dropped a pile of papers for the second time, Jake swung his chair around.

"Woman troubles?" he asked with a note of hopefulness in his voice.

Tony gave a mirthless laugh. "You wish, so you could pummel me with some more of your Dear Abby advice. I hate to disappoint you, but it's not woman troubles. It's little girl troubles."

"Penny?"

Tony nodded, retrieved the scattered papers, and then sat on the edge of Jake's desk. "Penny ran away last night."

Jake sat up straighter. "Is she okay? Did you find her?"

"She's fine." Tony laughed, this time with a little humor. "She ran next door to Millie's house."

"Next door?" His mouth quirked up at the corner. "Guess lack of imagination runs in the family." Tony threw him a deprecating glance. "So, why did she run away?"

Not at all sure he wanted to share this bit of information, Tony changed the subject. "Matt's sister, Lisa, showed up at the house. A few days later I got a letter from a lawyer. She wants custody of Penny." Just the thought started his blood boiling again. "I have to go to a hearing at the courthouse."

Jake blew out a gust of air. "You're not going to let her take Penny, are you?"

"Damned straight, I'm not."

"I play golf with a guy named Harry Jenkins. He's

a top-notch attorney, and he specializes in child custody cases. I'll be seeing him at the church Christmas party this weekend. If you want, I'll get his phone number for you."

"I'd appreciate it. I hadn't even thought of getting a lawyer, but I'm sure I'll need one." Picking up a pencil from his foreman's desk, Tony twirled it between his fingers. "Why the hell can't life be simple, Jake?"

"Because if it were simple, it wouldn't be any fun."

Tony laughed. "Well, if this is fun, then I hope I never have to come nose-to-nose with the part that isn't."

CHAPTER 18

A FEW TENSION-FILLED DAYS AFTER PENNY RAN away, Tony and Dora walked into the county courthouse, down the winding maze of halls and doors, and into the conference room.

Although he had no idea what to expect, the fact that the day was finally here came as a huge relief to Tony. The hearing had lain heavily on all their minds, and he knew living with him had been like living with a bear with a thorn in his paw. He'd barely spoken to anyone, and when he did, despite his best effort to be civil, his replies were curt and often sharper than necessary. It didn't take a rocket scientist to realize his frayed nerves were on the very edge. The least little thing set him off, and it hadn't escaped his notice that Penny and Dora had gotten into the habit of talking to him only when necessary and giving him a wide berth.

After deciding there was no need to worry the little girl, they'd kept everything from her. Dora had told her Tony and she were going to finish up their Christmas shopping when they left. Lying to her had not set well with Tony, but the alternative of upsetting Penny, perhaps without reason, held even less appeal.

Millie had said she'd pick Penny up at school and watch her until they got home. The last thing she'd said as they walked out the door was, "I have a good feeling about this." But Tony could see in her eyes that she was as apprehensive as he and Dora.

Anything could happen today. Tony's common sense told him that, but in his heart he prayed Millie's words would prove prophetic. Certainly if he and Dora told the judge they loved Penny and she had a good life, the judge would see she was better off with them.

He'd spoken to Henry Jenkins, the lawyer Jake had arranged for him, and he'd assured Tony his chances of winning looked good. They'd drawn Judge Collier for the hearing, and she had a reputation of being stern but fair. But what worried him most was that Tony was a single man raising a little girl. Lisa and her husband constituted a complete family. Would that sway the judge's decision in Lisa's favor? Only time would tell.

The cold, unwelcoming room seemed to mock Tony with its starkness. Gray, metal filing cabinets stood side by side, filling one corner, and in the center a long, shiny, dark wood table surrounded by a dozen or so chairs waited for people who didn't even know Penny, but who were about to decide her future.

Near the end of the table, a salt-and-pepper-haired man in an immaculate navy suit shuffled papers he'd taken from his briefcase. Beside him sat Lisa, her tailored suit shouting money, as did her professionally styled hair. The saccharin smile she offered Dora and Tony held as much sincerity as it had on the day she'd sat in Tony's living room.

When the door *thunked* closed behind them, the sound echoed around the room. The man looked up, smiled, then rose with his hand extended to Tony. "Mr. Falcone?"

Tony shook it. "Yes."

"I'm James Mayfield, Mrs. Randall's attorney." He gestured at Lisa, who, aside from the fake smile, made no move to acknowledge Tony and Dora's presence. She turned away and stared stoically straight ahead. "Please, have a seat." Mayfield pointed to the two chairs across from Lisa.

Tony had no desire to see Lisa until it was absolutely necessary and, if he could avoid it, not even then. "I think we'll just wait outside for—"

"Tony! Sorry I'm late. Damned car wouldn't start."

Both Dora and Tony turned toward the voice.

Henry Jenkins had entered the room, a jovial smile curling his lips. It was the only thing that came close to matching Mayfield's impeccable appearance. Henry's black suit, while clean and pressed, displayed the sheen a well-worn suit acquires after years of use. One side of his off-white shirt collar curled up, and his light blue tie had a dark spot in the center that spoke loudly of an accident at lunch. His briefcase was scuffed and as worn as his suit, and his hair looked as though he'd just exited a wind tunnel. All in all, not a terribly impressive sight.

"Hello, Henry." Tony stepped aside. "This is Dora DeAngelo, Penny's nanny."

Henry's grin widened. "Miss DeAngelo, I'm so glad to meet you." He pumped Dora's hand, then moved to the end of the table opposite his well-groomed adversary. "Mayfield." They shook hands.

Henry swung his briefcase onto the table. The catch popped open and papers slid in every direction over the highly polished table.

Everyone scrambled to retrieve them. Tony caught the this-is-going-to-be-a-piece-of-cake grin Mayfield flashed at Lisa. Taking a deep breath, Tony led Dora to a chair one seat away from Henry and took the empty seat between them.

While Henry struggled to right his papers, Tony sighed and bowed his head. Dora leaned close, laced her fingers with his, and squeezed. "It'll be fine," she whispered.

He sought her gaze and found understanding and compassion, but he also saw the same worry in her eyes that lay in a big lead ball in his stomach. Just having her beside him made him feel better; he didn't know what he would have done if he'd had to weather this alone.

Unwilling to upset her with his apprehension, he nodded. "I'm sure it will."

The door at the side of the room opened, and a woman in a black robe entered. "I'm sorry to have kept you waiting, but I had a case to finish up and came straight here from the courtroom."

She removed the robe and laid it over the back of her chair, then assumed the seat at the head of the table. Under the robe she wore a red blouse and a gray skirt. Without the formal garment of her office, she looked much less austere. She was middle-aged, and her auburn hair lay in soft waves over her shoulders.

She glanced at the people around the table. She had a heart-shaped, pleasant, somewhat plain face and a congenial smile. Her light-colored eyes were framed by dark-rimmed glasses that made her look like a small, curious owl. The smell of a flowery perfume drifted over the table from her direction.

A young man, presumably her court stenographer,

followed her into the room carrying a small machine on which Tony assumed he'd record the proceedings. He took a seat at a smaller table near the window, away from the primary group, but within hearing distance.

As the judge shuffled the papers, Tony noted a gold wedding band on the third finger of her left hand. Would that make her more biased toward Penny having both a mother and a father figure? Doubts churned in his stomach like fan blades laboring to cool the air on a sultry day.

Glancing up from scanning the file that had awaited her on the table, she announced, "I'm Judge Collier." She met the gaze of each person. "Everyone seems to be here, so let's get started." Again she consulted the file. "Penny Stevens is the child in question?"

"Yes, Your Honor," Henry said.

"And Mrs. Randall is seeking to remove the little girl from the custodial care of her uncle, Tony Falcone? Mr. Falcone has had legal custody of the child since the death of both her parents a little more than a year ago?"

"That's correct, Your Honor," Mayfield said. "Your Honor, Mrs. Randall—"

Judge Collier stopped Mayfield's words with a raised hand. "I'll hear your arguments in a moment, Mr. Mayfield." She continued to leaf through the papers.

Under the table, Dora squeezed Tony's fingers so

tightly he was certain the blood had stopped pumping through them. But he needed the reassurance of her touch and made no move to extract his hand from her painful grasp.

Finally, the judge laid the file aside and removed her glasses. "Mr. Mayfield?"

"Your Honor, my client feels that while Mr. Falcone's intentions are good, the child is being deprived of certain things that she and her husband could more readily provide."

The judge slipped on her glasses and once more studied the file. She removed her glasses and looked at Mayfield. "Such as?"

"Mr. Randall is a prosperous businessman in Texas and can provide a stable financial environment for the girl, send her to college, et cetera. It takes only a brief glance at Mr. Falcone's financial records to see that there is no comparison between his finances and those of my client's husband. Along with that is the fact Mr. Falcone is a bachelor, Judge, but with the Randalls the child would have a more . . . conventional home life, with the influence of both a mother and father."

Tony's heart dropped. That point was the only one he couldn't fight. He had to pray the pluses in his favor would be enough.

"Your Honor," said Henry, "Mr. Falcone has a full-time, live-in nanny, Miss DeAngelo"—he pointed at Dora—"who adores Penny."

"But," chimed in Mayfield, "Miss DeAngelo is not a permanent resident in the home. She is an employee who can leave at any time, or Mr. Falcone can fire her. Either way, her presence in the home is tenuous at best."

"I'm assuming that divorce is still a legal option in Texas, Mayfield," said Henry. "If the Randalls decided to dissolve their marriage, then Penny would once more be with a single parent. There are no guarantees."

Lisa glared indignantly at Henry. She opened her mouth, presumably to assure the judge she and her husband would not be getting divorced, but Mayfield silenced her with a hand on her shoulder.

Mayfield's chest puffed up like a peacock. "I can assure you that my client and her husband have a solid, loving marriage. Divorce is not even in their vocabulary."

"I'm sure Elizabeth Taylor and her innumerable husbands said the same thing."

"Your Honor," Mayfield protested, "I object."

"Mr. Mayfield, we are not in a courtroom, so hold your objections." She fought back a small smile. "However, Mr. Jenkins does have a point. I'm sure many marriages, Ms. Taylor's not withstanding, never began with divorce in their vocabulary, either."

A complacent smile curved Henry's lips. "Should

it enter their vocabulary, the end result would be the same—a single parent home. Right now, Mr. Falcone and Miss DeAngelo provide as secure and loving environment for Penny as any married couple could." He turned his attention to the Judge. "Your Honor, it's my hope that you'll judge my client on his present circumstances and not on what could be." He laughed. "Hell, the courthouse might explode in the next five minutes, and we'd all be dead. That doesn't mean the wheels of justice should grind to a halt today . . . just in case."

"Your Honor," Mayfield demanded, a vein in his neck pulsing wildly.

The judge smirked. "As crudely as it may have been stated, Mr. Jenkins has another valid point. Let's stick to the here and now, Mr. Mayfield, and Mr. Jenkins, please confine your arguments to the case at hand and not the imminent demise of the courthouse."

"Very well, Your Honor. The here and now is this. My client lives in a large house in a good neighborhood. Her husband has a lucrative business that provides a steady income, substantial enough to provide the girl with all the amenities to make her life more than comfortable. And they can offer the girl the benefits of having both a mother and father."

Tony's blood boiled. Mayfield referring to Penny as *the girl* infuriated him.

"Dammit! *The girl* has a name. Penny! Her name is Penny!" The judge started at Tony's angry voice. No sooner had he allowed his anger release than regret filled him. "I'm sorry, Your Honor, but she's a real, flesh-and-blood little girl, and she does have a name."

"So noted, Mr. Falcone." She turned to Mayfield. "Since you've stated your client's case, I'd like to hear from the other side." Henry opened his mouth, but she shook her head and nodded at Tony. "Tell me about Penny, Mr. Falcone."

All eyes turned to him. He hadn't planned on having to say anything. Henry had cautioned him to hold his tongue and said he would do all the talking. Fear froze his vocal cords. "I . . . uh . . . I . . ."

Dora leaned close to his ear. "Let your heart talk for you," she whispered, then smiled at him. Suddenly, he felt as though he could do anything.

He cleared his throat. "When I was just three, my mom and dad died. My sister, Rosalie, raised me—"

"Your Honor," Mayfield interrupted, his voice impatient.

"Mr. Mayfield, you had your say without interruption. Kindly afford the same courtesy to the others. If you find it impossible and interrupt again, I'll have you removed from the room." Mayfield shrank back in his chair. "Go on, Mr. Falcone."

"We didn't have a lot. Rosalie worked and kept a roof over our heads, clothes on our backs, and food in our bellies. No, we didn't have all the things that some of the other families had, but we had each other. We had determination. But most of all, we had love. I may have wanted for a special toy, but I never wanted for someone to talk to, to confide in, to be there for me. That's what I try to give Penny."

He lowered his head for moment. "I don't always do things right, and I didn't know that much about being a parent when I came into this. But Penny was my sister's first and only child, so neither did Rosalie. I'm learning just like she did. Every day gets easier." He turned to Dora and smiled. "And with Dora's help, I'm getting there. I know how my sister would want her daughter raised—with the same values she instilled in me. Nothing would make me happier than to be the one who watches over Penny as she grows up.

"I may not have a big bank account, but I have a business that's doing well and growing every day. No, we don't have a college fund yet for Penny, but when the time comes, if we don't have the money, I'll make sure she goes even if I have to borrow against everything I own to make it happen.

"Penny has spent a year adjusting to her parents' death. She's finally becoming a happy child again. If you tear her away from the only home she's ever known and the people who love her, there's no telling how she'll react."

"Thank you," the judge said. For a time, she stared down at the file and pushed her glasses around on the papers. Then she looked at Lisa. "Why exactly do you want this little girl, Mrs. Randall?" She glanced at the papers again. "According to Mr. Falcone, you never saw this child, Penny, until a few days ago."

"I think I can answer that, Your Honor." A man's voice came from the rear of the room.

CHAPTER 19

EVERYONE IN THE CONFERENCE ROOM WAS IN-
stantly alert. In unison, they turned toward the well-
dressed man at the back of the room. Well over six feet
tall, his shoulders strained at the material of his dark blue
business suit. His dark hair lay neat and sleek against his
head, and patches of white at his temples declared he was
not as young as Dora had first thought. As he closed the
distance between them, she could make out fine lines
around his mouth and across his forehead. But in his
eyes she saw kindness and wisdom.

Lisa's mouth fell open. "Leon? What are you doing
here?"

Dora's gaze swiveled back and forth between Lisa and
the man. Lisa seemed to know him, but who was he?

The judge frowned. "And you are . . .?"

He came forward and stopped behind Lisa. Resting

his hands on her shoulders, he said, "I'm Leon Randall, Lisa's husband."

A tense, expectant silence fell over the room. Tony's fingers gripped Dora's hand with such force she was sure her bones would snap.

"Well, Mr. Randall, please join us." The judge gestured for Mayfield to move over and make room for Lisa's husband. After he was seated, she continued, "Now, I believe you said you could tell us why Mrs. Randall wants custody of Penny Stevens."

He nodded. "For medical reasons, my wife is not able to have children." He took Lisa's hand and held it to his chest. "We both want children very much. A few months ago, Lisa went to visit her parents, whom she hadn't seen in some time. They told her her brother and his wife had a child. They also told her her brother and his wife had been killed last year in a traffic accident. When Lisa came home, she could talk of nothing else but this child, Penny."

Judge Collier stopped him. "Mr. Randall, why was your wife estranged from her family?"

Leon Randall glanced around the table. Dora's heart went out to him. The worry in his eyes told her that he feared losing Lisa if he said too much. Yet, he knew, if he was to make everyone understand, he had to tell the entire story to the judge.

"Until six years ago, Lisa was a drug addict. She put herself into rehab and spent a year and a half there. I met her after she got out. Six months later, we were married. She's been clean ever since."

The judge nodded. "Go on."

"She tried to get pregnant and, when we didn't have any luck, we went to talk to a doctor. That's when we learned that the chances of Lisa conceiving a child were slim." He looked at his wife, and Dora could see the love shining in his eyes.

"We don't want your pity," he said. "I just want you to understand what drove her to come here and try to win custody of Penny."

"There are other ways to get a child, Mr. Randall," Henry said, his voice gentle. "Artificial insemination."

Leon shook his head. "You don't understand. Lisa's reproductive system is too fragile to carry a child. Even if she had conceived our child, she would have miscarried within weeks of becoming pregnant."

"Adoption? Surrogacy?" Henry offered.

Again, Leon shook his head. "I'd even offered to use a surrogate, but she refused. Lisa wanted a child of my blood and hers, not another woman's, and she'd lost all hope of that ever happening. Adoption can take years, and she wanted a child right away. She became depressed and I worried that . . . well, that she'd revert to some of her old habits. But she didn't. She fought her way through it and came out stronger than before. When she found out about Penny, it seemed like a miracle to both of us."

Dora had been studying Lisa while her husband spoke. She seemed to have shrunk in size, and the arrogant woman who had occupied her seat before Leon showed up had vanished. Instead she had turned into a fragile child herself. She clung to Leon as though he were her lifeline, as though if she let go, she'd disappear.

Obviously, more than one of Lisa's facades was a fake. Because of her apparent need to cling to her husband for support, Dora had to believe the arrogant woman they'd met upon entering the hearing room was a front she'd put on for them. The fragile woman who occupied that same chair was the real Lisa Randall.

"I tried to talk her out of it," Leon went on, "but she wouldn't hear of it. When I learned she'd flown here, I immediately understood why and followed as quickly as I could."

Lisa began to sob quietly. Leon gathered her in his arms. "I just wanted to give you a child," she choked out.

"It's okay, sweetheart." Leon held the broken woman close.

Silence enveloped the room. Dora watched Judge Collier. She seemed deep in thought. Finally she spoke.

"I'm going to look over the information I have here." She gestured to the file. "I will also take into consideration everything everyone has told me. Your lawyers will notify you of my decision as soon as I've rendered it."

Tony leaned forward. "Your Honor, Christmas is only a few days away. Is there any way we could get your decision before then?"

Dora wasn't sure why he'd made the request, but if the judge agreed, it would mean they'd be out from under the unbearable strain of waiting for weeks for a decision.

"I understand your reasoning for wanting this settled quickly, but there are other cases ahead of yours." Judge Collier consulted a small black book she'd pulled from a pocket in her robe. "You're lucky, Mr. Falcone. This is a small jurisdiction. Evidently most of the attorneys are busy Christmas shopping instead of filing cases, which makes my schedule for this month pretty light." Once more, she consulted the book. "I'll see you all again on Friday morning at nine."

Supper that night was eaten in almost total silence. Dora's heart bled for Tony. Though he had managed to get the judge to agree to act quickly, the wait for Judge

Collier's decision was driving her crazy, and she could only imagine what Tony was going through. She'd tried very hard to read the judge's face, but had no luck, so she couldn't even make an educated guess what her final decision would be. Because the decision fell under the heading of free will, Dora couldn't even consult Gracie.

Tony laid his fork down, his food barely touched. Dora frowned. "You really should eat, Tony."

He raised a worried face to her, then pushed his plate away. "I'm not hungry."

Truth be told, neither was she. For the first time since coming to the mortal world, Dora's passionate interest in their food was absent. She, too, pushed her plate back. Thank goodness Penny was eating supper with Millie and wasn't around to witness the scene. Dora wasn't sure she would have been able to put on a happy face for the little girl.

The phone rang, breaking the silence. "I'll get it," Dora said, making her way to the wall phone. "Hello."

"Dora," Millie said, "I have a little girl here who is jumping up and down in fear of missing the Winter Carnival. She wants to know when you'll be leaving."

Dora's mouth fell open. In all the excitement of the custody hearing, she'd forgotten about Penny's essay reading tonight. "Let me check with Tony," she said, playing for time. Slipping her hand over the mouthpiece, she turned to Tony. "Penny's reading her essay tonight. What time are we leaving?"

From the look of total surprise on Tony's face, she knew he hadn't remembered, either. "Damn! What time is the carnival?"

Dora checked the flyer on the refrigerator. "Seven o'clock."

He looked at his watch. Five thirty. "She has to change, and we need to get dressed. Tell Millie to send her over now, and we'll leave in about an hour."

❖ ❖ ❖

The school was decked out in Christmas finery. Artificial trees covered in fake snow, lights, and shiny balls of every color flanked the stage at the front of the room where a snowman resembling the one standing in the Falcones' front yard stood sentinel. Piles of what looked like sheets draped over boxes to simulate snowbanks formed a perimeter around the stage. Scattered among them were brightly wrapped boxes of all shapes and sizes.

To Dora's intense delight, Christmas seemed to be everywhere in the room. Even the programs, decorated with a child's drawing of Santa and his reindeer, told of the holiday. Penny's teacher, who had greeted them at the auditorium doors, wore a bright red dress and a

Christmas corsage made of pine, holly, and white carnations, all held together with a shiny green ribbon.

Tony and Dora took a seat near the front where Penny, who had been taken backstage when they'd arrived, could see them.

"Did she ever let you see her essay?" Tony whispered.

Dora shook her head and chuckled softly. "It's been top secret. I don't think even Millie knows."

Tony's deep laughter told Dora his dark mood had lightened a little. "Then it has really been top secret, because there's nothing that Millie doesn't know."

Just then the lights dimmed and the auditorium went silent. Penny's teacher, Mrs. Johnson, walked onto the stage and announced the fifth- and sixth-grade class chorus would do a selection of holiday songs.

For the next hour they listened to a variety of choral pieces, several solos by both male and female chorus members, and a selection of Christmas carols. Despite the renditions sometimes being a little off-key, when Dora looked around her, she smiled at the pride glowing in the faces of the proud parents. Deep inside her a wish formed that she would one day sit in the audience and watch her own child perform. But the futile notion died with the last notes of the chorus. This would have to suffice and fill in for the family she would never have, only cherished memories helping to ease a future that would be bleak and lonely.

After the chorus shuffled from the stage, Mrs. Johnson took their place again in the spotlight. "Very well done," she said, applauding as she waited for the last chorus member to disappear behind the side curtains. "Now, we have a very special treat for you. My first-grade class was asked to write about the best Christmas present they had ever gotten. The essays were judged by all the first-, second-, and third-grade teachers. The first, second, and third place winners are going to read their essays for you tonight."

Mrs. Johnson glanced to the side of the stage. "First to read her third place essay is Amanda King."

A tiny girl dressed in a pink, flouncy dress and with long blond curls falling over her shoulders emerged hesitantly from the right side of the stage. She walked slowly to the center, apprehension written clearly on her face. Nervously, she peered out over the audience. Spotting her parents sitting in front of Dora and Tony, her nervousness seemed to vanish, and she gave a little wave with the tips of her fingers. She waited until Mrs. Johnson nodded for her to begin.

Amanda's essay was about a talking doll she'd gotten from her grandmother. Not only did it have a full wardrobe and long golden curls just like Amanda's, but it also talked, wet itself, and said "Momma." It even came with its own carriage. Her grandmother had sewed an entire wardrobe for the doll, as well.

The applause was exuberant, but no one applauded harder than Amanda's parents. As Mrs. Johnson reappeared on the stage to announce the next winner and Mrs. King pulled her husband back into his seat, Mr. King clapped one more time and then the auditorium went quiet.

Joseph Stein followed Amanda. He had written about a Hanukkah present, a Lionel train set his dad had given him that was a family heirloom and had been passed down through four generations of Steins. The engine whistled and blew smoke. There was a station house with a little man who came out and waved a lantern whenever the train passed by.

Again, the volume of the applause of Joseph's parents far outdid everyone else in the room. Joseph made a courtly bow and exited the stage.

At last it was Penny's turn. As she took her place in the center of the stage, she smiled shyly at Dora and Tony. Tony gave her a thumbs-up, and Dora waved. She looked so pretty in the dark green velvet dress Millie had given her just for this occasion. Dora had pulled her hair up, tied it with a white silk bow, and let her copper curls cascade down her back.

"Ladies and gentlemen, our first place winner, Miss

Penny Stevens," Mrs. Johnson said, then stepped off to the side of the stage.

Penny waited while the applause died down, then cleared her throat, and began to read.

The best Christmas present I ever got was an empty box. My mommy gave it to me. She said what was inside was special. She said the box was full of love. She said you can't see love. You can only feel it. Mommy's with the angels. My Uncle Tony and Dora take care of me now. This year, I'm gonna give the box to Uncle Tony. Uncle Tony always looks very sad because he misses my mommy, too. I think he needs lots of love.

Deafening applause followed. Tony couldn't move. He couldn't applaud. He couldn't talk. He could barely breathe.

Memories rushed at him with all the force of a hurricane. Rosalie had given him that empty box every year to remind him how much he was loved. The first time she'd given it to him was the first Christmas after their mother had died. Because their father had passed away a few years earlier, Tony had been feeling especially alone. He'd thought Rosalie had forgotten to put the gift in the box, but when he asked her where it was, she'd assured him the box was filled to the top with love.

Every year after that, right up until Tony moved away, Rosalie had given her brother the empty box. Until this very moment, he'd forgotten all about it. Evidently, she had kept the tradition alive by giving Penny the box.

Rousing from his memories, he realized Penny was standing at the edge of the stage staring expectantly at him. His heart swelled with pride and love for his niece.

He grinned, then started to applaud. Penny beamed.

Then Tony stepped to the edge of the stage, reached up, scooped her into his arms, and lifted her down to the floor.

"Let's go home." Taking Penny's hand, he smiled down at her. "We need to talk, and there's also something you and I need to do."

CHAPTER 20

By the time they got home, Penny was out for the count in the backseat. Tony carried her inside and headed for the living room. He laid her gently on the sofa, and Jack charged in from the kitchen and jumped up beside her.

"Poor baby. She's exhausted," Dora said. "She needs to go to bed."

"I'll take her upstairs in a few minutes." Tony looked at Dora with purpose in his eyes. "Why don't you make us all some hot chocolate?"

Penny, who, after Jack had enthusiastically licked her face and was now fully awake, sat up, and looked at Dora with pleading eyes. "Please, Dora?"

Relenting, Dora headed for the kitchen. She'd barely started down the hall when she wondered if they'd like cookies, as well. Heading back to the living room to ask, she overheard Tony talking to Penny, and paused in the hall to listen.

"When I was very little, I wanted to put the angel on top of the tree, but I couldn't reach, so your mommy would lift me up to do it. Every year after that, she lifted me up to put the angel on the tree. Now I think it's time, if you want to, for you put the angel up there."

Dora peeked around the door in time to see him hand Penny the angel tree topper.

Penny took the tree topper and then looked at Tony as if to verify that he was serious.

"Well," he said, "do you want to?"

Her face glowed as brightly as the lights on the tree. "Oh, yes. Please."

Penny stood and turned her back to her uncle. He gripped her tightly around the waist and lifted her high in the air. Very carefully, she placed the angel atop the tree. He set her back on her feet, and the two of them stood looking at it for a long moment.

"I told you this tree was special, Uncle Tony."

"That you did, and you were absolutely right, sweet-heart."

In the hall, Dora fought back the tears suddenly clogging her throat. She knew how much the ritual meant to Tony. The fact he had been willing to finally share it with Penny said much about his progress toward freeing himself from the emotional prison in which he'd locked his heart.

Tony sighed with relief. Letting go hadn't hurt at all. He'd been so sure that it would, that the pain would come rushing in, but it hadn't. Instead, the act of sharing the simple ritual with the child his sister had loved so much filled his cold, empty soul with a rush of consoling warmth.

The forlorn little tree was, indeed, special. It had played a big part in bringing him closer to Penny and his feelings than anything else could.

Now that he'd opened the door and let the feeling back into his heart, he knew he had one more thing to do. Taking Penny's hand, he led her back to the sofa and sat beside her.

He inhaled deeply, not totally sure about holding the conversation with his niece, but knowing he had to. "Penny, the night you ran away, you told me you thought I hated you." He brushed a stray hair from her forehead. "Do you think you can tell me why?"

Penny folded her hands in her lap and dipped her head. "B . . . because it was m . . . my fault."

"What was your fault, sweetheart?"

She took a deep breath, and in a voice that emerged as barely a whisper choked with tears, she said, "That M . . . Mommy and D . . . Daddy died."

Tony was stunned.

For a moment he couldn't think, couldn't even absorb what Penny had said. He'd always felt that of the two of them, Penny had come to terms with her parents' deaths much faster and better then he had. This particular thought had never entered his mind. That she'd been carrying the unbelievable burden astonished him and tore his insides to shreds. That he hadn't realized it made him feel ashamed.

Was this why she'd worked so hard to win his approval? Why she'd been afraid of disappointing him? Why she'd never complained about anything and obeyed him to the letter on everything? Had she been afraid that if she made what she saw as another bad decision, that he'd get hurt, too, or worse?

His heart twisted painfully in his chest. His whole body felt as though he'd been beaten, but he knew it was nothing compared to what Penny had been carrying on her slim shoulders for over a year.

With shaking hands, he drew her into his lap and wrapped her securely in his arms. For a time, he was too emotional to speak. Then he cleared his throat.

"Penny, you are not to blame. I'm so very sorry you even thought that. Whatever could have made you imagine such a thing?"

She buried her face against his chest. "B . . . because I wanted pizza. If we hadn't gone to get it, they w . . .

wouldn't have gotten into the a . . . accident."

The emotional knot in Tony's throat almost choked him. Tears trickled silently down his cheeks. "Your wanting pizza had nothing to do with the accident," he told her gently. "A man who had been drinking ran a red light and hit their car. It didn't have a thing to do with you."

She leaned back and looked at him. Her cheeks glistened with tears. "But—"

He laid a finger on her lips. "No buts about it. You were not to blame for the accident. You have to believe that. Okay?" She nodded hesitantly. He kissed her forehead. "And I could never hate you." He looked deeply into her eyes. "You are very special to me, and I love you, very much."

Something let go inside him when he said the words he'd been holding back for so long. He couldn't say what it was, but it spread a *good* pain throughout his entire body, as though a dam had been breached, and the pressure of the water pushing against it was suddenly released.

"You love me? Really?"

"Really." He caressed her cheek with the back of his fingers and kissed her nose.

Penny looked as though he'd just told her she could have the run of the local candy store. "You don't hate me?"

He shook his head, his heart suddenly feeling like it

was two sizes too big for his chest. "No, I don't hate you. And I promise I will always love you, no matter what."

Something told him he'd have to repeat that declaration often for a while to totally convince her, but at least they were on their way. For the first time in a long time, he could say the words, and he found the idea of having to say them over and over very comforting.

Jack jumped into Tony's lap along with Penny and began licking both their faces. Penny squealed.

"I think Jack's happy that you love me, too," Penny declared when she could catch her breath. Then she looked up at Tony. She brushed away the tears from his cheeks. "Don't cry, Uncle Tony. I love you, too."

In the hall, Dora smiled through tears that washed her face in happiness. Yes, Jack probably was happy. After all, with Tony's declaration of love to Penny, Dora's job was done. Her mission was complete, and Jack, aka Calvin, could go back to Heaven without fear of suffering reprisals for her messing up another job. Dora just had to come up with an explanation for his sudden absence that would not break Penny's heart.

Smiling, she went back to the kitchen. But the smile faded when she recalled that they still had one more hurdle to get over on Friday.

❖ ❖ ❖

Friday dawned with freezing temperatures and an over-cast sky spitting out a light, wet snow. The cold air seeped through Tony's sheepskin-lined coat and bit into his skin. Somehow, the dismal day was appropriate for what would to take place, and perfectly mirrored the gray fear that had enclosed his heart.

As he and Dora climbed the courthouse steps, Tony held her hand in a tight grip. He didn't care that the gesture transmitted to her that he was as terrified as she was that he'd lose Penny.

After all, he'd just established a new relationship with his niece, and in the last few days since the Winter Carnival they had grown steadily closer. He loved playing games with her, or coming home early from work so he could have an after-school snack with Penny and discuss her day, or taking them all out for burgers and a movie. He'd even laughed hysterically with Penny through an entire movie about a penguin tap-dancing his way through life.

Penny had taken on the life of a different child. She'd been happier than Tony could ever recall seeing her. Her ready laugh was genuine and filled with glee when she told Dora about what a lousy cook her uncle was. She'd stopped looking to him for approval about everything she did and had taken on her own unique personality. Her eyes sparkled with new life, and her attachment to him was heartwarming and unmistakable.

Was that all about to end with Judge Collier's decision? Were they going to have to go home and tell Penny she was leaving them to live with people she didn't even know? Was he going to have to watch while the child's newly mended heart broke wide open?

Tony didn't even want to think about what that might do to Penny's newfound lease on life, or to the house that had been transformed from a building into a home, or to the people who would be left behind. Or that once Penny was gone, there would be no reason for Dora to remain in his life.

With a sick heart and weighed down by an emotional burden heavier than he'd ever carried on his shoulders, he swung the door to the conference room open and stepped aside for Dora to precede him. Inside, Leon, Lisa, and the two lawyers were already gathered at the table. When they entered, the somber mood prevailing over the room was thick enough to cut. Everyone nodded at them, but no one said a word. They took their seats.

Tony avoided eye contact with either Lisa or her husband. Not out of fear of physical retribution, but because his fear had manifested itself in a way that left him feeling helpless, and he would not give Lisa the satisfaction of knowing it. To his dismay, Tony felt what could only be described as fragile, as though a big block of ice had formed around his body and any movement might break it open, and he'd shatter into a million pieces. After the pain he'd endured following Rosalie's loss, he wasn't at all sure that this time he could put the pieces back together again.

Finally, after what seemed an eternity, Judge Collier entered. She'd exchanged her red blouse and gray skirt for a plain, tailored navy dress. Her hair, pulled into a bun at the back of her head, made her look more severe. The fear surrounding Tony's heart thickened. He reached for the reassuring warmth of Dora's hand and squeezed it.

The judge laid a file folder on the table and took her seat. She opened the file and scanned it for a time, then raised her gaze to the people waiting expectantly.

"I've looked over the file and taken into account everything you've all told me." She paused. "To say I find some serious questions would be minimizing my concerns in this matter." She leaned forward and clasped her hands atop the open manila folder that held the secret to Penny's future happiness.

A dull ache formed in Tony's right temple. He had to physically stop himself from ordering Judge Collier to just tell them her decision. Dora must have sensed his impatience and gave his hand a gentle squeeze. He glanced in her direction, and she smiled encouragingly.

That one simple gesture from her eased the tension knotting in his gut.

"Over the last few days, I've read this file innumerable times, and one thing stands out in my mind."

Another maddening pause.

Tony's insides tightened. He clenched his jaw and he glanced at Dora. Nerves made his empty stomach heave. The seconds stretched into interminable minutes. Tension around the table was palpable and as thick as a London fog. Finally, the judge cleared her throat, took a deep breath, and turned to the Randalls.

"Mr. and Mrs. Randall, the argument you presented for the financial stability and the kind of life you could provide for Penny is admirable. One cannot argue that it's certainly beneficial for a child to live in a big house, attend the college of her choice, and be provided with anything she could ever desire. I have no doubt Penny would do well with you."

Tony's heart sank. He could feel the color drain from his face. Lisa and Leon exchanged a satisfied smile. The gloom from outside the windows seeped into Tony's soul. He'd lost Penny. His body went numb, beyond feeling anything but complete and utter despair.

"At the same time, however, Mr. Falcone presents equally persuasive arguments why Penny's continued residence with him would be in the best interests of the little girl."

The satisfied smiles vanished from the Randalls' faces. A tiny sliver of hope rose up in Tony, allowing the rays of sunshine to filter in and part the gray mist holding his soul captive. He fought it down, certain he wouldn't be able to stand it if that hope was dashed to the ground.

"There is, however, one glaring difference between the arguments the two of you presented." Judge Collier closed her file. Leaning her forearms on the table, she studied the people around her. "One word, which I found made all the difference, and it played a big part in my final decision."

Tony looked questioningly at Dora. She shrugged. Tony racked his brain, trying to think what that difference could be. Was it that the Randalls could provide both a mother and father for Penny? Was the fact that Dora was an employee too insubstantial to assure the same in Tony's home? Once more, the knot of apprehension took up residence in his gut.

"That difference is love," the judge said. "It's quite obvious to me Mr. Falcone loves this little girl very much. His main concern is for her emotional well-being, and to me, that's much more important than any of the material things anyone can buy her. Penny has been through one of the worst traumas a child can experience. She's lost both parents. Some children don't survive the loss of one parent, much less two. To put her through any more pain, in my considered opinion, would be unjust and cruel in the extreme. What she needs now is stability in a home that reinforces her emotionally and as such, plays a major role in helping her to heal. I believe that Mr. Falcone can better provide that type of home for Penny."

Tony held his breath, unwilling to allow himself to believe his ears. Dora's grip on his hand tightened.

"I am, therefore, denying the Randalls' suit and ordering custody of Penny Stevens remain with Mr. Falcone."

Breath she hadn't been aware of holding escaped from Dora in a rush. Tony's mouth turned up in a broad grin. He squeezed Dora's hand so hard she had to bite her lip to keep from crying out. Despite the dismal weather outside the windows, it seemed as though rays of blinding sunlight lit the room. Happiness bubbled inside her.

Judge Collier turned her attention to the Randalls. "I'm truly sorry for your plight, but wanting a child so you can shower her with gifts and possessions is wanting a child for all the wrong reasons. As for your interest in this little girl, I must tell you that you don't need to have custody of Penny to be a part of her life." She looked directly at Lisa. "She's your blood, your deceased brother's child. There is no reason you should not be a part of her life, but be a part of it because you love her, and not because you can give her things or because she fills a hole in your life. Love is a must. Possessions are a bonus. And there are a lot of children out there looking for the kind of love you seem willing to give if you just open your heart to them. Don't cross them off your list of possibilities because your blood doesn't run through their veins. Believe me, I've seen many families with damaged children come through my court. More often than not, they were blood related. Your DNA is a fact of nature, but it does not come with love built in." Judge Collier stood and shook Lisa and Leon's hands. "I wish you the very best life has to offer. Merry Christmas." Then she turned to Tony and extended her hand.

Tony rose and shook her hand vigorously. "Thank you."

The judge's smile reflected her benevolence. "Merry Christmas, Mr. Falcone. But then, I'm sure it will be."

Dora and Tony turned to leave, but Leon stopped them. "Congratulations . . . May I call you Tony?" At Tony's surprised nod, Leon went on, disappointment evident in his face. "We would like to be a part of Penny's life, if you'll let us."

Tony said nothing for a moment and then nodded, and stunned Dora by adding, "Why don't we begin with both of you coming to our house for Christmas dinner? You can get to know this remarkable little girl a bit better."

CHAPTER 21

When Tony and Dora walked into the house, Millie and Penny, clad in pink pajamas, were playing the little girl's favorite game of Chutes and Ladders on the living room floor. A fire blazed merrily in the hearth, warming the room and casting a yellow glow over everything. In the corner, Penny's tree stood proudly, the ornaments catching the glow of the fire, making them sparkle with added zest. Beneath it were three badly wrapped gifts, Penny's presents for the important people in her life.

At their entrance, Millie bolted to her feet as quickly as her arthritis would allow, rousing Jack from his lazy slumber next to Penny. Millie's face reflected the worry she'd been going through waiting for their return and news of the judge's verdict.

"Well?" she said, wringing her hands and glancing

apprehensively from one to the other.

Penny stopped arranging the pieces on the game board and got to her feet to stand beside Millie. Though she had no idea what was happening, her face plainly reflected the air of apprehension radiating from the adults.

Before Tony answered Millie, he had to feel the substance of the little girl, to make sure he really hadn't lost her. He scooped her into his arms and hugged her close. Burying his nose against the soft, fragrant flesh of her neck, he inhaled deeply. She smelled like freshly shampooed hair and the talcum powder he'd given her for her last birthday. Her arms encircled his neck, and he squeezed her tighter, making her squeal in protest.

"Uncle Tony, you're squishing me!"

"Sorry," he mumbled, unable to say more through his emotion-filled throat. "I just missed you, I guess." He kissed Penny's cheek, then set her on her feet.

"Well?" Millie repeated, still looking from Dora to Tony. "What's the verdict?"

"What's a verdict?" Penny asked, looking from one adult to another.

Tony's throat still filled with emotion; he could only nod and smile at Millie.

She expelled a long breath and sank onto the sofa as though her legs no longer had enough strength to support her body.

"Thank the good Lord," she said in a whisper.

Penny surveyed the adults, her face scrunched up in a frown. "For what?"

Tony glanced helplessly at Dora. Dare he tell Penny he'd nearly lost her? Did she need to know? As usual, Dora came to his rescue.

"For you," Dora interjected with a big smile and she kissed the child's cheek. "And for us all being together at Christmas." She took Penny's hand. "Now, let's you and I go get some cookies and milk for everyone."

Still looking confused, Penny nodded and obediently followed Dora from the room. Jack trailed behind them, his tail wagging happily. Ever since he'd tasted the chocolate chip cookies, Calvin's addiction to them had increased daily and the mere mention of cookies found him front and center, waiting for his share.

When the room was clear of all but him and Millie, Tony sank to the sofa beside his neighbor. Briefly he related what had happened in the judge's conference room and told her Lisa and her husband were coming for Christmas dinner.

Millie looked skeptical. "I don't trust that girl, but it sounds as though her husband is a very smart man. That little girl needs all the support we can give her, and if Lisa is truly interested in being a part of Penny's life, we should know if she means it soon enough."

Tony agreed. "I'm sure if she's less than sincere, she'll show her colors eventually. I just want to be sure she doesn't hurt Penny in the process."

Millie tilted her head and studied him. "If you don't mind my saying so, for a man who just won a custody battle, you don't look all that happy. There's something more bothering you," Millie said with her usual perceptiveness. "You want to talk about it?"

He could deny it, but he'd tossed the problem around all he could. It was time he asked someone else about it. He knew there was a great deal Penny discussed with Millie that she didn't talk about with anyone else. If anyone would know, it was Millie. "Has Penny ever told you that she feels responsible for her parents' accident?"

Millie's mouth fell open. She pressed a hand to her chest. "Oh, good heavens. That poor baby." She shook her head. "No. She's never mentioned it."

Millie's words helped to close a bit the chasm of guilt that had opened inside Tony the night Penny had revealed her belief to him. If Millie hadn't known how Penny felt, then no one had. But the heartache for his niece intensified. Because he'd been so wrapped up in his own grief, she'd been bearing this unspeakable burden alone.

"Whatever made you think she felt like that?"

"She told me the other night. She thought I hated her because of it. She said if she hadn't asked for pizza that night, they wouldn't have been there, and the accident wouldn't have happened." He sighed and leaned his head against the sofa back. "I tried to convince her it wasn't true, but to be honest, Millie, I'm not sure I was successful."

Millie patted his hand. "I don't think this is something you can explain away with words, Tony. Just love that baby with all your heart and soul, and she'll know. In my experience, love speaks louder than anything else on this Earth."

After they'd had their celebratory snack and Millie had gone home, Tony sat on the sofa alone while Dora put Penny to bed. Was Millie right? Would Penny eventually believe she hadn't been responsible for her parents' deaths? He could only pray it would be the case. In the meantime, he had a lot of time to make up for with Penny. He silently promised that from now on not a day would pass without Penny knowing how much he loved her.

Christmas Eve day dawned with clear blue skies and bright sunshine, a direct contrast to Dora's emotional state. This would be her last day with Tony and Penny, and although her heart was breaking, she planned on trying not to dwell on her departure from their lives instead of focusing on the joy of the time she had left to be with them. However, it was easier said than done. Keeping her feelings at bay got harder with each tick of the kitchen clock, and the time seemed to be passing with alarming speed.

Tony sat at the kitchen table overseeing the completion of a pumpkin pie and, as he'd been doing all day, he was studying Dora with unusual intensity. Penny had stirred the ingredients, and she and Dora poured the batter from the large mixing bowl into the unbaked pie shell. When the bowl had been scraped clean, Penny caught a drip on the tip of her finger and licked it up like a thirsty cat.

She grinned at Tony. "This is gonna be the best pumpkin pie ever, right, Dora?"

Dora heard Penny, but only nodded. She didn't trust herself to speak. Emotion had clogged her throat, and it seemed no matter how many times she swallowed to remove them, tears continued to threaten to break through. She could not, would not cry. Tony and Penny would inevitably ask what was wrong. What would she tell them?

I'm an angel, and I have to go back where I came from tonight. I'll be leaving both of you forever. I'll never see you again.

Once more, she swallowed back the tears and forced a smile to her lips. Carefully, she picked up the filled pie plate. "Let's get this in the oven," she said, thankful for a reason to turn away.

She'd just slid the pie in the preheated oven and closed the door when she felt Tony standing close beside her.

"Is something wrong, Dora?"

She pushed her mouth up in a smile and faced him. "No. Why would you think that?" Averting her gaze before he could see the lie in her eyes, she skirted around him and busied herself clearing away the floury mess she and Penny had made while assembling three pies.

He followed her. "Because you've seemed preoccupied, maybe even a bit sad, all day." He ran his fingertip down her cheek.

Making a conscious effort to tamp down the shudders of delight threatening to take over her good sense, Dora pulled away, bit her lip hard, and made her way to the refrigerator.

When it came to her moods, Tony had become far too perceptive of late. She had no idea how that had occurred, or why, but she did know she could not have him probing into the reason behind her mood.

"Okay, Miss Penny," she announced with false cheer, "are you ready to get the dressing ready for the turkey?" Dora returned to the counter with her arms laden and deposited celery, onions, sausage, a package of bread cubes, and several bright red apples in front of Penny.

Penny pulled up the stool, scooted a large, clean bowl toward her, and held up a clean wooden spoon. "Ready."

"Can't some of this wait until tomorrow?" Tony asked, reseating himself at the table, but continuing to eye Dora skeptically.

Tomorrow.

The word hit Dora in the gut with all the force of a battering ram. Tomorrow didn't exist for her. At least not in the world of mortals.

A sharp pain pierced her heart. She knew letting go of the only family she had ever and probably would ever know would not be easy, but she'd never imagined the agony that would accompany it.

For the very first time ever, and only for a fleeting moment, she questioned her desire to become mortal. The doubt passed quickly. In her heart she knew she'd suffer the ravages of hell if the Heavenly Council endowed her with permanent mortality, and she could stay with Tony and Penny forever. But they wouldn't and so she couldn't. Come midnight, her reason for being here would be no more, and she would have to return to her job in Celestial Maintenance.

"Some things just can't be put off until tomorrow," she said softly. She swallowed the newest threat of tears and began chopping celery for the dressing.

❖ ❖ ❖

Dora and Penny spent the rest of the day in the kitchen, preparing for the Christmas feast the following day. Dora was intent on getting as much done as she could. When Tony repeatedly told her some of it could be done the next day, she'd shrugged him off. He'd even tried tempting her with constructing a snowlady to keep their snowman company, but she'd turned him down.

Despite her denials that nothing was wrong, he'd detected an oddly poignant ring to her voice. When she continued to stick to the explanation for her strange mood, Tony finally passed it off as a remnant of the emotional upheaval of the previous days and her drive to make this a great Christmas in every way she could.

In contrast to Dora's pensive mood, Penny's laughter filled the house as they worked. By evening, exhaustion had laid claim to Penny, and she went to bed without protest, eagerly looking forward to what she'd find under the tree the following morning.

Dora tucked the lavender coverlet around Penny's slim body. "Good night, honey." She kissed Penny's smooth forehead as she always did, but this time, as she memorized everything about the child, she let her lips remain against the sweet-smelling skin for few moments longer.

This was one more in a long line of *last times* Dora

had faced all day. The last meal she would prepare for them. The last time she would listen to the sound of Penny's laughter filling her heart. The last time—

"Dora?"

Roused from her pity party, Dora sat up and gazed down into Penny's sleepy eyes. "Yes."

"Do you love my Uncle Tony?"

Coming out of nowhere, the question sideswiped Dora. "Uh . . . of course. I love both of you."

Penny propped herself up on one elbow. "I don't mean love like you love your mommy and daddy or your sister and brother. I mean real love like daddies and mommies have. The really special kind. Do you love him like that?"

Love him? Tony's face swam before Dora's eyes. His strong brow and square, determined jaw. That errant lock of black hair that fell across his brow when he was upset. The strength of his arms holding her close. The feel of his lips on hers. When she'd left to come down here, she'd never expected to experience such emotions taking over her thoughts and dreams. And even though she knew nothing could come of it, she would not have traded loving Tony for anything in this world or above.

She opened her mouth to answer Penny, but when she looked down, the child was sleeping soundly. Dora kissed her and rose to leave the room. Suddenly, she knew she had to leave Penny something of herself.

Tiptoeing, she left Penny's room and went to her own. Slipping the sheet from the mirror, she stood before it. Taking a deep breath, she allowed her wings to spread out behind her angel image. Reaching behind her, she plucked one feather.

She replaced the sheet over the mirror and made her way back to Penny's room. Careful not wake her, Dora slipped the feather under Penny's pillow where she would find it and maybe remember the angel who had loved her.

As she looked down at the sleeping child, Dora brushed a coppery strand of hair from her cheek. "Have a blessed and happy life, little one. May it always be filled with love and laughter." She swallowed hard and added hoarsely, "Take care of your Uncle Tony for me and always remember that he loves you with all his heart."

❖ ❖ ❖

Tony waited in the living room for Dora, determined to get to the bottom of her mood.

"She was exhausted. All that cooking must have taken the stuffing out of her," Dora exclaimed with forced cheer and collapsed with a tired sigh on the sofa beside Tony. The unrelenting drive she'd been caught up in all day had finally taken its toll. Leaning back, eyes closed, she yawned.

"Are you ready to tell me what's been bothering you all day?" Instantly, a frown drew her brows together. He waited for her to answer, but she remained silent. "Dora?"

Still, she said nothing. Instead she stared at the Christmas tree. Finally, she sighed. "I guess everything just caught up with me. You know, the hearing, Penny running away . . . all of it." She turned to him and smiled, but he could find little joy in her expression. "Don't tell me you didn't find it emotionally draining."

He couldn't deny it. The past few days had exacted a heavy emotional price from him. And Dora had supported him every step of the way. It was logical that she had been undergoing the same emotional strain. Taking that into consideration, he decided he was making more of this than need be. Tomorrow Dora would undoubtedly be her old self. Satisfied with her explanation, he let it pass.

"I want to give you your Christmas present."

She rolled her head sideways on the sofa cushion. "Shouldn't we wait until tomorrow?" For a scant second, something resembling pain shown in her eyes, but before he could analyze it, it was gone.

"No," he said simply. "I want you to open it now." He picked up a small, rectangular package lying on the end table beside him. It was wrapped in bright red foil and sported a green bow. Handing it to her, he smiled secretively and leaned back. "Go ahead. Open it."

Dora held the box as if it would break with her slightest movement. If he didn't find it absurd, he'd think this was the first time she'd ever received a gift.

As he watched, she carefully removed the ribbon and picked at the tape holding the wrappings closed. "Oh, good grief, please don't tell me you're one of those people who unwraps gifts with all the precision of a surgeon performing an open heart operation. For goodness' sake, just tear the paper off. I promise I'll buy you more foil, if you want it."

Dora giggled and tore into the wrappings. She lifted the lid and gazed down at the snowman charm attached to a fine gold chain. Her eyes grew large, and her mouth opened in a silent O.

"I thought it would help you remember the day the three of us made the snowman."

She picked up the necklace and held it against the palm of her hand. "It's beautiful, Tony. You couldn't have chosen a more perfect gift. Whenever I look at it, I'll think of you and Penny. Thank you so much." She held it out to him. "Please, put it on for me."

Taking it from her, he opened the clasp and looped it around her neck. She turned her back to him and held her hair aside so he could fasten it. His clumsy fingers skimmed her bare flesh, and as though he'd just received a jolt of high-voltage electricity, his body came to life. With concentrated effort, he managed to get the clasp fastened.

Covering the charm with her hand, Dora faced him. "You have no idea what this means to me. I'll treasure it always."

Tony heard what she'd said, but the only thing that registered in his brain was that he was here with Dora, they were alone, and he wanted her as he'd never wanted any woman in his life.

He drank in the beauty of the incredible woman at his side. What had he ever done to deserve her in his life?

His heartbeat hastened in his chest, filling him with the overwhelming urge to gather her close and never let her go. No matter how hard he tried, never in a million years could he envision his life without her with him. For a man who had sworn never to get into a serious relationship, it came as a startling admission. In some nebulous way he couldn't put his finger on, she completed him, made his life whole and full.

Not so nebulous, a little voice inside him said. *If you think about it, you'll know why she's become so very important to you, and it has nothing to do with Penny and everything to do with you and that vast, empty hole inside you reserved for someone to fill with their love.*

Love? As though he'd been struck by lightning, as

crazy as it seemed, he suddenly realized he'd fallen in love with Dora.

The idea left him speechless but elated. He knew having her around had given him a peace of mind he'd desperately needed, but he'd always thought it was because of her ability to relieve him of some of the burden of caring for Penny. Dora's presence in the house had definitely lightened his emotional load in that arena. Despite the truth of that, right now, he wasn't so sure it was the only reason for the surge of happiness.

It wasn't just Dora's outer beauty, though God knew she was as intoxicating as an expensive bottle of champagne. Neither was it because she'd come into his life and through patience, understanding, and love had changed it forever. It was more, a combination of things that put together made up the incredible woman beside him. Every time he'd needed an emotional crutch to lean on, she'd provided it. She'd been there for him . . . just like Rosalie had always supported him through every troubling time in his life.

He thought back to when she'd held on to his hand and helped get him through the hearing with the Randalls. How she'd given him hope the night Penny had run away. How she'd always seemed to be there for him, no matter what. How, when he'd hidden behind his protective wall, she'd fought for him to understand

and love Penny.

More than anything else, how she'd encouraged him to open his heart. And now that he had opened it, he was suddenly acutely aware that someone other than Penny had slipped inside it.

Dora. Dora had sneaked under his skin and relentlessly wormed her way past the icy wall he'd erected around his feelings. He was hopelessly and helplessly in love with Dora DeAngelo.

"Why are you staring at me?" she asked, titling her head so a swath of dark hair fell over her cheek.

"Thank you," he said simply.

Dora frowned. "For what?"

"For being there when I needed you." His hoarse voice was barely above a whisper. "For helping me through the custody mess with Lisa. For taking such good care of Penny. For—" The pressure of her fingertips sealing his lips stopped any more of what he would have said.

As though a hand had reached into her chest and squeezed it tightly in its strong fingers, Dora's heart fought to beat. The love she'd felt for this man for so long welled up inside her wanting to break free, but she couldn't allow it. She could not start something she knew had no hope of a future. She would not give Tony false hope.

"There's no need for thanks." She removed her fingers from his mouth, the tips suddenly feeling as though they'd caught fire. "It's my job." The words were out before she thought about what they might imply. But not knowing who she really was, their underlying truth went right past him.

Tony shook his head. "No, I hired you to take care of the house and Penny. You've gone way beyond what I pay you for. You've given both of us a new life. You've made me see that love is not something to be avoided, that it's a wonderful emotion that fills your heart and your life with meaning and purpose. You made me understand that no matter how much I wanted to stand alone, you and Penny were always there, always ready to be in my corner, even when I didn't want you there."

Dora ducked her head and squeezed her eyes shut. If he kept talking like this, she would find it impossible to conceal what lay hidden from him in her heart. That she loved him beyond any emotion she had ever experienced before. That everything she'd ever dreamed of having and being lay just beyond her fingertips and she couldn't reach out for it. That leaving him and Penny would be like dying.

Then he touched her. His warm fingers cupped her chin, and she felt him pressing them upward until he lifted her face so her gaze was even with his. His dark eyes bore into her, and what she saw there should have thrilled her. Instead it brought heavy regret to her already-aching heart. Then he said the words that tore holes in her soul.

"I love you, Dora. I want you to be here always with me and Penny."

Such a simple declaration and one that brought a surge of joy rushing through her, but one that also ripped Dora's heart to shreds. If only she could stay. If only she could love him freely and without fear of having to leave. If only . . .

She closed her eyes, unable to stand seeing the love shining in his. How could she tell him she loved him, too; but that theirs was a love that would be denied and there was absolutely nothing either of them could do to prevent it from happening?

"Look at me," he urged.

Slowly, she opened her eyes and did as he asked.

"Don't you have anything to say?"

She had plenty she could say, but it was not what he wanted to hear. Her heart broke wide open in her chest. Despite the fire's glow, the room dimmed, and a chill seeped into it, filling all the formerly warm corners with icy cold sadness.

When she didn't answer, he stood and walked to one of the large bay windows. For a long time, he stared out into the inky, dark night. Then he made a sound that should have been laughter, but sounded more the cry of a wounded man. "I guess I took too much for granted. I figured if I loved you that you must love me, too."

She sprang to her feet. "No, that's not it at all. I do lo—" She bit back the rest of the word. But too late. Tony had caught her words and completed the thought.

He spun to face her, his expression filled with hope. "You do love me, too."

Quickly, she looked away, hoping to conceal the truth from him. "That's . . . that's not what I said."

"But it's what you were going to say, isn't it?" He came to her and took her shoulders in his hands. "Look me in the eye and tell me you don't love me. Do that and I promise I'll walk away, and we'll never talk about it again."

Dora looked up at him. Everything inside her urged her to lie to him, for his own good. For Penny's good. For their good. A tug of war went on inside her. Tell him. Don't tell him. The longer she gazed at him, the harder it was to hold her tongue, to hold back the truth of her feelings.

All she had to do to stop this was to tell him a lie. She'd never lied to anyone before. It just wasn't part of who she was. And she couldn't start. She just could not tell him she didn't love him. But she couldn't tell him she did, either.

Out of the corner of her eye, she saw Jack slip into the room. He sat at the side of the sofa and stared at her with unrelenting, judgmental black eyes, telling her without words that she could not admit to the emotional attachment she'd formed for Tony.

Tony caught the direction of her stare. "Damned dog!" he said and released her shoulders. He walked to the dog, grabbed him by the scruff of the neck, and pulled Jack with him out of the room. Dora heard the slam of the laundry room door.

She collapsed onto the sofa and gathered her mental strength for Tony's return.

A few moments later he came back into the room. Sitting beside her, he swiveled to face her. "Well? Can you tell me you don't love me?"

She raised her gaze to his. Instantly, she knew what she had to do.

CHAPTER 22

———◆———

Taking a deep breath, Dora looked him in the eye. "No, I can't tell you I don't love you." A broad smile split his face. "But it doesn't change anything. As much as I want to, I *can't* love you."

His smile died as quickly as it had been given birth. "What do you mean you can't? There's not a thing in this world to stop you," he said, attempting to pull her into his arms.

No, not in this world. Dora pulled away. "Tony, this is much more complicated than you know."

"Then explain it to me. Make me understand."

"Even if I do, it won't change anything."

"Tell me. Let me be the judge."

She sighed, resigned to what she'd have to do. She gazed deep into his dark eyes. When he would have gathered her in his arms again, she moved away. "No. If you touch me, I won't be able to say what I have to say."

From the laundry room came the sounds of Jack clawing at the door to get out. She knew why. Calvin had read her thoughts, and he knew what she was about to do and he strongly disapproved. As if confirming her suspicions, Calvin's voice inserted itself in her mind.

Don't do this, Dora. Think what it will mean for you, for me. The Council will never forgive you. All hope of promotion will be lost. You've done what you came here to do. These humans are well on the road to a happy life. Your mission is complete. Telling him will only make it harder for him. For all of us.

Dora closed her mind to Calvin's warnings. For once, she didn't care that Calvin disapproved. For once, she was going to do what she knew she must to make this as easy on Tony as possible, and Calvin be damned, her future up there be damned. If she spent all of eternity sharpening lightning bolts, then so be it. At least, even if it didn't ease his pain, at least Tony would never wonder why she had walked away from a future with him.

She took a deep breath. "Tony, I didn't just happen to show up on your doorstep. I was sent here."

He nodded. "I know, by the agency. I asked them to send someone."

She shook her head and stared blankly at her clenched hands. She wanted to look into Tony's beautiful dark eyes, but she couldn't bring herself to do it, couldn't stand to see the pain her words would bring.

"No, I wasn't sent by any agency," she finally said, her voice so subdued even she could barely hear it. Forcing her gaze to meet his, she said, "I was sent by someone else."

Confusion marred his handsome face. "I don't understand. Who else could have sent you? I only applied to the Angel Guardians Agency."

Dora looked at the ceiling.

He raised his face to follow her gaze. "Penny?" he asked, confusion coloring his voice even more.

"No, not Penny."

Dora sighed. This was much harder than she'd expected it to be. She'd always believed that, if she had to tell Tony where she came from, she could just tell him the facts. But when she'd imagined having to reveal her true identity, she didn't know Tony loved her. Now it had become difficult. But not impossible.

Finally, she knew what she would have to do. Simply telling a mortal you were an angel wouldn't do it. She would have to *show* him the truth of who she was.

Millie laid down the green and yellow afghan she'd been knitting for Penny's bed and gazed off into space.

Her husband glanced at her and frowned. He knew that look; he'd seen it innumerable times before. "What is it, Mil?"

"I have a feeling something's gonna happen."

During their many years of marriage, Preston had been privy to his wife's *feelings*, and he'd never known her to be wrong. She had some sixth sense and though he had no idea what it was, he trusted it implicitly. He put aside his newspaper and waited for an explanation. "What kind of something, dear?"

She blinked, as though coming out of a dream. "I don't know. I only know that, when it does, nothing will ever be the same again for any of us."

Preston tilted his head. "That sounds kind of ominous, Millie."

She smiled wistfully at him. "I know, but I can't tell if it's good or bad, just that it will happen and soon." She smoothed her hand over the afghan. "I just hope that whatever it is, it's not going to disrupt that poor little girl's life again." She stood. "I'm going to make myself some tea. Would you like some?"

"Please."

She started toward the kitchen, then stopped and turned back. "Preston, how would you like to have a child?"

❖ ❖ ❖

Dora took Tony's hand and led him from the living room, into the hall, and up the stairs.

"Where are we going?"

She glanced over her shoulder. "For you to really understand this, words won't be enough. I have to show you something."

When she stopped outside her bedroom door, she heard Tony gasp. "In there?" He nodded at the closed door.

"Yes."

He peered over her shoulder at the closed door. "You don't have a wedding band stashed in a box in there, do you? Are you already married?"

Dora gave a halfhearted laugh. "No, nothing like that."

Opening the door, she tried hard not to think about the fact that she was about to violate yet one more condition of her trip to Earth. Besides, she'd already violated so many, surely one more wouldn't matter all that much. From downstairs came the sounds of a dog whining and scratching frantically at a door.

She shut it out, but not before making a mental note that when the time came, and it would, she'd make it clear to the Heavenly Council that Calvin was entirely innocent of transgressions she had committed while in mortal form. He should not have to suffer consequences because of her choices. Keeping her in line had always been his priority, and he'd worked very hard to make sure that happened. Due to her actions and no one else's, it just hadn't worked out that way.

The animal sounds coming from downstairs ceased. The house became as quiet as a tomb. As if it were holding its breath, waiting for the next moments to tick by.

Tony followed her into the bedroom. But before she could do what she'd gone there to do, he grabbed her arm, swung her around, and pulled her into his embrace. "If what you're going to show me is going to do anything to make it impossible for us, I don't want to see it." She opened her mouth, but he shushed her with a look. "I love you, and nothing in Heaven or on Earth can stop that." He cradled her against his broad chest.

How desperately she wished it were true. How she wished she could simply surrender to the emotions running rampant through her. For just a moment she allowed herself the luxury of imagining what it would be like to fall asleep in Tony's arms each night and wake in them every morning. What it would be like to know she'd be here when Penny grew up and got married and had babies of her own. What it would be like to grow old beside the man she loved.

It amazed her that the sound of her heart breaking into a million pieces could not be heard.

Tony tilted her head back. "If it's another man, then he should know I will not let you go without a fight."

"It's not another man, either."

Tony frowned. "I'm running out of options. Of course, there is always this." Then he lowered his lips to hers.

A mixture of an intense awareness of life, of every pore in her skin, of every hair on her head, of every beat of her heart, surged through Dora. Left with no choice, she might have to give up everything she'd come to hold dear, but she would not give this up. She would kiss Tony as though it were the last kiss they'd share, because, in truth, it would be. The memory of his lips gently caressing hers would be locked in her mind for eternity, and on those days when she couldn't bear the loneliness any longer, she'd take it out and absorb the love.

Dora tightened her hold on Tony's neck and molded her body to his. She allowed him to pry open her lips and delve into the moist interior of her mouth. Prickles of pleasure washed over her. Her limbs suddenly seemed incapable of supporting her limp body. She wilted against him.

Never before had she felt so alive, so full of an energizing need to— To what? She had no idea, but deep inside her the need was growing by leaps and bounds. The longer Tony kissed her, the stronger it became.

Then he ran his hand down her side and his thumb brushed her breast. Fire shot through her. Pleasurable fire. Fire that fed the nebulous need. Fire that planted a wanting in her so vibrant, so all-consuming, that she couldn't ignore it, couldn't deny it. Her body began to tremble uncontrollably. He circled her waist with his big hands and pulled her against him. Something hard pressed into her stomach.

Tony pulled his lips away and looked down at her. His dark eyes were smoky with desire. "Now, tell me you don't love me," he whispered, his lips a mere inch away from hers.

Dora opened her mouth, despite being certain she'd long ago lost the ability to speak. "I can't. I do love you. I love you more than you will ever know." Her voice was raspy and sounded strange to her ears.

What was happening to her? But Tony gave her no time to think, just feel.

"That's all I need to know," he said, and reclaimed her lips with his.

This time the kiss was hungry, demanding, and all-consuming. Emotion after emotion swamped Dora. Disconnected, scrambled thoughts raced through her foggy mind. The need, the hunger for that something without a name grew inside her. She curved her fingers into the flesh of his shoulders, straining for something solid to cling to, something to keep her head above the emotional waters threatening to drown her.

Desperately, she fought to clear her mind of the tangle of meaningless thoughts racing through it. She needed to get control. She needed to stop him and do what they'd come up here for.

"I'm afraid," she mumbled against his lips, "that—"

"Don't be afraid. There's nothing for you to fear," he whispered. "Just feel. Just let me love you."

And that's exactly what Dora did, until her mind closed down to anything except the feel of his hands on her, the caress of his lips, and those unnamed sensations crying out for fulfillment.

Tony's legs were threatening to fold under him. Before they could do so, he scooped Dora into his arms and carried her to the wide, canopied bed. Gently, he laid her down, then lay next to her. Gathering her close, he stared into her face.

She was so mind-stoppingly beautiful. Unlike some women, her beauty went far beneath the outer shell right down to her soul and, as a result, her inner glow radiated from her eyes. Gratitude for having her come into his life welled up in him.

He leaned forward and kissed her gently. To his surprise, her arms snaked around his neck and turned what he'd intended to be a butterfly kiss into a heat-seeking, sexual innuendo.

She looped a leg over his. The heat coming from the juncture of her thighs burned through the material of his jeans and into his flesh. He filled his lungs to bursting and then gritted his teeth in an effort to control his need as it teetered precariously on the edge of completion.

"You're playing with fire," he murmured into the luscious and tempting curve of her neck.

Suddenly, Dora stopped moving. She pulled back and looked into his eyes. "I don't understand."

At first Tony thought she was kidding, but the sincerity in her eyes told him differently. This was crazy. She couldn't possibly not understand what was happening between them, could she? Then it occurred to him that, as unbelievable as it was in this day and age, something he'd taken for granted might not be the case at all.

He propped himself onto one elbow and gazed down at her. "Dora, I have to ask you something." She stared up at him, waiting, wide-eyed, and tellingly innocent. "Are you a virgin?"

She blinked.

"Have you ever made love with a man before?" She frowned as though she had no idea what the words meant. Could she be that naïve? It was incomprehensible that she hadn't a clue what he was talking about. "Have you ever been intimate"——he searched frantically for the words that, without being downright crude, would clearly tell her what he was asking—"have you ever had sex with a man before?"

"I . . . I . . . I don't think so."

Tony laughed. "Honey, making love with someone is not something you're likely to forget."

"Well, then, I guess the answer is yes, I'm a virgin."

Tony groaned, released her, and turned away. He sat on the edge of the mattress with his feet on the floor. He couldn't believe he had a virgin in his bed. Well, technically, *her* bed, but no matter whose bed it was, Dora was still a virgin. What the hell did he do now?

He had had women before who had little experience, but never one who didn't even know what making love was. A virgin. Never in his wildest imaginings had he dreamed he'd one day have a virgin in his bed. Nor had he ever wanted to.

However, the idea that he'd be the first to make love to Dora sent a wave of pleasure over him. Not sexual pleasure, but a pleasure that made him feel honored, privileged.

Still, the nagging doubt that he didn't have the right to take this from her kept nudging him. Dora seemed to be more than just a virgin. She had an innocence about her that could be thought of as unusual. Even rare.

CHAPTER 23

<figure>✦</figure>

DORA WAS CONFUSED. SHE STARED AT THE BROAD expanse of Tony's back, trying to figure out what had happened. Had she done something wrong? Was being a virgin bad? Repulsive to him?

"Tony? What is it? What's wrong? Was it something I did?"

He turned back to her. For a moment he simply stared, then his mouth broke into a half smile. "No, something I almost did."

Dora was under the impression everything had been going very well for the past few moments. What could he have possibly done wrong? "What?"

He shook his head. "You're a virgin. That means I'd be your first lover. I very nearly steamrolled you into something you might regret tomorrow."

Regret? How could she possibly regret the feelings

Tony had given birth to in her? Never, ever before had she felt like that. Hot and cold all over, as if tiny pins pricked her skin. As if at any moment she would explode into a shower of rainbow colors. The sensations Tony had made her feel were glorious, unbelievable, mind-blowing, wonderful.

"I wouldn't have regretted anything that we did to-gether," she said in a soft voice.

"You say that now, but . . ." Again, he stared at her. "You do realize what we were about to do, don't you?"

"Kiss some more? I hope so, because I love kissing with you."

He laughed. "Well, I love kissing with you, too, but there's a lot more to making love than kissing, sweetheart."

"Like what?" This was so confusing.

She'd heard the word before, but the angels never actually talked about sex. Mostly because they weren't privy to that part of their charges' lives. In fact, whenever their charges moved into the bedroom, the Earth Pool always turned opaque. Evidently, her lack of knowledge upset Tony.

Tony sprang to his feet and began pacing the limited confines of the room. Several times he raked his fingers through his hair and looked at the ceiling. Dora felt helpless. She wanted to help him, to say something, to bring him back beside her, but how could she when she had no idea what the problem was or how to fix it?

"Tony—"

He swung to face her, his hands extended palms out. "No. Don't say anything." He glanced around the room as though looking for an escape route. "Listen, why don't you show me whatever it is you brought me up here to see?"

Dora froze. If she took the sheet off the mirror and showed him her true image, it would be the end of everything. There would be no going back.

But did she have a choice? Come what may, at midnight she would be called back up there. Disappear without a trace or explanation. Whether or not she revealed her angel image to Tony, whatever could have been between them would be over, done, irrevocably ended. However, if she did show him, at least he'd know why.

Slowly, she got to her feet. Without a word, she slipped the sheet from the mirror. Instantly, her angel image appeared, complete with white robe, golden curls, sky blue eyes, lopsided halo, and large, white, feathered wings.

Tony's pacing had stopped. He stood to the side watching her. "What are you doing?"

The sheet slipped from her fingers and landed in a white puddle at her feet, reminding her of the snowbanks that lined the front walk and the street outside. She smiled sadly at him. Summoning all her courage, she spoke the words that would effectively end her world. "Come stand beside me."

Puzzled, Tony came to her side, then looked at her directly in expectation. What was this all about?

"Look," she said, motioning at her reflection in the mirror.

He turned and gaped at the image standing beside him. "What the hell . . .?" He turned to her to verify she was the woman he remembered. The reflection didn't match. Where Dora should have been was a strange woman, a woman with wings, an angel. Then he looked back into the mirror. "Is this a trick mirror?" He looked behind the mirror, then inspected it, running his hands over the frame and the backing. But he found nothing to account for the strange difference in her image.

As he moved back to Dora's side, he tried to sort through the jumble of questions filling his mind. Being a man of logic who had been trained to rely on facts and figures, he found this beyond his comprehension. There was no possible explanation.

"Okay, I give up. What's the trick?"

"There's no trick, Tony. The person you see in the mirror is who I really am. I'm an angel. I was sent here to help you and Penny." Appearing surprisingly calm, she waited for him to say something. But he just kept looking at her, then back at her reflection. "They only allowed me to stay until tonight at midnight. Then I have to go back . . ." She looked at the ceiling.

Though he heard what Dora was saying, he didn't understand it. Inside his chest Tony's heart twisted and writhed in agony.

"I never meant to fall in love with you. In fact, they warned me not to form any emotional attachments to my charges. It . . . it just happened, and I didn't know how to stop it. In the end, it doesn't matter how much you love me or I love you. I *have* to go back. They gave me no choice. At midnight, I'll vanish from your life forever."

Everything inside Tony rebelled at the idea of Dora's leaving for good. "I don't know who the hell *they* are, but they can't do that." Tony snatched Dora from in front of the mirror, twisted logic making him believe that if *they* couldn't see her, *they* couldn't take her away.

"But, I'm an—"

He slammed his fist on the dresser top making the bottles jump, topple, and roll to the floor. "I don't give a damn what you are. I won't let them take you."

She sank to the edge of the bed. "Can't you see? You can't stop them. Whether or not I want to go back or you want me to stay doesn't matter. In the first second after midnight, I will be gone, Tony. Gone." He could hear the tears choking her voice.

If what she said was true, and he had to believe the

proof he'd seen with his own eyes, then he could do nothing but stand by and watch her go. It would have hurt less if they'd torn his heart from his chest. Damn it, it wasn't fair!

Anger boiled to the surface. Anger at Dora for deceiving him, for allowing him and Penny to fall in love with her. Anger at whomever the hell *they* were for playing with their happiness. Anger at himself for feeling so helpless.

If circumstances had been different, he would have done battle with Satan himself to keep Dora at his side. But how could he argue his case before someone he couldn't see, someone with whom he had no idea how to communicate? He could do nothing but wait for midnight.

He glanced at the crumpled, defeated figure sitting on the edge of the bed. Everything in him wanted to go to her, to hold her, to tell her everything would be all right. But he couldn't, because nothing would be all right again. It seemed he was destined to spend a lifetime losing everyone he loved.

He shifted his gaze from Dora to the alarm clock on her bedside table. Eleven forty-six. In less than fifteen minutes Dora would be no more. Suddenly, he knew that staying here and watching her leave would be more then he could stand. Living without the woman he loved, the woman who had become his best friend and companion, would be hard enough.

He went to her, kneeled down, and took her hand. "I have to go. I can't be here when . . . when it happens." She raised her tear-streaked face to his and nodded. With the pad of his thumb, he gently wiped the tears from her cheeks, and wished he could just as easily wipe the tears from his heart. "I love you, Dora. I always will. No matter where we are." He leaned forward and softly kissed her lips for the last time, then rose and left the room.

Silence surrounded Dora like an oppressive blanket. Unheeded tears cascaded down her cheeks and dripped on her hands. She made no effort to wipe them away. An unrelenting ache encased her entire body.

Absently she looked around the room that had been hers for a few short weeks. It had become so familiar, so right. From the first day she'd walked into it, she'd felt as though it truly was hers, as though she belonged here. But she'd been fooling herself from the beginning. Nothing on Earth would ever be hers. Quite simply, no matter how much she wanted to deny it, she just didn't belong here. She was an angel, and she knew the rules. Angels guided and protected the mortals, but they had no permanent place in their world.

Her gaze fell on a box Penny had planned to use to hold the angel she'd gotten Millie for Christmas, but the box had been way too big. Dora smiled as a mental picture of the little girl struggling to wrap her presents drifted through her mind. Following swiftly on its heels came a picture of Penny delivering her winning essay.

No sooner had it taken form in Dora's mind than her gaze shifted back to the empty box. She grabbed it, put the lid on, and wrote five words on a plain sheet of paper.

To Tony. Love always, Dora.

Careful not to make a sound, she tiptoed down the hall and set the box outside Tony's door. For a moment she remained there, tempted to open the door and fling herself into his arms. But she knew it would solve nothing and only prolong the pain of parting. She kissed her fingertips and laid them against the cold wood, then returned to her room.

By the time Dora got back, she could feel the changes beginning to manifest themselves in her body. She glanced at the clock. Eleven fifty-eight. Turning her attention to the other mirror over the dresser, the one in which she'd always appeared as she did to Penny and Tony, she watched as her reflection slowly morphed from Dora DeAngelo, the nanny, to Dora, the angel assigned to Celestial Maintenance.

The jeans and sweater she'd put on that morning

melted away like snow on a sunny day and were replaced by a long, flowing white robe. A golden cord encircled her waist. The ends of her dark hair lightened, and seconds later, her entire head was covered in blond curls. A soft popping sound preceded the appearance of a halo and wings. The transformation was complete. It made no difference what mirror she looked into. Dora DeAngelo was no more.

Oddly, she felt no differently inside. The love she felt for both Tony and Penny was still there, mixed with the agonizing pain of parting. If only she could wave her hand and make that vanish, as well.

A noise behind her drew her attention from her sad thoughts. She swung toward it, hoping it might be Tony coming to say good-bye again. But it was only Jack. She'd forgotten all about him. Forgotten what would happen when Penny awoke in the morning to find not only Dora gone, but also her beloved dog.

Jack sauntered into the room, head down, ears flattened, and his tail unusually still. With his nose, he nudged the door closed, then turned to Dora. A ball of blinding light appeared, obscuring him from her sight. It pulsed and shimmered for a few seconds, then vanished, leaving behind Calvin as Dora had always known him.

His sad eyes surveyed her from head to toe. "It's time, Dora. Are you ready?"

She shook her head. "I'll never be ready, but I suppose it doesn't matter." He shook his head and held out his hand, and she took a step toward him, then stopped. "What about Penny?"

He frowned.

"When she wakes up, she'll look for Jack."

Calvin smiled. "Not to worry. I've seen to it that Jack will be waiting downstairs for her, just as he always does."

Dora didn't bother to ask how he planned to do it. Knowing Penny would have one less disappointment, one less heartache, was all she cared about.

"We have to go," Calvin softly reminded her.

"I know." She looked in the direction of Penny's room. "You go ahead. I'll be there in a moment." Calvin arched an eyebrow. "Calvin, I know what I have to do, and I promise I will follow you shortly. Besides, do I have any choice?"

For a moment, he studied her, perhaps assessing her sincerity. "Don't be long." He shimmered out of sight.

Dora stared at the place where Calvin had stood seconds before. No trace of him remained. Just as in a few seconds, there would be no trace of her, no hint she'd ever lived here, loved here.

Before the tears could start again, Dora closed her eyes, readying herself to be torn away from everything she loved.

Tony lay on his bed staring at the ceiling, trying not to think or feel. But there was no respite from the pain. It tore at his soul and shredded his heart. If it was possible to bleed to death emotionally, then it was happening to him.

He'd thought the pain of losing his sister had been more than he could bear, but it was nothing compared to losing Dora. Rosalie was gone for good. Dead. But Dora was out there somewhere in the cosmos, alive. Yet even alive, she was beyond his reach.

He glanced at the bedside clock. Twelve-o-three. Dora was gone. The injustice of it burned through him. Who in hell was this phantom *they* who had decided to play god with his life?

How dare *they* do that? How dare *they* allow him such complete happiness, then snatch it away at their whim? How dare *they* let a little girl attach herself to Dora, only to subject her to the loss of another loved one?

The same helplessness he'd experienced in Dora's room swamped him. Frustrated at being left without a weapon with which to fight, he bolted from the bed and began pacing the floor.

There had to be something he could do. But what? He had nothing but words of protest, pleas to change their minds. But to whom did he go to voice the words? He was fighting a phantom enemy without a prayer of win—

Prayer. Part of *their* job was to listen to prayers, right?

Tony sat on the edge of the bed and folded his hands. His lips moved in the first prayer to pass his lips in many years.

I don't know who you are, and I don't really care. All I know is that you sent Dora here to help us, and she did. Penny and I fell in love with her. We want her here. You have plenty of angels up there, but we only had one Dora. Please, if you have one ounce of compassion in your hearts, send her back to us.

Over and over, he repeated the last five words. He had no idea if his words fell on deaf ears or if his pleas were so much smoke in the wind, but he didn't want to take the chance that they were. He didn't want any one of *them* to feel he hadn't bothered to plead for Dora's return. If there was the slightest chance he could change *their* minds, he'd sit here all night and repeat those five words.

When her transition back to heaven was complete, Dora was not surprised to find Calvin waiting for her on her favorite cloud. Her failures and her lost love riding heavily on her shoulders, she couldn't meet what she knew for certain would be Calvin's censuring gaze. Knowing how much the mere sight of her tears upset him, she fought to hold them back. However, the pain of leaving Tony and Penny was so sharp, she feared losing the battle and causing Calvin even more anxiety than he already had.

As she'd feared, before she could stop it, a lone tear slipped down her cheek. To her surprise, rather than becoming agitated, Calvin used the hem of his robe's belled sleeve to wipe it away. He smiled at her, the gentle curve of his mouth taking a bit of the edge off the excruciating pain radiating everywhere inside her.

He smiled weakly. "The Heavenly Council has ordered us to come before them in the Hall of Prayers as soon as you arrive," he told Dora, his voice filled with a compassion she'd never heard from him before.

Having expected the summons, she nodded. Normally, being called before the Council would have caused any angel great alarm. Only the Archangels and angels of the highest rank were allowed in the Hall of Prayers. When a lowly angel from Celestial Maintenance was summoned, it could mean nothing good.

However, today Dora didn't care. She'd expected the reprimands to come. The Council could do nothing to her that would hurt more than the separation from the people she loved.

The main worry that dogged her was what would

happen to Calvin. Would he be blamed for her failure, too? She must make sure the Council understood none of this was his fault. He'd given her explicit instructions not to allow anyone to see her as an angel and not to become emotionally involved with her charges, and he'd warned her of the dire consequences of not following those instructions. And what had she done? Not only had she let Penny see her angel reflection in the mirror and then told Tony who she really was, but also she'd fallen in love with Tony.

"I'm so very sorry, Calvin."

He patted her shoulder consolingly. His hand trembled slightly. "I know." Then he cleared his throat. "We'd better be going."

Dora nodded. Calvin took her hand, and they shimmered out together.

CHAPTER 24

✦

Outside the imposing, beautifully carved, double golden doors to the Hall of Prayers, Calvin straightened his robes, smoothed his ruffled wing feathers, and straightened his halo. Dora followed his lead. Not because she felt a well-groomed Dora would be less likely to feel the wrath of the Heavenly Council, and not because she cared, but because she wanted to look good for Calvin. After all, he'd done nothing wrong.

"Should we go in?" she asked in a soft whisper.

Calvin shook his head. "They'll let us know when they're ready for us."

The minutes ticked by with maddening slowness. Calvin had begun to pace in circles. Dora had found an out-of-the-way cloud to sit on. And they waited. Angels came and went through the big doors, but none of them even acknowledged Calvin and Dora's presence.

Suddenly, the enormous doors began to swing slowly and silently open.

"Enter," came a booming voice from inside. They both looked around and, seeing no one else, took their first steps into their uncertain future.

At first Dora couldn't see anything but white swirling clouds from ceiling to floor. The only sounds were those of the softly murmured prayers drifting up from Earth.

Gradually, the clouds dissipated to reveal golden walls, a floor of the fluffiest white clouds, and a ceiling of twilight, cerulean blue sky studded with sparkling stars. Directly in front of them, a raised platform holding throne-like chairs dominated the room. Two very intimidating Archangels—the Heavenly Council—occupied two of the chairs. The third was obscured from view by the massive wingspread of the two Archangels. Angels of a lesser rank stood on the floor around the platform.

"Raphael and Michael," Calvin whispered, using his eye movements to single out the two Archangels seated on the platform.

Both the angels on the floor and the Archangels on the platform were unlike any Dora had ever seen before. With the exception of one of the Archangels, they wore flowing, gossamer robes so startlingly white she had to squint against the radiating brightness. Unlike her generic version, their halos resembled small, golden crowns.

The wings of the angels surrounding the platform were three times the size of hers and Calvin's. But the impressive wings of the two Archangels spread so wide they blotted out everything else on the dais, including, if there was one, the occupant of the third throne, and they seemed to reach nearly to the ceiling.

Of all of them, the one Archangel who stood out most had to be Michael, one of the two highest ranking on the Council. The other angels who'd seen him had told Dora he was not like the other Archangels. Young, muscular, and very handsome, he wore a shining coat of mail and a sheathed sword. In his hands he held a shield and a spear. Despite his warlike dress, he was the Angel of Righteousness and Mercy. Dora hoped he'd remember that when he pronounced her punishment.

Dora absently noted that Raphael's robe wasn't quite as bright white as the others' and had three sets of wings that needed a trip to Celestial Maintenance for a good feather-grooming. But his smile and the mischievous gleam in his startlingly blue eyes took some of the edge off Dora's nervousness.

Just when she'd begun to feel a bit better about the whole situation, Michael and Raphael folded their glorious wings and stepped to the side. To Dora's surprise, the third and middle throne was occupied by her friend Gracie. In contrast to the splendor of the Archangels she looked small, out of place, and very forlorn. Hopefully, Gracie was not about to feel the wrath of the Council for her part in helping Dora from time to time, and that they'd only brought her here to bear witness to Dora's long list of transgressions.

Before Dora could even begin to guess at what that list would disclose about her ineptitude as an angel, a small ball of light seemed to burst from Gracie's chest. It swelled until its brilliance blocked out everything else in the room. Unable to look at it any longer, Dora closed her eyes. Still the brightness seeped through her eyelids. Then suddenly it faded, and she heard Calvin's whispered exclamation.

"Gabriel!"

Dora's eyes popped open, and she gasped at the change that had taken place on the platform.

The Archangel, who had taken form and replaced the diminutive Gracie, stole Dora's breath. Gabriel could have stepped from the heart of the sun. Her blinding white robes pooled around her feet, and her magnificent wings beat the air with a slow, deliberate rhythm. Instead of the instruments of war held by her counterpart, she gripped a snow-white lily in her hand. Though she was the lone female, she seemed to dominate the Council.

How could this be? What had happened to Gracie? Then it hit her. Gracie had never really existed. Gabriel had taken on the image of Gracie. Her friend had simply been a transformation conjured by the Council to keep watch on her.

"But . . . I—" Dora sputtered.

The Archangel raised her hand to stop Dora's disjointed protests. "You don't understand," Gabriel said kindly, easing the knot of tension that had gathered in Dora's stomach. "All your questions will be answered in good time, Dora."

"But—"

Michael stepped forward. "Patience, Dora."

His deep voice boomed out and echoed around the chamber like a clap of thunder. From the rumbling sound of it, Michael must have been the one who had bid them enter the Hall of Prayers. Dora shuddered and took a step back.

"You're scaring the poor girl out of her halo, Michael. Do turn down the volume." The third Archangel leaned forward and smiled benevolently at Dora. "I'm Raphael." He shielded his mouth with his hand. With the other he pointed toward Michael and Gabriel. "They'll tell you that I'm a bit on the unconventional side. And they'll be right," he shouted, and then burst into gales of laughter.

The other angels snickered behind their hands, but quickly sobered when Gabriel admonished them with a silencing glare.

Gabriel frowned at Raphael. "If you please. We have serious business to take care of. For once, try to contain your frivolity."

Looking suitably reprimanded, Raphael slouched back in his chair, his ruffling wing feathers reflecting his unhappiness with Gabriel's admonishment.

As Dora waited for the Council to exact whatever punishment they'd decided on for her, she realized the murmur of prayers coming into the Hall from below had grown in volume since she and Calvin had first entered. The Archangels seemed oblivious to the increase in noise.

Before Gabriel could say anything, Dora stepped forward. "If you please, I just want to say that none of what happened down there is Calvin's fault. He gave me the Council's rules about not becoming emotionally attached to my mortal charges and not allowing my real identity to become known to the mortals. Despite his warnings of dire consequences, I fell in love with Tony Falcone. Through my negligence, Penny saw me as an angel, and before I left, it was completely my decision to show Tony who I really was. Calvin tried his best to stop me." She stepped back, then she remembered something else. "I also admit it was my idea to pry into the Sullivans' future."

There, it was all said, all out in the open. All that

was left was for her to receive her punishment.

Gabriel rose and moved to the edge of the dais. Her robes floated around her like liquid silk. "As for the Penny thing . . . unfortunate, but not something that will bring about the end of time. Six-year-olds are known to have vivid imaginations, one of their more charming qualities. In any case, there is no harm done. Children often see us and, to their detriment, adults tend to dismiss their reports of those sightings as nonsense. Besides, it's not as if Penny can prove it now, is it?" Gabriel studied Dora intently. "As for the Tony incident . . . also unfortunate. But nevertheless not something we need be concerned with right now."

Dora shuffled her feet. "Well, I did leave one of my wing feathers under Penny's pillow . . . so she wouldn't forget me."

"Ah, yes, the feather," Gabriel said, and resumed her seat. She waved the lily in the air. "My guess is that the adults she shows it to will assume it came from . . . a bird perhaps, a treasure she found while playing and not something she got from any heavenly being. And, if you recall, my child, I . . . or rather Gracie, helped you get the information you needed about the Sullivans, so if you were in violation of some nebulous celestial law, then so was I."

Somehow Dora doubted anyone, with the exception of Him, would have the courage to call Gabriel on the carpet for what she'd done. Even though she now knew Gracie had actually been Gabriel all along, Dora was relieved her *friend* would not suffer consequences for her actions.

"As for the question of no emotional involvement"—Michael cleared his throat loudly and leaned toward Calvin—"we never stipulated that Dora should not get emotionally attached to her charges. So exactly where did this rule originate, if not with us?" He raised an eyebrow and glared at Calvin.

Calvin squirmed under Michael's scrutiny. His nervously shuffling feet stirred up wisps of clouds. "I . . . uh . . . I guess I sort of made that one up."

"Made it up? Made it up? You took it upon yourself to make up additional rules?" All humor had vanished from Raphael's face.

A deep red hue crept into Calvin's cheeks. He swallowed hard, and his pronounced Adam's apple bobbed up and down comically. Then his wing feathers shuffled into wild disarray. "You see, Dora has had her share of . . . mishaps, and I thought a few additional . . . uh . . . guidelines would be helpful to keep her on the right path."

"Guidelines? The right path?" Michael bellowed. His fists tightened noticeably around the golden spear. The Heavens themselves seem to quake with the volume of his angry voice.

Gently, Gabriel placed a restraining hand on Michael's arm, and then she spoke to Calvin. "Did it ever occur to you that, had we wanted such a condition added, we would have done it ourselves?" Though soft, her tone did nothing to disguise her irritation with poor Calvin.

"But I felt that emotional involvement would only hamper her success, distract her from her mission. I had to stop her from falling in love—"

Raphael's laughter rang out through the Hall and all eyes turned to him. He slapped his knee. "You poor, deluded man, you can't stop love from happening. Once it's created it cannot be destroyed. As the Angel in charge of Love, Joy, and Light, I know. I did that on purpose so mortals wouldn't pick and choose and end up making terrible mistakes." He cleared his throat. "Of course, it doesn't always work out that way, but for the most part, it works very well." He patted his chest. "Even if a few wrong turns are taken along the way, the heart always knows best."

Michael stood. His massive wings beat the air with an agitated rhythm, churning up the clouds covering the floor into small whirlwinds. Though his voice still had the ability to fill the room, he tempered the angry tone he'd used earlier. "You have overstepped your authority, Calvin. As a result—"

Instant alarm filled Dora. He was going to punish Calvin. She couldn't let that happen. It just wasn't fair. It was her fault, not his. He'd warned her, and she couldn't let him take the blame. In the end, Calvin had been right to warn her against emotional involvement. Look what had happened. Though it hadn't been their ruling, she could see what harm falling in love with a mortal had already caused.

"No. Please don't punish him." Dora took several steps toward the dais. "He was thinking of me. Everything he did was to make sure I succeeded in my task. Don't punish Calvin because I failed."

Gabriel studied Dora for a long moment. She looked to the other members of the Council. One by one they nodded. "Very well, Dora. Only because you asked, we won't punish him." Then she turned to Calvin. "This will *not* happen again. Am I clear?"

He shook his head vigorously. "Yes. I mean, no. No. It won't . . . happen . . . again. You have my word."

For a long moment, Gabriel stared at Calvin, her brows knitted as though to further reinforce her warning, then she returned her attention to Dora. "Now, Dora, what makes you think you failed?" Gabriel's quiet voice had lost the edge it had acquired when speaking to Calvin. "You brought Tony and his niece together into a loving family. That was your mission, and you accomplished it."

Please send her back to us.

The level of noise filtering into the Hall from the Earthly prayers had risen considerably. Dora had barely heard Gabriel's last words. "But I fell in love with a mortal. And it complicated . . . everything." She choked back a sob.

Please send her back to us.

"You simply followed your heart, and I don't see complications arising from it, unless you consider *this*." She raised her hands to indicate the burgeoning noise level in the great room.

Please send her back to us.

"Had you not, we would not now be bombarded with this deafening din." She clapped her hands over her ears. Beside her, Michael did likewise and grimaced. Raphael smiled.

"I don't understand." Dora had to yell to be heard. The noise had risen to a level that hurt her ears.

Please send her back to us.

"Raphael, please." Gabriel's face twisted as the noise increased. "Can you control this for just a while?"

"Oh, all right." Raphael waved his hand, and the noise subsided to a faint murmuring of voices. He grinned devilishly at the other two Archangels casting stern looks his way. Then he shrugged innocently. "Just trying to make a point."

Dora looked from one to another of the Archangels. She had no idea what any of them were talking about. "What's going on?" she whispered to Calvin.

"Not a clue."

"That noise," Michael said, "has been growing in intensity and persistence since you left Earth. I'm afraid it's Tony. For hours, he's been praying for your return, and quite vigorously, I might add."

Now Dora felt even worse. She bowed her head, her remorse almost beyond bearing. It was all her fault that Tony was so despondent and in such pain. The ache clutching her heart increased tenfold. "I never should have let him fall in love with me."

Raphael slapped the arm of his chair and leaned in her direction. "Did you not hear what I just said, young lady? You have no control over whom you love or who loves you. It happens"—he snapped his fingers—"like that. No control. None. Nada. Zilch. Zip. Zero—"

"All right, Raphael, we get the picture." Gabriel took her seat again, rearranged her robes, and looked up at Dora. "Despite Raphael's overly exuberant display, he's right. The heart *always* wins out. Now, let us get on with things. Perhaps, once we do, you'll understand more." She raised her chin and gestured with the lily to one of the lesser angels standing at the side of the dais. "Lailah has something to tell you." The petite, very motherly looking angel who stood to Gabriel's right stepped forward.

Dora frowned. She'd never heard mention of this angel before. "Lailah?"

Gabriel laughed lightly. "She's not one of the better known angels, but nevertheless, a very important one." She glanced lovingly at the angel. "Lailah guards the Well of Souls. That's where the souls of both angels and mortals are stored in separate chambers until they are ready to be assigned a body. When a mortal soul enters the womb of a woman, Lailah stands guard over the babe until birth. During the time it resides in the mother, Lailah tells the child what its life will be like. When the child is ready to enter the world, she flicks it on the nose and removes all memory of what she's told it." She nodded at Lailah. "Please tell Dora what happened."

The little angel took a deep breath. "The last Guardian of the Well was . . . well, shall we say, a bit less than efficient. She didn't keep good watch on the souls and one of the mortal souls slipped in with those of the angels." She glanced hesitantly at Gabriel.

"Go on, Lailah. It's time she knew."

"That soul was yours, Dora. You were destined all along to be a mortal." She smiled broadly, obviously relieved to have the burden off her shoulders at last.

Dora didn't know what to say. A joy unlike anything she'd ever known swept through her. Her heart raced faster. She clutched at the sides of her robe, hoping she could keep her knees from buckling. Mortal? She was actually a mortal? This explained so much: her ineptitude at being an angel, her inexplicable interest in the mortals in the Earth Pool, and most importantly, her strong desire to go to Earth. And all this time . . . they had known.

"Why did no one ever tell me?"

"We wanted to tell you, but we thought it better to wait until you asked to go to Earth. We knew you would eventually. It was inevitable. Your mortal instincts were getting stronger each day. But it had to be your decision, not ours. When Calvin came to us with your request, we were ready to grant it immediately." Gabriel left the dais and seemed to float across the floor to Dora. She took both of Dora's hands in hers and looked deeply into her eyes. A contented warmth invaded Dora's body. "Your trip to Earth was to see how well you could blend in with the mortals. If you could adjust." She smiled. "I'm happy to announce that you passed with flying colors, my dear. Now, you can reap your reward for a job well done."

"Reward?" Dora fought to keep at bay the hope of,

until now, an unattainable dream. Could it be that she . . .?
No. It would be too much to expect.

"Because you were so successful with the Falcones,
we're promoting you to Guardian Angel."

CHAPTER 25

✚

GUARDIAN ANGEL? LIKE GLASS SMASHING AGAINST a wall, all hope of going back to Earth splintered into tiny, irretrievable fragments around Dora.

Dora didn't want to be anyone's Guardian Angel. She wanted Tony and Penny. She wanted to go back. But she'd known all along it would be impossible. Still, the disappointment of the finality of being stuck in Heaven hurt more than she could express.

"Thank you," she mumbled, but even to her own ears the words lacked sincerity.

With a gentle finger, Gabriel raised Dora's chin. "Or you can return to Earth as a mortal."

Dora couldn't believe her ears. Suddenly, the sun threatened to blind her with its brilliance, the sky had become even more blue, and the sound of her heart beating rapidly in her ears nearly deafened her. Joy flooded every corner of her being. She had to force herself to stand still and not jump up and down and shout with happiness.

"You mean I . . ." She was almost afraid to say the words. Afraid Gabriel would tell her she'd misunderstood. But she forced them through her trembling lips. "I can go back to Penny and Tony?"

Gabriel nodded. "If you want to."

"If I want to? I've never wanted anything more. When can I leave?"

Gabriel smiled and glanced at the other Archangels. They were grinning broadly. "Just as soon as we can arrange it. The Council still has a few . . . ah . . . loose ends that need tending."

Dora tried to restrain herself from hugging Gabriel. After all, one didn't go about hugging Archangels. But the joy racing through her made it impossible to adhere to decorum. She launched herself at Gabriel and flung her arms around the highest ranking Archangel in the cosmos.

"Oh, my!" Gabriel squeaked in surprise, her celestial demeanor thrown into disarray. Nevertheless, she returned the hug.

Over the Archangel's shoulder Calvin grinned at Dora, his smile spreading from ear to ear. Dora had to wonder if it was because of true happiness for her or because he would at last be free of his most troublesome angel. Either way, she couldn't help returning his grin.

Finally, she released Gabriel and, a bit embarrassed at her spontaneous show of affection, whispered, "Thank you."

"There's little to thank me for, my child. You've earned this. Your deep concern for everyone, even those who might not deserve it"—she cast a glance in Calvin's direction—"while you put yourself second, was most impressive. Only someone with a big heart could have done it. Not many mortals have the capacity." She patted Dora's hand. "As for your thanks, none are necessary. We are simply righting a terrible wrong."

A troubling thought occurred to Dora. "What about Tony and Penny? Will they remember me as . . . as an angel?"

"Tony's memory will be wiped clean of anything related to your being an angel. It's better this way. Adults seldom handle things like this well. However, Penny will be allowed to retain hers. She will recall seeing an angel, but she won't make the connection to you."

Real fear prevented Dora from speaking immediately. Finally, her need to know overpowered her fear of what Gabriel might answer. "Will Tony remember he loves me? That I love him?"

❖ ❖ ❖

The early Christmas morning sun danced on the rippling surface of the Earth Pool, sprinkling the pristine robes of the angels gathered around it with splashes of rainbow colors. As each angel stepped forward in turn, Gabriel oversaw the solemn process.

Raphael, his face unusually serious, sprinkled the surface with a fine, silver powder. "I give Dora love, joy, and the light of a new life." He stepped back as the surface swirled and the powder disappeared beneath its surface.

Zadkiel, a rather wiry angel, was next. He sprinkled the pool with a pale blue powder. "On you, sweet Dora, I bestow the gift of forgetfulness and in its place present the gift of memories of a life fully lived and filled with love, family, and happiness." Taking another pinch from his pouch, he repeated the action. "On you, Millie and Preston Sullivan, because of your unselfish benevolence, I bestow the gift of a life produced from your love of each other and for your fellow man." Again the surface swirled and swallowed the offering.

"For you," said the next angel, Matatron, a large man with a gentle smile and hands the size of a small star, "I wipe the slate of time clean and record the birth of a family steeped in love and bound by understanding." The sunshine yellow grains that trickled through his large, thick fingers were quickly sucked beneath the waters.

Michael was next. His massive wings beat the air

gently, stirring up wisps of clouds and sending them floating off into the cosmos. In a surprisingly quiet voice, he spoke into the pool as he scattered red dust over the water. "As a mortal, your life will be filled with happiness and, at times, turbulence. I give you the courage to face the trials yet to be. May you do so with mercy, wisdom, and righteousness."

At last, it was Gabriel's turn. She'd long pondered over her gift to Dora. Having been closer to the young woman than the others, she felt a deep responsibility for her happiness. After much thought, she was certain what would serve her best.

Pure white sand fell from Gabriel's outstretched hand. "I give you the strength and wisdom of the women who came before you. Use it wisely. Temper it with understanding and administer it with love."

Gabriel swirled the contents of the pool with her fingertips to make sure all the gifts were fully absorbed and reached their destination intact. When the water had once again settled into a motionless shiny surface, she peered down into Dora's bedroom at the Falcone house.

Good-bye, little Dora. Be happy.

Gabriel waited until she saw a shimmer of rainbow-colored light appear, then turned to the others.

"So be it."

The group of angels disappeared one by one into

the clouds.

Nearby, a small angel, who had remained at the back of the group, opened her wings to take flight. "Lailah," Gabriel called, "please remain with me. We have some additional business." Lailah nodded and folded her wings.

When the shimmer died away, Dora looked at herself in the big mirror standing in the corner of her bedroom at the Falcone house. When the familiar image of Dora the angel looked back at her, disappointment flooded through her.

Had they lied to her? Was this some kind of sick joke played by the Archangels for their collective amusement? Perhaps raising her hopes only to dash them to the ground was her punishment for the mistakes she'd made.

Despondent, she sank to the edge of the bed and stared at the angel gazing back at her. Then, clinging to the last glimmer of hope, she looked down at herself. The image in the mirror this time was not a transformation of her mortal form, but an actual reflection of her as she really was. To confirm it, she looked in the dresser mirror. Dora the angel looked back at her.

Something had gone terribly wrong. She wanted to

go to Tony, but she couldn't go like this.

Hurrying back to the big mirror, she called for her friend. "Gracie! Gracie!"

Then she remembered that the Gracie who had been her confidant and friend wasn't Gracie at all, but actually Gabriel, the highest ranked Archangel. What made her think Gabriel would come running at the beck and call of a lowly angel like herself? Besides, if this was her punishment, then Gabriel had been instrumental in conceiving of it, and for her to reverse a decision was almost unheard of.

Before Dora had a chance to dwell on the thought, the mirror suddenly came to life with splashes of silver, gold, red, pale blue, yellow, and white. In the center of the rainbow of color was Gabriel's smiling face.

"Yes, Dora?"

Holding her arms out to show Gabriel her robe, Dora asked, "What happened? I'm still an angel."

Gabriel chuckled. The multitude of colors surrounding her face swirled in a crazy dance. "Be patient, little one. Be patient." She moved her hand in a circular motion. "For now, go to sleep, Dora. Go to sleep. Tomorrow you will begin a new life."

The colors on the mirror's surface began to swirl and then blended into a smear of all the colors. Gabriel's face began to shimmer and fade, then it vanished like melting snow.

Suddenly, Dora's eyes grew heavy. Though she fought against sleep, she found it impossible to stay awake. Curling up on the bed, she closed her eyes and drifted off.

Lailah turned away from the slumbering image of Dora in the Earth Pool and faced Gabriel. "Now?"

"Now."

The Archangel and the diminutive Lailah disappeared into the cosmos and seconds later reappeared on either side of Dora's sleeping form.

Lailah glanced at Gabriel. She nodded. "It's time," she said, smiling gently at the sleeping woman. "Because of our negligence, she has been robbed of something very precious. It's time we gave it back to her. All of it."

Smiling, Lailah leaned forward, pressed her lips to Dora's ear, and in a voice so soft even Gabriel couldn't hear it, whispered to the woman like she whispered to the babies snuggled warmly in their mothers' wombs.

In her dream, Dora saw herself as a dark-haired child running through a field of wildflowers into a woman's open arms. A man sat near her on a blanket scattered with the remnants of a picnic.

"Momma!" Dora cried. "Look!" She pointed heavenward. "There's an angel in the cloud."

The man laughed, a deep, rumbling sound filled with delight. "You and your mother and your angels."

"Really, Daddy. Look. She's right there." Dora pointed a chubby finger toward a large white cloud.

The man opened his mouth to speak, but the woman silenced him with a frown. Gathering Dora close, the woman looked up. "I see her, Dora. She must be watching over our little girl for us."

"But you and Daddy take good care of me. I don't need an angel."

The woman laughed this time. "We all need an angel in our lives once in a while, Dora. It's good that you have yours."

Dora stared at the cloud. It shifted slightly in the breeze. A smile formed on the lips of the image. She waved a white lily at Dora, and then vanished.

Dora's dream faded and a new one took its place. This time, she was standing in the foyer of the Sullivans' house dressed in a frothy, pink dress. Beside her was a very nervous young man in a baby blue tuxedo. He was slipping a corsage onto her wrist.

"Smile, kids." An older Preston Sullivan aimed a

camera at them and clicked.

"Isn't our daughter the most beautiful thing you've ever seen?" Millie's eyes flooded with moisture.

Preston patted his wife's shoulder. "She certainly is." Kissing his daughter on the cheek, he ushered the couple out the door. "Have fun." Then he grabbed the young man's arm and pulled him backward. "Not too much fun," he whispered in the boy's ear.

For a moment, the young man looked confused, and then, as comprehension dawned, he blanched. "N . . . no . . . sir. Ab . . . absolutely . . . not."

Again the scene faded.

What followed in the next few hours was a panoramic parade of the high points of her life drifting in and out of Dora's dreams. Soon she had relived every significant moment from birth to the present—except one.

The final scene emerged.

She and Tony were sitting on the floor in front of the blazing fireplace in his living room. The flames in the hearth warmed her skin, but not nearly as much as the loving look shining in Tony's eyes. In his hand was a small, square box with a gold bow. Her eyes misted over. She felt as though she'd waited eons for this moment.

Taking her hand, he put the box in her palm. She slowly lifted the lid. Nestled against a bed of black velvet was a diamond ring.

"Marry me," Tony said.

The scene vanished.

Dora bolted upright, blinked, and looked around her familiar bedroom.

Shelves her father had made and hung above the window were lined with the dolls from her childhood. The frilly curtains that her mother had insisted were perfect for the two bay windows filtered the winter sunlight before it spilled across the multicolored, braided rug beside her bed. Relieved it had all been a dream, she turned toward the dresser and its large oval mirror. Looking back at her was a young woman, hair tousled from sleep, her dark eyes bright with excitement.

Her gaze shifted to the dresser. On it sat a framed photo of her, Penny, and Tony.

Tony!

An overwhelming urge to see him and Penny overcame her. Jumping from the bed, she threw on her robe and slippers, dashed from the room, and down the stairs. Not caring about the six inches of fresh snow that had fallen the night before, she raced across the snow-covered back lawn to his house.

Throwing open the back door, she hurried through the kitchen to the living room. Penny and Tony sat next to the tree. Beside them was piled a colorful heap of torn, discarded gift wrap and ribbon.

"Dora!" Penny exclaimed and ran to her, her new doll clutched under her arm.

Dora picked her up off the floor and into her arms. She hugged her slight body close, overcome by a feeling that she'd come very close to losing her. "Merry Christmas, sweetie." She kissed Penny's warm cheek and set her on the floor.

Tony had gotten to his feet. Holding her gaze, he walked slowly in her direction. "Morning."

Mesmerized, she could only think to answer his question from her dream. Before she could stop them, the words slipped past her lips in a rush. "Yes, I'll marry you."

Tony's laughter filled the room. "Well, I hope so, since you already accepted my ring." He lifted her hand to show her the engagement ring encircling the third finger of her left hand.

Heat rose in Dora's cheeks. How had she forgotten one of the most important moments of her life? She tried to make sense of it. How could she not remember? Carefully, she replayed the dream. "I had a dream that you asked me to marry you, but I never answered. I thought—"

He stopped the cascade of words with his lips. He lifted his head and gazed down into her eyes. The same love shone from them she'd seen in the dream. Intense, deep, and everlasting. "You answered. Trust me, if you hadn't, I'd remember."

Dora smiled up at him, then rested her face against his broad chest and hugged him close.

"Where's Jack? He has to open his presents," Penny said. Her face was stained with the chocolate Santa she'd been sampling. In her hand she held a red and green stocking that read *Dogs Need Christmas, Too.* "Jack? Here, Jack." She made a clucking sound with her tongue. "Where is he, Uncle Tony?"

Just then they heard scratching at the front door, followed by a sharp bark.

"I guess that answers your question, kiddo." Tony went to the front door and opened it.

A shaggy white dog trotted past him and jumped on Penny. She immediately sat down, and the dog climbed into her lap, licking her face and wagging his stubby tail. Tony put his arm around Dora, and they watched as Penny tore into Jack's stocking and began feeding him the contents.

❖ ❖ ❖

"So, you finally asked our little girl to marry you," Preston Sullivan said to Tony from the far end of the dining table.

"Yes, sir, and she said yes." Tony grinned at Dora, and her heart flipped over in her chest.

"'Bout time," Preston said, holding his plate out for another piece of pumpkin pie.

Millie frowned at him. "You've had enough pie. Besides, I made an extra and you have your own at home." She pushed her chair back and stood. "Now, as soon as I help Dora clean up these dessert dishes, we'll go home and you can have your second piece."

Dora laughed. She loved her mother and father's good-natured sparring. "No. Tony will help me. You take Dad home before he wastes away to nothing."

Millie laughed this time. "Not likely. I had to let out his pants last week."

Then she scanned the table. "You sure you don't want me to help?"

Dora opened her mouth to say she was sure, but her father stepped in between his wife and daughter. "Millie, my love, can't you see these young people want to be alone?"

Tony grinned. Dora slipped under his arm and nestled against his side.

Looking a bit embarrassed, Millie gathered up the shopping bag with her presents and Preston's, kissed her daughter's cheek, then started for the door. Preston followed.

Dora let the silence of the house close around her. It had been a long day. Lisa and Leon had made good on their promise to come to dinner, and to Tony and Dora's amazement, Penny had liked them instantly. Lisa appeared to be very taken with her niece and promised to come for another visit before they returned to Texas.

After they left, Penny had had her dessert. When she nearly fell asleep at the table, Dora had taken her upstairs and put her to bed. Now that her parents had gone home, she and Tony finally had the house to themselves.

"Tired?" he asked, kissing the top of Dora's head.

"Exhausted." She snuggled her face against his chest and leaned against him.

He pushed her back and looked into her face. Love shone from his eyes. He winked. "Well, Soon-to-Be Mrs. Falcone, how about we go upstairs and I give you one of my famous massages?"

Standing on tiptoe, she kissed him long and suggestively. "Just a massage?"

"For starters."

Their shared laughter could be heard throughout the house as he carried her up the stairs.

The Archangels were once again gathered at the Earth Pool. Lailah stepped from behind Michael's massive wings and took her place at the rim of the pool. From the small white pouch she held, she drew a handful of sparkling, gold powder. As she let it drop into the pool, she said, "I give you the precious gift of a new life." She smiled at Gabriel and stepped back.

Don't miss Elizabeth Sinclair's next novel:

Garden
of the Moon

Elizabeth Sinclair

ISBN# 9781933836980

US $7.95 / CDN $8.95

Mass Market Paperback

Paranormal Romance

DECEMBER 2009

www.elizabethsinclair.com

THE
DREAM
THIEF

HELEN A. ROSBURG

Someone is murdering young, beautiful women in mid-sixteenth century Venice. Even the most formidable walls of the grandest villas cannot keep him out, for he steals into his victims' dreams. Holding his chosen prey captive in the night, he seduces them . . . to death.

Now Pina's cousin, Valeria, is found dead, her lovely body ravished. It is the final straw for Pina's overbearing fiancé, Antonio, and he orders her confined within the walls of her mother's opulent villa on Venice's Grand Canal. It is a blow not only to Pina, but to the poor and downtrodden in the city's ghettos, to whom Pina has been an angel of charity and mercy. But Pina does not chafe long in her lavish prison, for soon she too begins to show symptoms of the midnight visitations; a waxen pallor and overwhelming lethargy.

Fearing for her daughter's life, Pina's mother removes her from the city to their estate in the country. Still, Pina is not safe. For Antonio's wealth and his family's power enable him to hide a deadly secret. And the murderer manages to find his intended victim. Not to steal into her dreams and steal away her life, however, but to save her. And to find his own salvation in the arms of the only woman who has ever shown him love.

ISBN#9781932815207
Mass Market Paperback / Paranormal
US $6.99 / CDN $9.99
Available Now
www.helenrosburg.com

Amy Tolnitch

A Lost Touch of Bliss

Five years ago, Cain Veuxfort, Earl of Hawksdown, followed duty and broke Amice de Monceaux's heart. But now he needs her. Desperately.

For Amice has a very special talent. She is a Spirit Goddess, able to help restless souls move on. And Cain has a very restless ghost he wishes fervently would leave his castle. Anxious to regain order in his chaotic life, Cain offers Amice the one thing he's sure she can't resist; an Italian villa on the sea in exchange for her unique services.

Although Amice's wound is deep, and as fresh and painful as ever, she agrees to help her former lover. Life on the Italian coast will be the start of a new life for her. Perhaps then she will finally be able to put the past behind her as well as an importunate Highland lord who wants nothing less that her hand in marriage. But there is more going on at Castle Falcon's Craig than a simple haunting, and more than one tragic tale of unrequited love. Yet to set things right, for both the living and the dead, Cain must find the courage to shed his mask of indifference, Amice must move beyond her pain to forgive . . . and long dead, star-crossed lovers must lead them all on the path to. . .

A Lost Touch of Bliss

ISBN#9781932815269
Mass Market Paperback / Paranormal Romance
US $6.99 / CDN $8.99
Available Now
www.amytolnitch.com

Into the Mist

Elizabeth Sinclair

In this sequel to *MIRACLE IN THE MIST*, Karrie Henderson, the amnesiac victim of an abusive marriage, finds herself alone in a blizzard wandering the streets of the village of Tarrytown, NY. Guides from the misty village of Renaissance—the town where miracles happen, find her and take her to Renaissance. Living with Clara Webb, the village weaver, and healing in the security of a new love, Frank Donovan, Karrie is guided through her memories a bit at a time until she emerges a stronger woman, sure of who she is and what she wants.

Frank is enchanted with Karrie from the first time he sees her, but he knows she's a wounded soul, and he doesn't trust himself not to hurt her further. He also must come to terms with his own demons, the ghosts of his dead wife and child. Until that time, he cannot hope to help Karrie or love her as she deserves to be loved and cherished.

But Renaissance has a way of healing the soul and opening the heart to all kinds of possibilities. All they'll need is faith and trust to give birth to the miracle of love.

ISBN# 9781933836423
Mass Market Paperback
US $7.95 / CDN $9.95
Paranormal Romance
Available Now
www.elizabethsinclair.com

First, there is a River

Kathy Steffen

A family conceals a cruel secret.

Emma Perkins' life appears idyllic. Her husband, Jared, is a hardworking farmer and a dependable neighbor. But Emma knows intimately the brutality prowling beneath her husband's façade. When he sends their children away, Emma's life unravels.

A woman seeks her spirit.

Deep in despair, Emma seeks refuge aboard her uncle's riverboat, the Spirit of the River. She travels through a new world filled with colorful characters: captains, mates, the rich, the working class, moonshiners, prostitutes, and Gage-the Spirit's reclusive engineer. Scarred for life from a riverboat explosion, Gage's insight into heartache draws him to Emma, and as they heal together, they form a deep and unbreakable bond. Emma learns to trust that anything is possible, including reclaiming her children and facing her husband.

A man seeks revenge.

Jared Perkins makes a journey of his own. Determined to bring his wife home and teach her the lesson of her life, Jared secretly follows the Spirit. His rage burns cold as he plans his revenge for everyone on board.

Against the immense power of the river, the journey of the Spirit will change the course of their lives forever.

ISBN# 9781932815931
Trade Paperback
US $14.95 / CDN $18.95
Available Now
www.kathysteffen.com

For more information
about other great titles from
Medallion Press, visit

www.medallionpress.com